swishing sound as a sapling bent back on itself, whipped back into place, and six sharpened bamboo stakes, each eighteen inches long, impaled both Domingo and Laframboise where they stood. Holliday saw that the sapling was weighted at the end by a small, curved rectangular object that he recognized instantly: it was an MMI 'MiniMore,' a smaller version of the much larger Claymore fragmentation mine.

'Hit the dirt!'

Holliday dropped, the gentle pinging as the second trip line pulling the ring on the mine tinkling melodically before the main charge exploded and its load of shrapnel burst in a twenty-foot arc at roughly waist level. It sounded like a small sharp thunderclap followed by an acrid cloud of smoke and then something like the pitter-patter of hail as the projectiles within the mine hit the jungle. Then there was silence . . .

Valley of the Templars

PAUL CHRISTOPHER

PENGUIN BOOKS

PENGUIN BOOKS

Published by the Penguin Group
Penguin Books Ltd, 80 Strand, London WC2R 0RL, England
Penguin Group (USA) Inc., 375 Hudson Street, New York, New York 10014, USA
Penguin Group (Canada), 90 Eglinton Avenue East, Suite 700, Toronto, Ontario, Canada M4P 2Y3
(a division of Pearson Penguin Canada Inc.)
Penguin Ireland, 25 St Stephen's Green, Dublin 2, Ireland
(a division of Penguin Books Ltd)
Penguin Group (Australia), 707 Collins Street,
Melbourne, Victoria 3008, Australia (a division of Pearson Australia Group Pty Ltd)
Penguin Books India Pvt Ltd, 11 Community Centre,
Panchsheel Park, New Delhi – 110 017, India
Penguin Group (NZ), 67 Apollo Drive, Rosedale, Auckland 0632, New Zealand
(a division of Pearson New Zealand Ltd)
Penguin Books (South Africa) (Pty) Ltd, Block D, Rosebank Office Park, 181 Jan Smuts Avenue,
Parktown North, Gauteng 2193, South Africa

Penguin Books Ltd, Registered Offices: 80 Strand, London WC2R 0RL, England

www.penguin.com

First published in the USA by Signet, an imprint of New American Library,
a division of Penguin Group (USA) Inc. 2012
First published in Great Britain in Penguin Books 2013

1

Typeset in 13.25pt Garamond MT Std
by Palimpsest Book Production Ltd, Falkirk, Stirlingshire
Printed in Great Britain by Clays Ltd, St Ives plc

ISBN: 978-0-718-17727-0

www.greenpenguin.co.uk

ALWAYS LEARNING   **PEARSON**

In memory of my old friend, NHL player
and stand-up comedian
Pete Laframboise
January 18, 1950–March 19, 2011
who squirted ink from a trick pen into his
grade 7 teacher's face at York Street Public School
and got away with it.

'The Chinese use two brushstrokes to write the word "crisis." One brushstroke stands for danger; the other for opportunity. In a crisis, be aware of the danger, but recognize the opportunity.'

John F. Kennedy

'Capitalism is the legitimate racket of the ruling class.'

Al Capone

'I think that a man should not live beyond the age when he begins to deteriorate, when the flame that lighted the brightest moment of his life has weakened.'

Fidel Castro

'Caesar turned in his bed and muttered,
With a struggle for breath the lamp-flame guttered;
Calpurnia heard her husband moan:
"The house is falling,
The beaten men come into their own." '

John Masefield,
The Rider at the Gate

PART ONE
Countdown

I

Room 212, Hart Senate Building,
Washington, D.C.
Committee Investigating the use of Paramilitary
Corporations, Private Armies and Private Police
Forces both within and without the Continental
United States, Senator Fulton J. Abernathy, Dem.,
Wisconsin Chairman
February 20, 2012

Room 212 in the Hart Senate Building was a
multimillion-dollar chamber for interrogation people
from Enron executives to possible appointees to high
positions in government. There was a single massive
wall of marble behind the senators' dais, which
stretched around three walls of exotic wood paneling
with cutouts for press boxes like some political baseball game; a single long table faced the senators on the
carpeted floor and room for two hundred or so specta-
tors behind. There was plenty of room for press
photographers to kneel or squat beneath the senators'
dais and a large UNITED STATES SENATE seal on
the marble wall with a convenient swing door beneath
it to allow for a television camera to get reaction shots.

The two men and their several lawyers being spitted

that particular day were Major General Atwood Swann, president of Blackhawk Special Forces Corporation, and his second in command, Colonel Paul Axeworthy. Swann was dressed in the uniform of a U.S. Marine major general, his chest resplendent with medals from Vietnam and both Iraq wars, as well as Afghanistan. Swann was a big man, square-faced, his marine buzz cut going from blond to gray. Axeworthy was wearing Blackhawk Battle Dress Uniform, or BDUS, consisting of green-on-green camouflage shirt and trousers tucked into spit-shined combat boots, a bright blue scarf at his throat and a dark green beret bearing the black bird on a gold background that was the Blackhawk logo. The beret was tucked into the left epaulette of his blouse. He wore an identical gold-and-black patch on both shoulders. The two men's five lawyers were dressed like lawyers.

Senator Fulton J. Abernathy, the committee chair, wore a dusty suit twenty years out of date, a psychedelic tie that wouldn't have looked out of place on the *Sgt Pepper's* album cover and a face like a wrinkled apple. His eyes were bright blue and extremely alert behind a pair of bright green half-framed bifocals. The grilling had already been going on for two hours, but Abernathy was still in top form and Swann hadn't flinched once.

AB: What is your annual salary at Blackhawk, General Swann?
SW: I was informed that there would be no questions regarding personal matters.

4

AB: Well, I'm telling you otherwise and I'm the boss here, so answer the question.

SW: One million seven hundred and eighty-five thousand plus bonuses.

AB: What kind of bonuses?

SW: Bonuses for successful missions.

AB: Such as?

SW: Katrina for one.

AB: Katrina as in the hurricane?

SW: Yes.

AB: What, pray, was your mission there?

SW: We were hired as an adjunct to local forces to maintain order.

AB: What about your mission in El Salvador?

SW: I'm not sure I understand the question.

AB: Were you or were you not hired by the government of El Salvador to 'relocate' several villages and their occupants in the interior for the purposes of a major gold mining corporation owned by the same person who controls the multinational corporation known as the Pallas Group, which in turn owns both Blackhawk Security as well as Blackhawk Special Forces – one Kate Sinclair, mother of the late Senator William Pierce Sinclair who recently took his own life?

SW: That's a complicated question, Senator.

AB: I'll try to pay attention when you answer it. El Salvador, in particular the village of San Diego de Tripicano and the village of Cuscatleon, which according to my information simply do not exist anymore. In fact, the only thing left of both places is a scattering of burnt-out ruins and a few charred bones. How did you manage that little trick, General, and what kind of bonus were you paid for slaughtering two hundred and thirty people, men, women and children?

sw: I'm afraid the El Salvador mission is a matter of national security, Senator.

AB: El Salvador's national security? Ask me if I give a tinker's fart about El Salvador's national security.
Pause.

sw: My counsel advises me to plead the Fifth Amendment.

AB. I'll just bet they do. One more question before we break for lunch, General Swann. Have you ever been hired by any U.S. government agency to invade the territory of a sovereign nation?

sw: My counsel advises me –

AB: We get the picture ... General. Let's break for lunch.

Four miles off Cayo Largo, Cuba
Phase of the Moon: New
April 21, 2012

It was midnight and it was raining. The four ancient, rusting fishing trawlers puttered slowly northwest along the coast offshore from the long archipelago of cays and islands that stretched along Cuba's Caribbean shoreline. Most were uninhabited strips of sand and

6

coral occupied by a few windblown palms, though a few had been turned into sportfishing resorts to entice tourists. But it was the end of the season and even the resorts were almost empty. If anyone was listening that night, they would have assumed that the engine sound came from the rock lobster and shrimp fleet that plied the banks of the *Bahia del Pedro* farther south and were now heading for one of the main fishing terminals like Matanzas or Cienfuegos.

At ten past twelve the engine of one of the four old boats in the group sputtered and died and the three others stopped their own engines to see what they could do to help. Some wit in the head office had decided to name one of the boats *Bahia* and another *Cochinos – Bay of Pigs –* but under the rust and the filth and the piles of empty nets hanging over the derrick and the mast, it was unlikely that anyone was going to notice on a dark rainy night four miles out to sea. Even if Cuban radar was in good enough repair to be working that night, the four boats were wooden and so low in the water they would likely have been invisible.

As soon as the engines stopped, the crews of all four boats surged into action. Instead of shrimp and lobster the trawlers carried ten five-by-six bags, each containing a seven-meter inflatable Zodiac boat, and another set of bags contained their silenced electric motors, hardly neccessary tonight because the tide was rushing strong inshore. Each of the trawlers also carried thirty men, all fully equipped with weapons bags and LAR V Draegar bubble-free rebreathing apparatus, suitable for the shallow depths and warm waters inshore and with a ninety-minute useful breathing time. Within twenty minutes the boats and all one hundred and twenty men had been off-loaded and were heading toward a GPS point between two uninhabited cays sixteen miles northeast of Cayo Largo. The four trawlers continued their journey, their course slowly changing to a more northeasterly one and their staging point on the southern tip of Little Cayman Island.

Ninety minutes later, their Zodiacs sunk in seventy feet of water, the four-hundred-and-eight-man unit landed on a rocky abandoned beach twenty miles west of the town of Trinidad. They stripped off their rebreathing gear and stowed it in the waterproof knapsacks where their camo gear had been kept. The weapons bags were unsealed, each man armed himself according to his role in the mission and at three fifteen in the morning the company-handpicked men from the Blackhawk Special Forces elite Special Boat Unit moved off the beach in double time, and within another hour they had vanished into the deep jungles covering the slopes of the Escambray Hills. They were the third such unit to be landed successfully on the empty beaches of Spiritus Sancti Province, and there were three more to come over the next six weeks. Operation Cuba Libre was in full swing.

2

Holliday's stay at Ramstein Air Force Base lasted much longer than he'd wanted, and both Christmas and New Year's had come and gone before he was released along with Eddie. The Cuban had been keeping in erratic touch with his aging mother and father, but there was still no news of the vanished Domingo, Eddie's older brother, or at least no news his mother or father wanted to share with the listeners at the Signals Intelligence Base just south of Havana.

In early spring, Holliday's still-healing wound and battered brain pan leaving him unable to drive and Eddie never having been behind the wheel of a car in his life, the two friends took the high-speed ICE train from Mannheim to Amsterdam, then checked into the Hotel Roemer on the Visscherstraat. The snowbanks were melting, the canals were thawing and the first leaves were appearing.

'I have to see a guy about something,' Holliday said cryptically when they had settled in. 'I'll be back in an hour. Order something from room service.'

'I think I will sleep instead,' said Eddie. 'I will dream of the beaches near my home in Alamar.'

'Alamar?'

'Fidel's great gift to the people of Havana.'

'What is it?'

'A slum, built with Russian concrete.' The Cuban smiled. 'But very close to the sea.'

Holliday left the hotel and made his way to Nieuwmarkt on the edge of De Wallen, Amsterdam's red-light district. The place he was looking for was squeezed in between a sex shop and a bierhaus. A green neon sign in the blacked-out front window read DARBY'S AMERICAN BAR, EST. JUNE 16, 1969 – the day its owner, Danny Farrell, finished his second and final tour in Vietnam, Holliday knew. After seeing the way things were upon landing in San Francisco, Farrell slipped into civvies in the toilets, caught the next plane home to New York and then kept right on going, opening the bar in Amsterdam that had always been his dream in-country.

Holliday stepped in and let his eyes adjust to the dim light. The bar was on the right, a row of vinyl-covered booths on the left. A big TV was mounted on the wall behind the bar, playing CNN with the sound turned off. Holliday sat down at the bar and checked the grimy plastic-coated menu. Burgers, fries, BLTs, Denver sandwiches and Reubens on dark rye. All the foods that Farrell had talked endlessly about in the hooch.

The bartender made his way down the bar to where Holliday was sitting. He was thin, no more than five-six, bald, with oversized ears a huge, broad nose, and wearing wire-rimmed glasses. He was dressed in a wrinkled white shirt with sleeves rolled up, blue jeans and a barman's short apron. There was a fading tattoo of a skull backed by a parachute and a sword on his right forearm. Holliday would have recognized him anywhere, mostly because of the lumpy, jagged scar that ran from just under his right ear to his chin. It was lumpy and jagged because Holliday only had the needle and thread he used to darn his socks with him when the piece of shrapnel from the tin plate mine opened up Farrell's face. It wasn't easy to do a great job of battlefield surgery on the slope of a hill with the enemy popping mortar shells your way and screaming 'Yanqui, you die!' over their bullhorns.

'Help you?' Farrell said, his voice bored.

'BLT, easy on the mayo, and a double Maker's Mark if you wouldn't mind, Beagle.'

Farrell called out something unintelligible in Dutch toward a closed door at the far end of the bar, then turned slowly back to Holliday, a suspicious look in his eyes. 'What did you call me?'

'Beagle, just like everyone else.'

The man involuntarily reached up with one finger and touched an ear. 'Am I supposed to know you or something?'

'November 1967, Hill eight eighty-two, Dak To. I was the one who sewed that up,' said Holliday, pointing at the scar. 'You called me Frankenstein after that.'

'Doc Holliday! I'll be screwed, blued and tattooed! It's been, what, thirty-five years or something?' The ex-Ranger grinned from one big ear to the other, turning the scar into a curling snake slithering across his face.

'Closer to forty-five.'

'You're not still in, are you?'

'I was for a long time.'

'You look like you took a few hits of your own.'

'Here and there.'

'So, what you been up to lately?'

'Wandering around the world, getting into trouble.'

A Chinese cook appeared with the BLT, dropped it in front of Holliday and retreated. Farrell made a generous double of Maker's Mark and set it down on the bar. 'What kind of trouble?'

Holliday took a bite of the sandwich, which was delicious, and sipped his drink. 'The kind of trouble that might require some new documents.'

'What kind of documents?'

'Passports, drivers' licenses, birth certificates, the works.'

'You been getting into serious trouble, then, Doc.' Farrell shook his head. 'Not the Doc I knew.'

'Not the Doc I knew, either,' said Holliday. 'Don't worry, though, Beagle. I'm still on the side of truth, justice and the American way.'

'Well, that's okay, then, Doc.' Farrell smiled. 'None of us are the way we were back then. All of us are missing parts of one kind or another.'

'Can you help me out?'

'I think I got a name and an address somewhere, but this guy is bad news, Doc. He does good work, but he'd slit your throat for a dollar if he could get away with it.'

'Nice friends you have.'

'Nice friends don't forge passports.'

'True enough.'

Holliday stayed and finished his sandwich and whiskey, talking about old times with his scarred buddy from a lifetime ago, but old times weren't necessarily good times and he left with both of them promising to stay in touch and both of them knowing they were lying.

Holliday called the number Farrell had given him, and he and Eddie arrived at the appointed address shortly after eight o'clock the following evening. Kostum King was located between a Christian bookstore and a Braun café on Raadhuisstraat between the Herrengracht and the Singel canals in the center of Old Amsterdam. It was a narrow building with a tattered blue awning and four dusty-looking Michael Jackson Thriller costumes complete with shoes and rubber masks dangling in the window from what looked suspiciously like meat hooks. The sign on the door said CLOSED, but Holliday rang the bell anyway.

The man who answered was short, scraggly-haired, clubfooted and with a large hump on his back. The suit he wore was as dusty as the Michael Jackson costumes.

'*Ja?*'

'Dirk Hartog?'

'*Ja.*'

'Darby sent us.'

'Ah yes, come in.'

They stepped into the shop, bypassing the hunchback, who closed and locked the door behind him. The shop was long and narrow with costumes of all kinds hanging in gloomy rows. None of them looked as though they'd been rented in years, and the most modern U.S. president mask they appeared to have was Richard Nixon. There was even a Jane Fonda mask and a set of long-haired Beatles masks lined up on a shelf. The hunchback led them to a door at the back of the room and opened it, ushering them inside. It was an office, crammed with filing cabinets and a large wooden desk with a vinyl-covered office chair. There were two other chairs for guests and a coffee machine on top of one of the filing cabinets. The only picture on the walls was a framed Rembrandt cigar ad from a magazine. To the right of the hanging picture was another door, probably leading into some sort of storeroom. The hunchback sat down at the desk, slipped out of the hunchback jacket and the scragglyhaired wig and slipped off the clubfoot shoe.

'Much better,' sighed the man happily. 'Now, what can I do for you gentlemen?'

'Identity papers.'

'*Ja*. Any particular type?'

'Passports, driver's license, birth certificate.'

'Any particular country?'

'Canada. My friend in the Dominican Republic.'

'You have pictures?'

'Yes.' Holliday and Eddie handed over sets of passport photographs they had taken earlier in the day.

'It will be expensive.'

'How expensive?'

'Five thousand euros. For each of you.'

'No problem.'

'Half now and your original passports.'

'Fine.' Holliday had already hit the bank machine and withdrawn money from one of the hundreds of accounts in Helder Rodrigues's secret notebook. Having expected something like this, he took ten five-hundred-euro notes out of his wallet and put them in front of the man. He and Eddie put their real passports on the desk. Hartog swept them up. '*Goed*,' he said. 'Come back in three days. Same time.'

They spent the three days sightseeing, going to most of the big museums like the Rijksmuseum, the State Museum, newly renovated, and of the course the world-famous Rembrandt Museum. They watched a diamond being cut and even took a boat ride through the city's canals. At five past eight, three days after their first meeting, Holliday knocked on Hartog's door. This time he was wearing a plain dark suit and a Richard Nixon mask. He met them at the door with the famous V for Victory sign the ex-president had given from the door of *Marine One* before making his long trip into purgatory, and then led them into the back office. There were fresh documents laid out on the desk. Holliday picked up his passport and Eddie picked up his.

'Very nice,' said Holliday.

'They are blanks from a friend I have at the consulate. If anyone ever matches the holograms, your names are on file. I even managed to get you Ontario Health Cards. Unfortunately, although the cards are real they are not in circulation, so if you are breaking your leg you are on your own, *ja*.' Hartog laughed behind the Nixon mask.

'That only accounts for three photographs; we gave you four. And where are our original passports?'

Hartog snapped his fingers. 'I must have left them in the workroom downstairs.' He got to his feet, made the V sign again and disappeared through the rear door of the office.

Eddie frowned. 'This has fish in it.' He leaned over the desk and twisted Hartog's phone around. It had three buttons on it and one of them was lit.

'You're right.' Holliday nodded, standing up. 'It is fishy.' They pocketed their new documents and headed for the rear door of the office.

Behind the door was a small plain foyer lit by a single bulb and a set of heavy plank stairs leading downward. Holliday went first with Eddie right behind him.

The room was low ceilinged, dark, with a makeshift darkroom in one corner, a long table fitted with a laminating machine, a drafting table and a large color Xerox in one corner. Hartog was sitting at the long table talking in Dutch when Holliday and Eddie appeared. There was a fuming pipe in his mouth and a lighter on the table beside him. On seeing them he muttered something into the phone and hung up quickly. He put down the pipe.

'Talking to someone?' Holliday asked.

'My friend.'

'How long before your friend shows up?'

Hartog suddenly pulled out a desk drawer in the table and reached inside. Eddie took one step forward, grabbed the ten-foot-long oak table and overturned it, dumping Hartog off his stool. Holliday stepped over the table, bent down and picked up a compact little automatic pistol off the floor. A Walther PPK, the James Bond gun. He pointed it at Hartog. 'The passports and the pictures.'

'In the drawer,' replied the Dutchman. Eddie checked the drawer and came up with the documents.

'Who were you talking to?' Holliday asked, pointing the gun roughly at the center of Hartog's face, now devoid of its Richard Nixon mask.

'A lawyer.'

'What's his name?'

'Derlagen.'

'Why?'

'He has contacts.'

'Who is he sending?'

'Some people.'

'How many?'

'Two, three, I don't know.'

'They're coming to kill us?'

'Yes.'

'Once upon a time it wouldn't have occurred to me

to do this,' said Holliday. 'But people change.' He squeezed the trigger on the Walther and put a bullet into Hartog's head just above the bridge of his nose.

He looked around the room, found a gallon tin of acetone for cleaning the press and spread it over everything, including Hartog. He dribbled a train of acetone to the bottom of the stairs and then used the lighter to start the fire.

'Come on,' said Holliday. 'We better get out of here before the bad guys arrive.' He stood for a moment at the foot of the stairs, watching the fire gain strength; then he followed Eddie back to the main floor.

By the time they reached the store itself, Holliday realized they were too late. Someone was rattling at the door. There was a quick, brittle sound of glass breaking and then the door was unlatched. Holliday motioned Eddie to the left as the two men slipped in between the hanging racks of costumes.

Holliday could already smell the smoke from the fire downstairs, and it wouldn't be long before the whole store was consumed. As the two men approached, he tensed, waiting for the right moment. He had the flat little Walther, but small caliber or not, it still made a lot of noise.

When it came, it came without thinking for both men. As his man passed him by, Eddie stepped out into the aisle, grabbed the man's right wrist and bent it back toward his shoulder blades, forcing him to drop his weapon, a large-caliber automatic with a suppressor on it. That accomplished, the Cuban kicked the man's legs out from under him, put a knee in his spine and wrapped an arm around his head, pulling sharply until he heard the bone at the base of the intruder's skull snap.

Holliday's man wasn't much different. Holliday used the butt of the Walther to punch him in the throat, swept his legs out from under him and broke his neck. The smell of smoke was very strong now, and Holliday could see flames behind the glass in the office window. He flipped his man over and checked in his pockets.

'Shit.'

'*Qué?*' Eddie asked.

'They're company men. CIA Philpott's put a hit out on us.'

'A hit?' Eddie asked. '*Como un golpe en la cabeza? No lo entiendo.*'

'A kill order. We've got to get out of Amsterdam, fast.'

3

They took the six fifty a.m. KLM flight the following day and arrived in Toronto in the late afternoon. Holliday used his new passport and driver's license to open up an account at the Royal Bank of Canada Airport branch; then he and Eddie took a town car into the city. They booked into the Park Hyatt at Avenue Road and Bloor Street, which was kitty-corner to the University of Toronto's Centre for Medieval Studies, had a room service steak and then Eddie bailed out and was asleep on the couch within five minutes. Holliday gathered up his key card and went down to the business center.

Using the account codes he'd long ago learned from the notebook the monk Helder Rodrigues had given him, Holliday transferred one hundred and fifty thousand dollars in U.S funds from the Royal Bank of Canada's main branch in Nassau in the Bahamas to his newly opened account in Toronto. He booked off the hotel computer, the online fees charged directly to the suite, then went back upstairs, had a quick shot of Scotch from the minibar, listening to Eddie snoring on the couch while he looked out at the lights of the city, then went to bed himself, giving in to the fatigue he'd endured in Ramstein's hospital and his much more recent jet lag. He was asleep within a minute of his head hitting the pillows.

The next morning he and Eddie went to the hotel concierge, asked a number of questions and got satisfactory answers. Their first chore was a taxi ride to a store called Save More Surplus on the western edge of a public housing project ten or eleven blocks from the flying saucer shape of Toronto City Hall. Eddie bought a battered knapsack with a faded Canadian flag sewn onto the flap, and Holliday bought two black Samsonite F'lite hard-shell suitcases. They then had the taxi do a U-turn and take them west along Queen Street until they reached a store called Henry's Photo. While the taxi waited Holliday went into the big store, bought a Nikon D2X camera body and every lens and accessory that was available as well as a large block of cutout hard foam to protect it all.

They dropped their purchases off at the hotel, then took a second taxi to the local Walmart, where they bought a commercial-grade Weston Vacuum Sealer with an eighteen-inch seal, a box of one hundred large bags, two bottles of Krazy Glue and a black yoga mat.

They took the sealer and their other purchases back to the hotel, where Holliday dropped off Eddie and continued on to Royal Bank Plaza at the foot of Yonge Street, Toronto's version of Broadway. The main branch of the bank was housed in a somewhat ostentatious skyscraper with gold-tinted faceted windows. Banks, never really liking the idea of people withdrawing money, balked slightly at Holliday requesting a hundred thousand dollars in American twenties, but eventually and after a few phone calls to the Bahamas they complied, giving him the money in a white cardboard box with a discreet lion rampant logo in one corner. Holliday immediately took the money back to the hotel, and the real labors began.

'You really think this is going to work, *mi colonel*?' Eddie asked, staring at their purchases spread out across the dining table in their suite.

'If what you tell me about customs at Jose Marti Airport is right, it should work like a charm,' Holliday said, smiling at his friend.

One hundred thousand dollars in American twenty-dollar bills weighs almost exactly eleven pounds. Each bill is approximately six inches by two inches, which means that a total of twenty-seven stacks of forty-seven twenties, or one hundred thousand dollars in total, can be vacuum-sealed in a single eighteen-by-eighteen-inch bag a little less than a quarter of an inch high. With the black lining of the Samsonite carefully removed, the bag could be glued to the back of the suitcase, covered with a carefully cut piece of black foam from the yoga mat and then the black nylon lining replaced. Which is exactly what they did.

At the concierge's suggestion they had an excellent dinner of osso buco at a restaurant simply called Grace and returned to the hotel. Back in their suite, Holliday trimmed the camera foam to the exact dimensions of the doctored suitcase, then cutouts for the camera body, the lenses and accessories. With that complete,

Holliday went down to the business center and within half an hour he had cut and pasted off the Internet to make himself fifty 'engraved' business cards, using the name on his passport and driver's license:

UNESCO WORLD HERITAGE CENTER
JOHN LEESON
SENIOR STAFF PHOTOGRAPHER

He made another set identifying Eddie as his assistant and printed those out, as well. Considering the fact that Havana was a Unesco World Heritage city, it made sense that they would send a photographer assistant around every few years to document and project on the restoration of historic buildings in the city, and all the camera equipment in the suitcase would easily disguise the added eleven pounds of weight.

'That's about it,' Holliday said. 'Tomorrow we buy some clothes and a few guidebooks in the morning, have our meeting down the street in the afternoon and the next day we fly to Cuba.'

'And pray that everything goes as we have planned when we get there,' added Eddie.

Dr Steven Braintree's office at the University of Toronto's Centre for Medieval Studies was located on the third floor of a large, stodgy-looking neo-Georgian building kitty-corner to the hotel on the southern side of Bloor Street. The office was pretty much the way Holliday had remembered: piles of papers on piles of file folders on piles of books with a few overflowing filing cabinets and more files, papers and books piled on his wide windowsill. Braintree hadn't changed much, either; there were a few flecks of gray in his long dark hair now, but the trendy Prada glasses, the sneakers and the jeans were just the same. This time the message on his black T-shirt said FREE GIGI'S! PIZZA GIGI'S, BEST PIZZA IN TORONTO – PICKY POT-HEADS PICK PIZZA GIGI'S.

Holliday made the introductions and they sat down in what little space was left. 'Been a while, Colonel. I was a little surprised to hear from you,' said Braintree. Holliday had been following clues to the origins of the Templar sword he'd found hidden in his uncle Henry's house, and Braintree had been on the list. 'You ever find what you were looking for?' asked the history professor.

'Too much, when you get right down to it,' Holliday replied. It had never occurred to him that there would be a litter of bodies left behind him on his search or that the monk Helder Rodrigues would pass along the best-kept secret in seven hundred years before dying in his arms.

'So, what can I do for you now?' Braintree asked.

'Tell me everything you know about the Templars in Cuba.'

Braintree glanced at Eddie. '*Te Cubana?*'

'*Sí, Doctore.*' Eddie nodded.

'Miami?'

'*Alamar,*' responded the Cuban with a smile. Braintree laughed.

'*Un cubano real, entonces,*' said Braintree.

'*Sí,*' said Eddie.

According to Braintree, after the dissolution of the Templar order by Pope Clement in 1312, its remnants fled in all directions, some across the English Channel into England and Scotland, some – as Holliday well knew – to the Azores and some to Portugal and Spain. The ones who crossed the Pyrenees Mountains into the Catalonian Province of Spain enjoyed a brief life as the Christ Knights of Catalonia, but they were quickly rooted out by the Catholic king of Spain. Those who traveled by sea and landed in Portugal fared much better and came under the protection of King Diniz under the name the Order of Christ in 1319, which led directly to Emmanuel I and Christopher Columbus.

'*That* you'll have to explain,' said Holliday.

Braintree did. Although virtually every school history text in North America identified Columbus as an Italian from Genoa, there was virtually no real evidence of this at all. It was far more likely that he was born in either Spain or, even likelier, Portugal.

By 1492, the year Columbus sailed west to what he thought was the Indies, both Columbus and Emmanuel I were members of the *Ordem Militar de Cristo*, or the Military Order of Christ, the present incarnation of the Knights Templar in Portugal at the time. Although Columbus soughts funds from Isabella of Spain for his voyage of discovery, he already had a secret pact with Emmanuel that any information about his voyage that he gave to Spain should also be given to Portugal. Columbus agreed and the Templar cross on the sails of his famous ships, the *Nina*, the *Pinta* and the *Santa Maria*, were a signal to Emmanuel that their secret bond would be kept.

Columbus spent very little time on the island of Cuba before moving on to Hispaniola, or what is now known as Haiti, and the Dominican Republic. One of the crew members on the first voyage, a man in his midtwenties and of prominent birth, Diego Velázquez, caught Columbus's eye and soon after they settled in Hispaniola, Columbus ritually made Velázquez an officer in the *Ordem Militar de Cristo*, an honor the young Spaniard took very seriously. Nineteen years later in 1511, Velázquez, now known as Don Diego Velázquez de Cuéllar, was ordered by Diego Columbus, Christopher Columbus's firstborn child and now viceroy of the West Indies, to occupy and conquer the island of Cuba. For the next five years Don Diego Velázquez established a number of settlements, including, most notably, Santiago de Cuba and San Cristóbal de Havana, a small town just west of present-day Havana. For these efforts Don Diego Velázquez was made governor of Cuba by Diego Columbus. To commemorate the discovery of Havana, Don Diego built *La Templete*, a small neoclassical temple, which would soon become the headquarters for Don Diego's version of the *Ordem Militar de Cristo*, which he named the Brotherhood of the Knights of Christ, *La Hermandad dos Cavaleiros de Cristo*. Very soon after this, at least between its members it became known simply as *La Hermandad* or the Brotherhood.

'Does it still exist?' Holliday asked.

Braintree shrugged. 'There've been all sorts of rumors over the years, just like the never-ending rumors of the original Templar, but soon after conquering Cuba, Velázquez fell out of favor with Diego Columbus during Cortez's conquest of Mexico, and stripped of authority, he died in Santiago de Cuba in 1524. Most probably the Brotherhood died with him.'

'Or maybe not,' said Eddie quietly.

4

The Air Canada A320 came in low over the sea, reaching land in the early afternoon. The gently rolling countryside below could just as easily have been rural France – fields, farms and small villages crouched in broad valleys or perched on low hills, all connected by country roads that led to broader highways.

'*Mi patria precioso,*' whispered Eddie with a choke in his voice as he stared down at the landscape from the window seat of the narrow-body jet.

'Let's just hope we get out of the airport,' said Holliday.

'We will, *mi colonel*, but remember, after that you must listen very carefully to what I tell you about how things work in this place.'

'I promise to obey every command.' Holliday smiled. Eddie raised an expressive eyebrow. An instant later the slightly ominous whir and thump of the flaps lowering filled the interior of the aircraft and they began their final approach to Jose Marti International Airport.

Terminal 3 at Jose Marti was built specifically for international arrivals and departures, showcasing Cuba as a modern twenty-first-century country, which everybody, especially the Cubans, knows it is not. The architecture was slick: glass, steel and open-beam high ceilings with crisscrossing assemblies of pipe and I-beams, some of them hung with large versions of the world's flags, including the Stars and Stripes. The Cuban government might hate American foreign policy and politicians, but they love American tourists. Although there have been no sanctioned flights to Cuba since 1960, the Cubans found ways around the problem almost immediately. Americans could reach Cuba by first going to Canada, Mexico or the Bahamas and flying onward from those countries. Instead of passport entry and exit stamps, Cuban customs provided the tourist with a small separate visa slipped into the passport on arrival and removed on departure. Although each tourist who visited Cuba from the United States could technically be arrested under the Trading with the Enemy Act, it didn't stop more than one hundred and fifty thousand tourists a year from going there, although most of the guidebooks suggest that they shouldn't announce their American citizenship too loudly and might even go so far as to wear a Canada pin, or a Canadian flag patch, on their knapsacks. On the other hand, there is a regular St Patrick's Day on O'Reilly Street in Havana, complete with a pipe band, green beer and a choir singing 'Danny Boy' in a Spanish accent. After all, it was rumored that even Che Guevara had Irish-American roots, and of course, even Castro himself had an American connection – in the late 1940s Fidel had been offered a five-thousand-dollar signing bonus by the New York Giants.

Holliday shuffled toward customs in the big, noisy terminal trying to figure what the impact on the world would have been if Castro had signed with the team and had a career as a major league pitcher. Perhaps there would have been one Batista after another for the next fifty years, all with a cozy relationship with the United States. American sugar, fruit and tobacco interests would have flourished, and so would the Mafia. Cuba could have stayed as corrupt as any of its neighbors to the south, or its slightly wackier compatriots in North Africa and the Middle East. American servicemen from Guantánamo on leave in Havana, picking up hookers in the bars and clubs and gambling in the casinos like the Riviera, the Capri or the Sans Souci. Blacks still unemancipated, working as cane cutters or in the tobacco fields, the vast majority of the country illiterate and poor.

He reached the head of the line, put both bags on the big industrial scales and waited while the weight figure was computed, paying the fee in U.S. dollars. Then he was signaled to the customs counter.

'Passport, senor,' demanded the uniformed customs agent. Behind him sat two men in suits and dark glasses, both reading *Granma*, the official newspaper. These would be the airport police that Eddie had warned him about.

Holliday handed over the blue-covered Canadian passport identifying him as John Leeson, smiling pleasantly.

'You are Canadian?'

'Yes.'

'You have traveled to a great many places, senor,' said the customs official, flipping through the pages. Holliday had been very specific to Hartog the forger about the stamps he wanted, including five countries with UNESCO Preservation sites, among them India, Japan, Peru and New Zealand.

'So I have,' said Holliday, keeping his tone genial.

'You are here on business or pleasure, senor?'

'A bit of both, mostly business.' He handed over the business card he'd made at the Hyatt in Toronto.

'You pay to fix our great buildings, yes?'

'I just take the pictures for the bosses. All of us have our bosses, right?'

'That is correct, *sí*.' The customs official smiled. 'We all have our bosses. Please, senor, put your suitcases on the counter and open them.'

Holliday did as he was told. Once the cases were on the counter, he unlocked them and pulled them open. The customs official rummaged through the clothes, felt the sides, bottom and back, then indicated that Holliday could close the first up. The customs man checked the second suitcase.

'A lot of camera equipment,' commented the official. At some invisible signal the two men reading newspapers stood up and stood beside the suitcase. As well as the camera case, there were round slots for thirty metal film containers. The taller of the two security men opened a few of the film containers at random while the other watched for a reaction from Holliday.

There was none. The tall security man then told Holliday to take out the hard foam insert. Holliday handed it to the man, who checked the bottom before setting it aside; if things could be inserted into the foam from above, it was logical that they could be inserted from below. He turned his attention to the red nylon lining, poking at it with a long finger.

'It is . . . soft,' said the taller man in the dark glasses. 'Why is this?'

'I put a foam pad behind the lining as more protection for the camera equipment.'

'Show me,' said the man.

Holliday did so, pulling aside a four-inch section of the nylon lining that he'd left loose after gluing the section of yoga mat into the suitcase. It was the mark of an experienced traveler who had to explain the same thing to other customs and security people at airports all over the world.

'Why do you not use one of those aluminum suitcases, the square one?'

'That's the best way I know to get your equipment stolen. The only people who use Halliburton cases do so because they've got valuable stuff inside or because they're trying to look cool. I prefer any old suitcase myself.'

The security man gave Holliday a long look, then nodded to himself. 'What hotel are you staying at, senor?'

'The Nacional,' answered Holliday. 'Where else?'

'Of course,' said the security man. 'You may close the suitcases now, senor. Welcome to Cuba.'

And that was that. He closed the suitcases, found his way to the exit and stepped outside into the blistering heat to wait for Eddie. He spotted half a dozen taxis, including a 1949 Ford Victoria, a '41 Dodge four-door sedan in powder blue and a Cadillac El Dorado convertible in bright pink. There was even a '31 Ford Model A in two tones of green with cream-colored wheels, whitewall tires and a steel luggage rack at the back.

'They have friends in Miami who send them the money to fix them up,' said Eddie, his voice quiet. He stared right ahead. 'And remember – half the drivers work for secret police.'

Holliday chose the '49 Dodge – his uncle Henry had driven one all through Holliday's childhood and his early adolescence. It reminded him of the smell of rubber on a hot day and egg salad sandwiches when he and Henry and his cousin Peggy went on camping trips.

Like many things in Havana, the Hotel Nacional was definitely a blast from the past. It had been built in the '30s by the famous New York architects McKim, Meade and Wright, and bore a strong resemblance to the Breakers, the Beaux-Arts hotel in Palm Beach. It wasn't surprising since the Breakers architects, Shultze and Walker, were contemporaries with

McKim, building such well-known hotels as the Pierre, the Waldorf-Astoria and the Sherry Netherland.

Stepping into the narrow lobby, its high ceiling done in dark coffered oak, the walls a pale creamy yellow, Holliday was uneasily reminded of the scene in *The Shining* when Danny Torrance was rumbling down the halls on his Big Wheel, Stanley Kubrick's camera looking over his shoulder.

They booked the Rita Hayworth two-bedroom suite and settled in. It was no five-star hotel as advertised, but it wasn't too bad; somewhere above a Best Western but not as good as the Waldorf. The suite had a balcony that looked out over the Malecon seawall to the ocean, and that was certainly something. Eddie did a cursory check for electronic bugs – usually not used in places like the Nacional according to Eddie – unless the Special Brigade had some interest in you, in which case it would have been likely they'd be taken to the dungeons under Morro Castle on the other side of the harbor and fed to the few remaining rats in the city – you don't have rats where there is nothing for them to eat. When Eddie was satisfied they ordered a bottle of Havana Club Rum, some ice and some Cokes and a Cohiba Behike 52, if they had it. When the rum, the Cokes and the cigar arrived on its own small silver serving platter with a cutter and a small silver receptacle full of matches, Holliday and Eddie sat out on the balcony to watch the sun go down and figure out the next step in the plan to find Eddie's brother, Domingo.

'You must remember, Doc, this is not the Cuba of my youth,' cautioned Eddie, puffing on the aromatic cigar. He sipped his rum and stared thoughtfully out over the Malecon and the darkening sea beyond. 'In my early days, when I was in the Pioneers, they were my best days, you understand? Everything was ahead of us. We went out into the fields each year to gather vegetables and to cut the cane and pick the fruit and it meant something. Fidel would lead us to better times, better days ahead. Everything was about the future, and for a while it was true. Before Fidel a black man could never have gone to university. Most didn't even go to school at all, but now we were equal, all of us, men, women, black, white, mulatto . . . none of that mattered . . . as long as we listened to Fidel and to Che.'

'So, what happened?' Holliday asked, enjoying the faint but cooling onshore breeze coming up from the ocean and riffling the curtains behind them.

'The lies began. Fidel would blame the "embargo" for everything . . . there was a food shortage because of the "embargo," a clothing shortage "embargo," always the same, but we could see it – a ten-ton truck packed with tomatoes rotting in the sun because no one had organized transportation or distribution. . . . There were rumors that all was not well among *El Comandante* and his friends. Have you ever heard the name Manuel Piñeiro Losada?'

'I don't think so.' Holliday shrugged.

'He was Fidel's head of the Dirección General de Inteligencia, DGI. Cuban intelligence. Between Losada and Fidel they convinced Che that the next step in the socialization of the Americas lay in Bolivia, of all places. Bolivia is more than four thousand kilometers from Cuba – what did it have to do with us? But Fidel and Losada told him the Bolivian Communist Party would rise to his aid. It wasn't true, just like it wasn't true for the poor *bastardos* at the Bay of Pigs. He left Cuba with his little group of less than twenty men in the middle of February, and by April he was dead, his guerrilla force wiped out, betrayed to the CIA by Losada.'

'Interesting piece of history, but what does it have to do with right now?' Holliday asked, cracking an ice cube between his teeth.

'People stopped believing in the lies. How do you say, the people and the government became . . . isolated from each other. First the Russians came and brought their KGB, then the Chinese and then finally we had no one. Nothing worked. There was no food, no coffee, no parts to replace the aircraft and the tanks. There was only the black market and the generals smuggling drugs. We traded doctors and engineers to Venezuela for gasoline, but that was all. No one cared about Fidel or Raul. They only believed in the Secret Police in their big houses with swimming pools in Atabey. Like a famous writer said . . . *"El emperador ya no responde a su teléfono."* The emperor no longer answers his telephone. Fidel is over. There are two Cubas now, the people and the generals, each general with . . . *su propio pedazo de la torta.* His own piece of the pie, yes? There is no government at all.'

'The Middle Ages,' said Holliday quietly. Eddie was telling him that Cuba had collapsed into fiefdoms, lords and vassals, masters and slaves; it was the ultimate expression of rich and poor; *Blade Runner* where the technology stopped dead in 1959. A *Clockwork Orange* in a 1958 Edsel. Anarchy.

'*Sí,*' answered Eddie with a sneer, 'and not one black man among them.' He shook his head sadly. 'This is not a revolution I can believe in. It is not a revolution *anyone* believes in anymore. Fidel speaks, but there are no ears to listen.'

'So, what do we do?'

'Just remember that anyone who walks behind you who looks like he is eating well is probably Secret Police, and bring a great many of those American dollars with you. . . . There will be lots of *soborno* to pay.'

'Bribes?'

'*Sí, mi colonel,* lots of bribes.'

5

They met the man at La Taberna de la Muralles, a café and bar on a small cobbled plaza in Old Havana, the following day at lunchtime. He was in his fifties, with a rugged, clean-shaven face that had seen a lot of sun. He wore a porkpie hat that made him look a little bit like Gene Hackman in the *French Connection*, dark glasses and he had a napkin tucked into his white silk guayabera shirt as he ate a plate of assorted *pastelitos* – Cuban puff pastry stuffed with savory fillings. His gleaming hair looked too perfectly black to be true.

'Who is he?' Holliday asked as they approached his table on the crowded outdoor patio.

'His name is Cesar Diaz. He is a policeman, a detective, in fact,' said Eddie.

'We're buying information from a *cop*?' Holliday asked.

'He is the brother of my sister's husband,' explained Eddie.

'Still . . .' worried Holliday.

'The police are as poor as the people they're supposed to serve. Five pesos a month doesn't buy anything on the black market. They have to make their way just like everyone else.'

They sat down and Eddie did the introductions. Diaz offered them pastries from his plate, but they declined. He ordered coffee for them all, wiped the crumbs off his lips with his makeshift bib and sat back in his chair. He really was beginning to look like Popeye Doyle.

'Eddie Cabrera, it has been a very long time,' said Diaz, speaking slightly accented English.

'Africa,' said Eddie. 'Other places more recently.'

'There are some people in the *Dirección de Inteligencia* who would be interested to know you are back in Cuba. You must know that, of course.'

'And if you so much as whispered my name, you must know what would happen to your brothers and your uncles and your aunts and your good friend Tomas who you play dominos with, even that dog of yours – what is his name?'

'Romeo.' Diaz smiled. 'You have turned very hard, Eddie. I must say this.'

'Try fighting with Ochoa Sánchez in Angola – that would make you hard, too.'

'Ochoa was executed in the Tropas Especiales.'

'Everyone is executed eventually who disagrees with Fidel. Which is why I stayed in Africa.'

'Probably a wise move.'

'I thought so.'

'But now you are home again,' said Diaz. 'And you want something.'

'That's right.' Eddie nodded. The coffee arrived, the real thing in tiny cups – thick and strong and black.

'So tell me,' said Diaz, sipping. He took a red-and-white package of Populars from the pocket of his guayabera and lit one with what looked suspiciously like a gold Dunhill lighter, or at least a pretty good knockoff. Holliday noticed that the detective was wearing a stainless steel Omega Constellation on his left wrist. Whatever the detective was doing for money was clearly quite lucrative.

'My brother, Domingo, has disappeared,' Eddie said flatly.

'A lot of people are disappearing these days.' Diaz shrugged, smoking. 'You have been away too long, Eddie; things have changed. Fidel gives lectures on the television about robots and Mars and how atomic bombs all over the world are leaking their radiation into the air, which is causing the hurricanes to get worse each year. He thinks American drones fly over his house all day looking for ways to poison his food. Raul dreams of his farm in Spain. The generals fight to see who will be the next *comandante*. The rest of Cuba thinks it wants to go to Miami.' He shrugged again. 'Not to mention that Domingo had the misfortune to work for the Operations Division of the Ministry of the Interior and who knows what that means? There was even a rumor he worked at Lourdes and at Mantanzas.'

Holliday had heard of Lourdes; it was a giant signal intelligence operation built by the Russians and completed by the Chinese. Effectively it was the Cuban version of the NSA, a giant ear, listening to America. He'd never heard of Mantanzas, so he asked.

'You know the CIA operates a training camp for new agents called the Farm?'

'I think I've heard of it,' said Holliday evasively. In fact, he'd once been an instructor at the installation at Camp Peary in the Virginia countryside. He didn't dare mention it.

'That is what Mantanzas is,' said Diaz, stubbing out his cigarette. 'Carlos the Jackal trained there in 1962.'

'You have no idea where he is?' Holliday asked.

'No, senor,' said Diaz, shaking his head.

'Can you ask questions, perhaps?'

'Careful questions. For a price.'

'What price?'

'A thousand. U.S dollars, of course, to start.'

'How about five hundred?'

'For now.'

Holliday took ten fresh twenties out of his wallet and laid them neatly on the table. Diaz covered them with his big hand and slid them out of sight.

'That is not five hundred dollars, *senor*,' said the cop.

'No. It's two hundred. Another three when you bring us some information we can use.'

'How do I contact you?'

'Tell my sister you wish to talk. She will know how to reach me. I will choose the place,' said Eddie. '*Vamos a necesitar armas.*'

'What kind of weapons?' asked Diaz blandly, lighting another *Popular*.

'*Pistolas,*' said Eddie.

'Makarov?'

'Two, with fifty rounds and an extra clip each.'

'A thousand.'

'*Mierde,*' scoffed Eddie. 'I can get an AK-47 for a hundred and eighty dollars in Mozambique and still with the greased paper on it. Do better, Cesar, and maybe there will be more business we can do together. Two hundred each, pay when we get them.'

'Are you sure we can trust this guy to get us guns?' asked Holliday. 'Maybe he's setting us up.'

'This is not America, senor. We do not have – what do you call them? Stings? We are all on the same side here, senor.' He rubbed his fingers together and winked. 'The side with cash in its pockets, *comprendez?*' Diaz frowned. 'Once upon a time Cuba was a paradise, senor. Now it is a jungle and the only object is to survive.' He stood up abruptly, pushed back his chair and walked away.

'What now?' Holliday asked.

Eddie watched Diaz go, a thoughtful expression on his face. Holliday looked around the square. From where he sat and from what he'd seen, there was nothing but music, cafés, good food and pretty women in Havana; it was a museum piece, a country caught in amber, a giant tourist trap, perhaps, but so far he hadn't seen much of Diaz's jungle.

'Now?' Eddie said at last. 'We must go to see my mother and I must pay my respects to her and tell her I am here.'

Eddie's mother lived in a second-floor apartment on the Calle Maloja, a narrow street well off the Avenida

Salvador Allende to the north. This was no place of cafés and tourists but something akin to a run-down backstreet somewhere in the French Quarter of New Orleans.

The colored stucco was broken and old, showing the water-stained limestone beneath, there was a maze of wires and cables running up and down the outer walls and sagging over the street to the other side, and the sidewalks beneath were cracked and broken and clearly hadn't been repaired since they were put down.

There were one or two ancient vehicles parked, pulled haphazardly off the street and the archways at the main level, which might once have been home to small businesses that were long since shuttered and locked. Oddly, on the ornate wrought-iron balcony that ran the length of the second story, there was more than one satellite TV dish, poking its seeking parabola toward the bright blue, blazing sky.

By comparison the inside of Anna Margarita Alfonso's apartment was pleasant, well appointed with a few pieces of old Victorian-style furniture, framed photographs of her children, grandchildren, nephews, nieces, aunts, uncles and other ancestors displayed on one pale blue wall.

Eddie's mother wore a blue housedress and slippers. She was very slim, her face dark as chocolate, with her son's aristocratic cheekbones and a narrow patrician nose. Her hair was snow-white and done up in a scrap of cloth. Eddie compared her to the pictures on the wall. Two photographs in particular caught Holliday's eye – a wedding photograph of a young man in his early thirties, very dark, and his even darker-skinned bride in a blazing white dress standing on the steps of some official-looking building, both figures looking ecstatically happy.

Parked to one side at the foot of the steps was a gigantic black 1960 Cadillac Special with whitewall tires and a raised wheel well set into the front fender, dating the photograph easily enough. The other picture showed the same striking black woman in a dramatic pose, backlit and wearing the maid's costume of Dolores in the Spanish opera of the same name.

On the other wall was a large plasma TV. A silent man in his seventies or eighties wearing a grimy wifebeater was sitting in what looked to be the original Barcalounger drinking from a tall brown bottle of Bucanero beer and smoking cheap *veguero* cigarettes. He was watching Miami channel 7.

'My *teo*, Fidelio. He used to work for the garbage, but he was let go two years ago. He comes here because my mother has a big TV and the satellite.'

'How the hell did she get a plasma TV? I thought the whole country was starving to death.'

'Her nephew Victor, my cousin, works for Air Cubana. They can bring back anything. In Cuba you have to know people,' Eddie explained.

Eddie embraced his mother. '*Madre*,' he said softly.

'*Mi niño hermoso!*' she wailed, and burst into tears. They stood like that for a moment and then she pushed

Eddie away and slapped him lightly across his broadly smiling tearstained face. '*Whay no han visitado a su madre en tan largo tiempo?*'

Holliday didn't need a translation. Teo Fidelio noticed nothing. Eddie's mother turned to Holliday.

'*Y qué es su amigo?*'

Eddie made the introductions. His mother answered in excellent English.

'You are a doctor?' Anna Margarita Alfonso asked.

'*Se trata de un apodo, Mama,*' explained Eddie.

'You were a soldier? You look like you were a soldier,' she said, eyeing him carefully, especially the eye patch and the new slash of gray above the scar on his temple.

'I was.' He nodded.

'An American?'

'Yes.' He nodded again, glancing at Eddie.

'You come here to fight Fidel?'

'He is my friend, Mother. He has saved my life more than once.'

'*Tranquillo, niño,*' the old woman said, admonishing her son. She turned back to Holliday. 'You come here to fight Fidel?'

'I came here to find Eddie's brother, Domingo.'

'Aye, Domingo!' wailed the woman, and launched into another bout of tears. She slumped down on an old overstuffed couch against the wall full of pictures and dropped her head into her hands. Eddie sat down beside her and put a comforting arm around her shoulder.

'Mama, Mama, we will find him,' he soothed.

'Your brother was a fool!'

Teo Fidelio broke wind, lit another cigarette and switched to channel 6. *America's Got Talent*.

'Why was he a fool, Mama?'

'Because he thought working for them would protect him when . . . the *Comandante* died.'

'Who is *them*, Mama?'

'The people who run this country, Edimburgo. The people who have *always* run the country. Fidel was one, Raul another, and Domingo thought they'd let him join if he worked for them. When the end came we would all be protected.'

'Who, Mama? You must tell us who these people are if we are to find Domingo.'

'The families.'

'What families?' Eddie urged, exasperated.

'The old families. The families going back to Diego Velázquez de Cuéllar. The Ten Families.'

'How do you know all this, Mama?'

'Because when I was a girl I did the laundry in the house of Ramon Grau and many other wealthy families in Havana. A black laundry girl was invisible. I saw and heard a great many things and I remembered. The Ten Families might have different names now, but they still rule Cuba with an iron fist.'

'The Knights of the Brotherhood of Christ,' whispered Holliday. 'The Spanish Templars!'

Eddie's mother made a hissing sound and waggled her long, gnarled fingers in some strange ritual motion, then quickly crossed herself on both chest and forehead. 'There is no Christ in these people – they go to La Templete to make their three circles around the ceiba tree. They are devils!'

'Ceiba tree?' Holliday asked.

'I will explain later,' said the Cuban. The old lady looked as though she was going to have a fit. Eddie laid a calming hand on her shoulder. 'It's all right, Mama, *tranquillo, tranquillo . . .*' He turned to Holliday. 'It is like your friend in Toronto said, Doc. Fidel's family were named Vazquez. They came from Lancara in Galicia. Galicia borders Portugal. They were sailors and conquistadores.'

'*Sí.*' The old woman nodded. 'The devils met at La Templete. Domingo thought they would protect us. The fool, the fool!' she wailed again.

'What happened?' Eddie asked.

'I do not know,' said Eddie's mother, weeping openly. Teo Fidelio appeared not to notice. He lit yet another cigarette and sighed a huge cloud of smoke toward the plasma TV. Eddie's mother wiped her tears away on her apron and spoke again. 'I only know that Domingo said if there was any trouble you were to go and see Leonid.'

'Leonid?' Holliday asked.

'Leonid Maximenko,' said Eddie. 'Which means my brother is in *very* bad trouble.'

6

Leonid Maximenko lived in Atares, a barrio, or slum, on the western edge of a low hill that overlooked the southeastern end of Havana Harbor. The barrio was named for the stone fort that still stood on the summit of the hill. The bottom of the hill was skirted by the multiple tracks and switch points of the Christina Railway Station.

The barrio itself was enclosed by Avenue de Mexico Cristina on the east, Arroyo Atares on the north, Avenue de Maximo Gomez on the west and Calzada de Infanta to the south. Fifty square blocks or so encompassed some of the poorest and most wretched people of Havana; it was not a district often mentioned in any of the guidebooks.

Maximenko lived on Calle Fernandina, roughly in the center of the area. The residence was a *barabacoa*, a word originally meaning *grill* or *barbecue*, but in the barrios it meant a two- or three-story building subdivided with extra wooden floors and rooms that are invisible from the street. Maximenko's room was on the top floor of a crumbling building reached by a narrow set of stairs that wound its way upward, past a dark shared toilet with no cover and a pile of torn pieces of newspaper on a bench beside it and an open area that was clearly some kind of communal kitchen. Smoke from a makeshift brick stove and oven went up through a series of rusted stovepipes directly through a rough-sawn hole in the wooden floor, presumably venting outdoors. Several older women were cooking simultaneously while a gaggle of crying, laughing children dressed in scraps of clothing milled around their skirts playing some kind of game. In one corner of the room an old iron bed had been set up with a thin mattress and was occupied by an elderly man in a grayish diaper and nothing else. His eyes were the blind white of cataracts and the right side of his face sagged like putty.

Eddie and Holliday kept climbing.

'*Viva la revolución,*' snorted Eddie.

'I thought Fidel made sure everyone was equal in his great society.'

'Some of us were more equal than others,' said Eddie.

'Where do they come from?'

'They've always been here, *mi colonel,*' sighed Eddie.

Maximenko's room had bare walls, the plaster rotted down to the stone and mortar that had made up the outer shell of the building for two hundred years. The floor was covered in small, cracked and broken diamond-shaped ceramic tiles that were a faded turquoise color. There were four pieces of furniture in the room, a bed like the one on the floor below, a sagging couch with no feet, a wooden card table that held a green-labeled half-empty bottle of Santero Aguardiente, a cloudy plastic drinking glass, a package of

Populars, a book of matches and a tin ashtray. Beside the table was an ancient-looking Victorian cracked green leather chair that looked as if it might have belonged in a men's club a hundred years ago. There was a small window at the far end of the room that looked out on a courtyard crisscrossed with hanging lines of laundry.

Sprawled in the chair, asleep and snoring, his head thrown back and his mouth open, was a large man in his late sixties with the ruddy complexion of a heavy drinker, presumably Maximenko. He was wearing a pair of filthy cotton pants, a stained and equally filthy guayabera and a pair of bright pink rubber flip-flops. His toenails were crusted and thick as horns and his feet were dark with grime. His hair, what Holliday could see of it, was long, stringy and gray. Bad hygiene or not, the man had a barrel chest, bulging biceps and huge ham hands that looked as though he could have cracked walnuts with them. Once upon a time Maximenko had been a powerful man.

'Leonid!' Eddie said sharply. Maximenko didn't move. 'Leonid!' Eddie called again. Holliday saw the man's eyelids flutter and his snoring changed its rhythm slightly. 'Leonid!' Eddie called a third time. One of Maximenko's hands slipped between his heavy thigh and the side of the chair and came up holding an ancient-looking Tokarev semiautomatic. He sat up, coughing up something nasty and then swallowing it again. '*Pochemu vy ne mozhete pozvolit' starym spat' chelovek?*'

'Because you're not sleeping – you are drunk,' said Eddie, speaking English for Holliday's benefit.

'*Kto poluslepo odin?*' Maximenko growled, looking at Holliday. The Russian expatriate poured half a glass from the green bottle, swallowed it like medicine and lit a cigarette.

Eddie spoke. 'He is my friend, Leonid, and be polite. Speak English.'

'Who are you?' Maximenko asked Holliday, wetly clearing his throat.

'A friend of Eddie's.'

'You sound American.'

'I am.'

'You fought in wars, yes? You look like you fought in wars.'

'A few.'

'What happened to your eye?'

'Afghanistan,' said Holliday, not bothering to explain the idiotic accident that had taken the sight from his right eye. Besides, with the scar from the attack at Sheremetyevo Airport in Moscow, the wound looked much fiercer than it really was.

Maximenko grinned around the fuming cigarette and used one hand to pull the Cuban shirt up over his expansive belly. The Tokarev didn't waver in his other hand. A thick keloid scar snaked through the wiry gray hair from his navel halfway to his armpit. 'Fucking mujahideen and those Stinger missiles you gave them,' he said, smiling. 'A piece of the Flying Tank I was sitting in did that,' he said almost proudly.

'An illiterate peasant with a goat for a wife shoots down the most sophisticated helicopter gunship in the world.' He pulled down his shirt. 'The Taliban are still using them.' He laid the Tokarev on the table beside the bottle as though the comparison of war wounds had made them friends. 'What is your name?'

'Holliday. My friends call me Doc.'

Maximenko nodded sagely. 'The dentist gunfighter with tuberculosis. Best episode of *Star Trek* ever. "Specter of the Gun," twenty-five October 1968, Gene Roddenberry and Gene L. Coon. Very surreal, like a Chekhov play. You see it?'

It was Holliday's turn to smile. 'In reruns a hundred times. I was in Vietnam when it aired originally.'

'Vietnam!' Maximenko said with a barking laugh. 'In 1776 the Americans are the guerrilla fighters and the British are the imperialist colonial war machine. Two hundred years later the war is fought again but with the Americans as the imperialists and the Vietcong as the guerrillas. We never learn, do we?'

'It seems that way,' said Holliday.

There was a short silence. Finally Maximenko spoke up. 'You didn't come to this shit hole to talk to me about old war wounds and tell stories. Why are you seeing Leonid Maximenko in his retirement home?'

'Domingo,' Eddie answered.

'Domingo is an idiot,' said Maximenko.

'You were KGB in Cuba until 1989 – you know people,' Eddie insisted.

'I defected,' said Maximenko. He poured another

glass of Aguardiente and swallowed it down noisily as though he were drinking mouthwash. He butted his cigarette and lit another. 'I retired. I saw the handwriting on the wall, but I saw it too late – call it what you want, but I cannot help you now. I'm too old. I'm out of touch.'

'What do you know about the Ten Families, about the Knights of the Brotherhood of Christ?' Holliday asked.

'I know enough not to say their name too loudly,' the Russian answered.

'My brother has disappeared, Leonid. I must find him,' pleaded Eddie.

'Forget Domingo. Forget he ever existed,' said Maximenko. 'Believe me, it would be better for all of us.'

'You know I can't do that, Leonid. I must find him. You worked with him at the Ministry of the Interior. You worked with him at that place in El Cano . . . you must know something.'

'What were you doing, listening at keyholes? No one was supposed to know about the El Cano unit.'

'I was only a *niño*. No one paid attention to me, but I had ears. And none of this matters. What matters to me is my brother, Domingo. I must find him.'

'I cannot help you.' The Russian shrugged.

'Can't or won't?' Holliday said. Maximenko threw him a dark look, then turned back to Eddie.

'All I can tell you is this – his last job at the ministry was as bodyguard and driver for Deborah Castro Espin.'

Eddie looked horrified. '*La madre que te parió!*'

'Who's she?' Holliday asked.

'I tell you later, *compadre*,' answered his friend. Eddie turned back to Maximenko. 'You still have your *moto-cicleta*?'

'In the courtyard.'

'We need to borrow it.'

'Take it; that much I can do for you.' He dug around in the pocket of his grimy cotton trousers and then tossed Eddie a set of keys. By the time they left his room, he was snoring again.

The motorcycle turned out to be a massive Soviet Ural Cossack with a sidecar. The bike was a nonde-script army gray-green and it was so old it still had the mount for the MG42 ShKAS machine gun and a cra-dle for the sidecar passenger's Mosin-Nagant rifle.

'We're really going to ride around in this?' Holliday said, trying not to laugh.

'There are hundreds of these in Havana. Leftovers from *la Invasión Rusa*. They are very often seen on the streets of Havana. We need something to give us . . . mobility? As I told you, taking taxis is dangerous.'

'We can't park this at the Hotel Nacional.'

'I know a waiter there. Give him twenty dollars and he will protect it better than he would his own mother.' Eddie grinned and climbed onto the heavily sprung saddle. He fitted one of the keys Maximenko had given to him into the ignition, stood up on the starter pedal and then slammed down on it. The eight-hundred-cubic-centimeter engine roared into life. 'Into the sidecar, my friend, and I will take you for a ride.'

'I was afraid you were going to say that,' said Holliday.

The sleek pearl white Piaggio P180 Avanti turboprop landed on the private paved airstrip a mile from Lake Carroll, Illinois, and taxied to a stop. As its two Pratt & Whitney engines spooled down, the door behind the cockpit opened, the automatic steps hissed down into place and a uniformed steward silently assisted a thin and aging Katherine Sinclair to the ground, then opened the door of the waiting Escalade and helped the woman inside. The black SUV with the dark-tinted windows quickly pulled away, leaving the steward on the tarmac. A few moments later the Escalade turned behind the rudimentary automated control tower and disappeared. The pilot of the executive aircraft joined the steward on the tarmac, and both men lit cigarettes.

'What a bitch,' said the steward.

'No kidding,' agreed the pilot.

The northern corporate headquarters and training facility for Blackhawk Security Systems was located eight miles from the airstrip. It was a six-thousand-acre parcel of land in the hill country north of Mount Carroll, Illinois, and was almost completely uninhabited.

Officially known as the Compound, the facility comprised five separate shooting ranges, three outside and two enclosed, a live-fire course, three obstacle courses, a rock wall-climbing course, four 'conflict reproductions,' including a war-torn urban area, an underground bunker and an Afghani-style hilltop fire-base.

There were helipads, an artificial lake, a six-mile defensive driving course and enough accommodation and supplies for twenty-five hundred men. The Compound was surrounded by a twelve-foot-high double chain-link fence fitted with a razor wire core, three hundred and sixty-two surveillance cameras, its own emergency generators and solar power units, a dedicated cell tower and its own radar system.

Both the inner perimeter and the outer perimeter of the Compound were patrolled by armed guards on a twenty-four-seven schedule. In the center of it all, occupying its own hilltop site, was the Grange, a massive four-story log-and-stone 'hunting lodge.'

The Grange had offices and sleeping accommodation for all of the Northern Division executives, conference rooms, a huge dining hall and large commercial-scale kitchen and a belowground 'War Room,' which was equipped with a direct-link satellite feed to every area of operations currently being run by Black-hawk around the world.

The offices of Major General Atwood Swann and his second in command, Colonel Paul Axeworthy, were located on the top floor of the Grange, with several large picture windows looking out over the lake and the forested area beyond.

Swann and Axeworthy met with Katherine Sinclair in the large conference room that separated the two men's offices. The centerpiece of the room was an immense, curving black granite table polished until it gleamed. In the middle of the table, carved into the native stone, was the aggressive Blackhawk that served as the company's logo. The table, like the rest of the compound, had been purchased with funds from the Department of Defense, Blackhawk's major client, and provided by Katherine Sinclair's untiring lobbying efforts in the hidden halls and private dining rooms of Washington.

Sinclair sat at the head of the table, flipped open the ostrich document case she carried and withdrew a red-covered file, which she opened in front of her. 'Tell me about Operation Cuba Libre,' she said.

Swann nodded to Axeworthy, who got to his feet and went to the huge flat-screen that took up most of one wall. He tapped the screen with one expertly man-icured finger and instantly a relief map of Cuba appeared. He tapped the screen again and a section in the center of the map enlarged to show a central spine of hills and steep valleys that ran through the middle of the island.

'These are the Escambray Hills. During the "revolu-tion within a revolution" that took place shortly after Castro took power, this was where Batista supporters, major criminal elements and anyone else who defied *El Comandante* went. It took Castro almost three years to clean them all out, including a team of eighty-five or so CIA advisers. If they'd had any real sense back then, Escambray was where the Bay of Pigs should have taken place – not a swamp.'

'If I wanted historical analysis I would have asked for it. Get to the point,' said the woman at the head of the table.

Axeworthy cleared his throat and went on. 'We used the old CIA runway for the Tucanos. So far we've managed to bring in four of them. In two weeks we'll have the full complement of eight, ordnance included.'

'I thought the Cubans had good coast guard radar?' Sinclair asked.

'They do,' said Swann, sitting on Sinclair's right. 'But they go dark when the Colombian cocaine flights come in, and we've got good intel about when that happens. The Colombian flights are usually Beechcraft King Airs or other midsize cargo planes; the Tucanos coming in from the Navassa Island Base read like fishing trawlers if they read on the radar at all.'

'Where is Navassa Island?' said the elderly woman. 'I've never heard of it.'

'It's a tiny island between Jamaica and Haiti. It's about a hundred and twenty miles from Cuba.'

'Whose territory is it?'

'Ours.' Swann smiled. 'Under the Guano Islands Act of 1890. It's uninhabited. The island is about two miles long, flat with a lot of scrub brush, an abandoned lighthouse and one palm tree. It was perfect. We burned off some scrub for a runway, camouflaged a refueling station and that was that. The Department of the Interior will never know we were even there.'

'Are eight aircraft enough?' Sinclair said. 'It's not as

though they're fighter jets and you're taking on the entire Cuban air force.'

'It's very much like the Soviet Union before the collapse – an illusion; the props are all there, but none of them work. The Cuban air force, for example,' said Axeworthy. He tapped the screen in three separate places and they blossomed into aircraft symbols. 'There are only three operating airfields left – Holguin, which was originally designed to defend against an attack from Guantánamo and which is now almost entirely civilian, San Antonio de los Baños, a little west and south of Havana, and Playa Baracoa, for Havana itself. Recent satellite and drone surveillance shows seven transport aircraft and five helicopters at Playa Baracoa and eleven MiGs at San Antonio de los Baños but only six that appear to be in operation. At San Antonio de los Baños the hardstands for the MiGs were overgrown with grass. I doubt that there are enough spare parts or even aviation fuel to fly more than a sortie or two a month. New storage buildings have sprung up at both Playa Baracoa and Los Baños. It is our opinion that they are using the buildings to cannibalize parts from one MiG to another.'

'How many aircraft do they have officially?' Sinclair asked.

'Supposedly one hundred and thirty-four,' said Axeworthy, 'of which the majority are trainers, cargo planes, VIP flights and transports. They list a total of seven attack helicopters and only six MiG 29s, a fighter which was developed in the midseventies and has a very limited range. I think we could conservatively cut that list in half – I doubt they have more than a dozen fighters in flying condition and most of those will be MiG 21s from the midfifties. At a guess the transports and the helicopters are for counterinsurgency use – the Cuban people rising up against Raul and his brother. They simply don't have the strength to mount an attack against Tortugas, let alone the continental U.S.'

'And the Tucanos?'

'They're armed with four Hellfire Air to Ground missiles; a flight of half a dozen Tucanos could take out the MiGs at Los Baños from five miles away.'

'What about coastal patrols, the navy?'

'It barely exists, ma'am,' said Axeworthy. 'Most of what they had is at the breakers yards at the old Cienfuegos Naval Base. They used to have a bunch of Osa-class missile boats, but they stripped off the Styx missile platforms and put them on land-based mobile launchers. Most of what they have are a dozen or so Zhuk-class coastal patrol boats mounted with a couple of manually operated machine guns and some even older Soviet P6 torpedo boats with antiaircraft guns bow and stern. The torpedos are long gone and their radar is totally out of date. Useless. The coast guard will take you to Mexico for a fat fee and the Zhuks make regular runs to the twelve-mile limit off Puerto Bolívar in Colombia to pick up product from the go-fasts. Most of the money, minus the Raul and Fidel Tax, finds its way into the pockets of one Rear Admiral Carlos

Alfonso Duque Ramos, whose daughter is married to none other than Raul Castro's bodyguard.' He tapped the screen and a photograph of a handsome man in his midforties appeared.

'Is that supposed to mean something to me?' Sinclair asked.

'His name is Major Raúl Alejandro Rodriguez Castro; he's Raul's grandson and Fidel's grand-nephew. It's like a Cuban version of the Gotti family.'

The elderly woman ignored the comment. 'The army?'

'Another joke. They have thirty-eight thousand men and women of all ranks, and half of them are employed as waiters and housekeeping staff for GAESA, the holding company for the Cuban Defense Ministry. Since the death of Julio Reugeiro, the Cuban minister of defense, in 2011, the CEO of GAESA is Major Luis Alberto Rodriguez Lopez Callejas, who just happens to be married to Deborah Castro Espin – Raul Castro's eldest daughter. It's organized crime run by the military and all in the family – Castro's family.'

Katherine Sinclair sat back in her expensive leather executive chair and smiled thinly. For the first time since arriving at the Grange, she seemed impressed.

'Well, I'll be damned,' she said.

7

Dr Eugenio Selman-Housein Sosa was desperately frightened. His blood pressure was rising into danger-ous numbers, his pulse rate was at least a hundred and thirty beats per minute and his breath was coming in short, painful gasps. If he wasn't careful he was going to go into ventricular fibrillation and drop dead on the front step of Dublin's Shelburne Hotel.

As Cuba's senior cardiologist, Dr Eugenio Selman-Housein knew this was no exaggeration, and at seventy-seven years of age he was painfully aware that one incidence of VF would probably be his last.

He cursed silently. If only he'd taken the two days he needed at the Swiss conference two years ago, he would have had the cardioverter-defibrillator implanted at the Lindenhofspital in Bern and he wouldn't be in this situation. Dear God, if only he hadn't decided to walk back from the Trinity College campus, he wouldn't be in this situation.

The doctor composed himself as best he could, nod-ded to the top-hatted doorman in the red frock coat and stepped into the front lobby and confronted the staircase that led up to reception. He forced himself to climb without relying on the old-fashioned double wooden banister and made his way up to reception. He picked up his key, climbed into one of the refurbished cage elevators and waited as the white-gloved operator took him up to the top floor.

By the time he reached his room and stepped inside, he was gasping for air. He made his way to one of the upholstered club chairs in the sitting room of his one-bedroom suite, picked up his medical bag and dropped it into his lap. He found his bottle of bisoprolol, swallowed a ten-milligram tablet of the beta blocker dry and waited for his adrenaline levels to drop. At the same time he took out his portable battery-operated blood pressure machine, fitted on the cuff and hit the START button. He sat back in the chair and closed his eyes. He was carrying around the most terrifying secret in the world and it was literally killing him.

It took the better part of an hour. When his pulse had slowed to a more tractable eighty beats per minute, he called down to the Horseshoe Bar and ordered a bottle of Pyrat Cask dark rum. When it arrived he poured three fingers of the expensive liquor into a Scotch glass and drank it slowly. He poured a second drink, then picked up the telephone. It was time. To carry the secret any longer was to invite death, and not just from ventricular fibrillation. Two bullets from El Tuerto, the One-Eyed's famous silver-plated Type-92 Chinese semiautomatic, was just as likely. The phone rang twice and a somewhat nasal voice with a distinctly London accent answered.

'British embassy. How may I direct your call?'

*

63

William Copeland Black walked down the carpeted hallway of the principal floor of the British embassy on the Merrion Road in the Ballsbridge suburb of Dublin, home to most of the diplomatic missions in Ireland. He turned into the cultural attaché's office, a small room with two desks and a tiny window that looked out onto the low-profile embassy's courtyard, the last place on the property you were allowed to smoke. The only other person in the office was Anabel Bonet, who had supposedly been seconded to the cultural attaché's office from Scotland Yard's Art Theft and Forgery Squad to deal with the rash of art thefts that had been plaguing Ireland for the last few years.

The truth of it was that Anabel Bonet had never seen the inside of New Scotland Yard and anything she knew about art came from a first-year course she took at Cambridge. William Copeland Black was no cultural attaché, either, and everyone who was anyone in the embassy knew it, right down to Eva Burden, the woman who answered the telephone. Both Anabel Bonet and William Black were MI6, tasked with keeping track of any potential terrorist action against the United Kingdom originating in or passing through the Republic of Ireland.

Black sat down behind his desk, pulled open the middle drawer and stared at the yellow packet of Carrol's Sweet Afton cigarettes. He closed the drawer and looked across at Anabel. 'I've just had the most intriguing telephone call.'

'Not here, you haven't,' said Anabel.

'No, it came through the inquiries desk. When he gave them my name, they patched it over to my cellular while I was coming in to work.'

'After a very long lunch, I might add.'

'I went into Dubrays on Grafton Street to hear that writer.'

'Which writer?'

'Simon Toyne, the one with the funny hair. He's rather good.'

'The phone call?'

'Right. It was from someone named Dr Eugenio Selman-Housein Sosa. He's staying at the Shelbourne. He wants to defect, of all things. I didn't think anyone did that sort of thing anymore. Cold War stuff, you know?'

'Who on earth is Dr Eugenio Selman et cetera, et cetera?'

'He's Fidel Castro's personal physician.'

'Bloody hell!' Anabel frowned. 'What's he doing in Dublin?'

'He's a cardiologist. There's a big convention at Trinity this week.'

'And he wants to defect?'

'That's what he said.'

'Tell him to get into a cab, then.'

'He's being watched, or so he says.'

'Do you believe him?'

'It's possible. The Cuban DGI has a very long arm and he's a VIP.'

'You can't authorize this on your own.'

'I know. He's only here until Friday. That's three days. I'll have to get on my trolley and visit Babylon tonight.'

'Good luck, mate.' Anabel grinned.

'I should be able to catch the diplomatic flight. No sense in traveling with the great unwashed on Ryanair or something equally disgusting.'

'No sense at all,' said Anabel somberly, then laughed.

At seven p.m. Black climbed into the waiting BAE 125 executive jet and settled back into one of the six cream-colored high-backed leather chairs in the narrow passenger section. Except for the diplomatic bag, he was the aircraft's only passenger. He felt a little foolish, but under the circumstances time really was of the essence. If Selman-Housein was serious about his intentions, it meant that something big was up. With Venezuela's Hugo Chavez's bowel cancer metastasizing to his liver and his lungs, the thought of one or the other of the two elderly Castro brothers casting off this mortal coil was the kind of thing that precipitated coups and revolutions. The world was in enough trouble without the Caribbean being hit by a political hurricane.

A white-jacketed RAF steward appeared from the front section of the jet and offered him coffee and biscuits. Black accepted and the steward disappeared again. Black ate the biscuits and drank the coffee, then dimmed the light and sat in the darkness, looking out at the night. The black featureless slab of the St

George's Channel slid by forty thousand feet below their wings. Black smiled. Once upon a time his father had told him a story about crossing the same channel on his way to finding an assassin hell-bent on murdering the king and queen.

Morris Black, his father, had taken a certain ironic pride in being the only Jew working as a detective at Scotland Yard, although he had been fully aware that he would never rise any higher in the force because of that fact. Perhaps because of that he'd become the foremost murder investigator that organization had ever seen and was called in to deal with the most difficult cases. One of those cases, which he wouldn't ever discuss in detail until the day he died, had involved him in the intrigues of World War Two intelligence, initially landing him in the Special Operations Executive and eventually, after the war and for the rest of his life, with MI6. Somewhere early along the way, his father, already a young widower by then, had met, become involved with and eventually married his mother, Katherine Sanderson Copeland, who'd been OSS posted to England under Wild Bill Donovan during the war and a CIA officer under Hillenkoetter, Bedell-Smith, John Foster Dulles and John McCone after the war.

He'd loved both his parents very much and had been devastated when both died within a year of each other when he was in his late twenties, but they'd left him with an enduring affection for both the United States and England, an Oxford education, dual citizenship and a legacy's introduction to the intelligence establishment of both countries. For that very reason he'd spent the last ten years as Washington liaison between MI6 and the CIA. Ireland was just a respite and he knew it – he had too many contacts in the agency not to be posted back there rather than the normally benign intelligence backwater Dublin had become. He could hardly wait. His estranged wife, Chelsea, lived in Anacortes, Washington, quite successfully working on her third marriage, but at least he'd convinced her to let their young teenage son, Gabe, go to the British School of Washington in Georgetown. If he was posted back to the States, he'd be able to see his son on weekends. Whoever said that spies shouldn't have families was right – there was no doubt that his marriage had been broken into matchsticks on the jagged rocks of his uncommunicative work as an intelligence officer, but in the end his son had been worth it. He sent up a silent prayer that the kid wouldn't want to get into the spying business – sheet-metal work or refrigerator technician would be a better career.

The government jet landed at Northolt, a queen's messenger in an armored Range Rover picked up the diplomatic bag and Black climbed into the waiting Augusta Westland helicopter that would take him to the London Heliport on the banks of the Thames. After that it would be a quick ride upriver in a Targa 31 Marine Unit cruiser, which would drop him off at the Thames security gate of the ziggurat-like headquarters of MI6.

Almost exactly three hours after leaving the embassy in Ballsbridge, Dublin, he was sitting in the expansive office of Sir John Sawyers, pronounced 'Saws,' the fifty-six-year-old, dashing James Bond-ish director of the Secret Intelligence Services. He even *looked* like Pierce Brosnan: dark hair, blue-green eyes with a hundred-dollar haircut, square jaw, square face, six-two or so and dressed by his own tailor on Savile Row. Also in attendance was James Wormold, the gray-haired, overweight and slightly slovenly old guard Section officer who had eventually come to head the Caribbean Section simply by attrition.

Sawyers had been educated at the University of Nottingham, St Andrews, in Scotland and at Harvard. He spoke with a clearly upper-crust accent, but not plummy enough to be offensive. He and his wife, Shelley, had three children, including the twenty-three-year-old Connie, who was famous for posing with a gold-plated Kalashnikov in front of the family Christmas tree on her Facebook page.

Black had been surprised that his call to the Caribbean Section earlier in the day had been taken seriously enough for a meeting with Sawyers, but nevertheless, here he was.

'You confirmed that the man was actually Dr Eugenio Selman-Housein Sosa?' Wormold asked. The Section head had the accent and attitude of a fifth-form English grammar teacher.

'Yes, sir.' Black nodded. 'I checked with the Shel-burne and he is registered there. He's also registered at the Trinity convention. Just to make sure, I had one of our people take a file photograph over to the registration clerk at the Shelburne and he confirmed it, as well.'

'Why do you think he wants to defect?' Sawyers asked mildly.

'I think it's probably a case of shoot the messenger, Sir John. If Castro is dying I think he's afraid that he's going to be blamed. In Cuba that means a bullet in the head, a plane crash or a "sudden heart attack."'

'Mr Wormold?' Sawyers asked.

'It's quite possible.'

Sawyers sat back in his expensive-looking leather chair and surveyed the George Stubbs painting hanging there – *Mares and Foals in a Landscape*. One of the perks of the job was to pick paintings for your office. Finally he spoke.

'Do we really want him?'

'I beg your pardon?' Wormold said, his eyes wide with surprise.

'Do we really want him?' Sawyers repeated. 'If that's all he's got to offer, it doesn't really amount to much – everyone knows Castro is ailing; he's had cancer and a bout of divirticulitis that almost killed him. He's frail and he probably has some sort of dementia.'

'And his mother was something like a hundred and three when she died,' said Wormold sourly. 'The man could live forever.'

'His mother was barely sixty when she died,' corrected Black. 'And his father was eighty. The whole Castro family longevity story is a myth.'

'So, what do you suggest?' Wormold said, a vague suggestion of a sneer in his tone.

'Call Younger Brother and tell them what we've got. They're probably more interested than we are,' Black answered promptly. For intelligence purposes during World War Two, Younger Brother had been the code name for the United States, while Older Brother was England.

'I like it.' Sawyers nodded. 'We'll let him defect, then send him off to Washington for interrogation.' He smiled. 'With you in tow, of course, just to keep them honest.'

'As Caribbean Section head, don't you think – ' began Wormold.

'No, I don't,' said Sawyers. 'Set it up, Black. I'll make the necessary calls to Langley.'

8

El Templete is located close to Havana Harbor on Avenue Carlos Manuel Céspedes, sometimes called the Avenida del Puerto. The neoclassical building constructed in 1828 is situated exactly in front of the Palacio de los Capitanes Generales, which today is the City Museum of Havana. Across the street is the Hotel Santa Isabel, the grandest of the old hotels in Havana and in the 1700s the home of the counts of Santovenia.

La Templete is surrounded by a wrought-iron fence and looks out onto the Plaza des Armas, a sixteenth-century square once used to assemble and inspect troops and that dates back to the original settlement of San Cristóbal de Habana by Don Diego Velázquez.

The cut-stone frieze below the simple peaked-roof cornice of the building is decorated with arcane symbols of skulls, crosses and intersecting circles that are usually associated with the Holy Trinity. One symbol, exactly in the center of the frieze and directly above the heavy bronze doors of the building, shows four triangles, points facing inward – a Templar cross separated into four distinct parts.

Most of the detail of the frieze is covered by two hundred years of lichen, mold and city grime. Alongside

El Templete stands a beautiful and thick ceiba tree in the place where on November 16, 1519, the Villa de San Cristóbal was founded. The tree was highly revered by the natives, who attributed it with great magical-religious powers.

On November 16 each year, Habaneros and people from all over Cuba line up for their chance to take three turns around the magic tree and leave offerings between her huge bulbous roots. For the Indio natives who were here long before Columbus set sail for the New World, this was the Mother Tree, a virtual god that solved all problems and healed all wounds.

Eddie drove the old motorcycle up onto the curb and switched off the engine. On their left was the low wrought-iron fence that surrounded the tree-shrouded Plaza des Armas. On their right, across the broad street, was El Templete, so small it looked more like a mausoleum than a temple. It, too, was surrounded by a wrought-iron fence, this one much higher. Between the fence and the building was a tall, heavy-trunked tree with widespread branches spread like a protective umbrella; this had to be the ceiba tree, the devil tree Eddie's mother had mentioned. There was also something that looked like a ticket booth on the pathway leading to the old building.

There were tourists milling around inside the fence, some taking pictures of the huge shade tree while others roamed around the tiny windowless building. Other people went in and out of the Museum of Havana directly behind it, and more tourists stood and read the menu and the prices posted for the restaurant inside. Most turned away shaking their heads, but a few actually went in.

Directly in front of them, shaded by an umbrella of her own and seated behind a flimsy-looking card table on a padded stool, was an ancient black woman, her rake-thin body encased in a formless, faded print dress. Her face was a mass of wrinkles and the skin was stretched like leathery parchment over her bony arms. Her feet were bare and she was smoking a narrow cigar. On the table in front of her was a cooler, a large deck of cards, a few silvery trinkets and some strange-looking leather thong necklaces with small cloth bags hanging from them.

'Who is this woman?' Holliday asked.

'Mama Oya,' said Eddie.

'Does she have a real name?'

'If she ever had one, even she has forgotten it,' replied Eddie. They approached the woman behind the card table. Holliday was surprised to see what appeared to be an old-fashioned six-ounce bottle of Coca-Cola lying on a bed of crushed ice in the cooler.

'*Hekua hey Yansa,*' said Eddie, bowing slightly.

'*Hekua hey* yourself, Eddie Cabrera, the child who used to be called *El Vampiro.*' She spoke almost perfect English.

'*El Vampiro?*'

'It is nothing, Doc,' said Eddie.

The old woman gave a brief cackling laugh as she looked up at Holliday. Her eyes were ice blue and clear with no hint of age. They could have been the eyes of a young girl. 'When he was a little boy Eddie would take off all his clothes and walk around the streets of Old Havana in the middle of the night,' said Mama Oya, grinning around her cigar. She turned back to Eddie. 'You come about your brother, the white-haired one.'

'You knew this?'

'Mama Oya knows everything. Just like I know your friend is American and was once a soldier.'

'Canadian,' said Holliday.

'*No mientas a Mamá Oya, gringo,*' said the old woman sharply. 'You are an American, you were once a soldier and then you taught soldiers. You hated your father and love your wife still even though she has been gone for many years.'

My God, thought Holliday, literally taking a step back. The wizened creature in front of him couldn't have known all that. Unless Eddie had somehow managed to tell her. He turned and looked at his friend, the question clear in his expression. Eddie shook his head slowly.

'I know this in the same way as I know that Eddie has crossed an ocean to search for his brother, Domingo, so he might ease his mother's pain. I know because Mama Oya sits here and sees many things.'

'You have seen Domingo?' Eddie asked.

'I saw him driving Raul's daughter, the one married to Espin. They came to this place more than once for their meetings in the night.'

'Who came, Mama?' Eddie asked.

'Luis Alberto Rodriguez Lopez Callejas, Luis Perez Rospide, Lieutenant Colonel Rojas.'

'The man who runs Tecnotex SA,' explained Eddie. 'They import anything technological ... computers, satellite phones – all for the top people only.' He turned to Mama Oya. 'Any others, Mama?'

'Jesus Bermudez Cutiño,' said the old woman.

'Director of Military Intelligence.'

'Juan Almeida Bosque.'

'He oversees all real estate transactions and builds hotels exclusively for the use of foreigners.'

'Colonel Brito.'

'CEO of Aerogaviota. It has its own fleet of helicopters based at Baracoa Air Base. The personnel are all military. It is supposed to be for tourism and rentals to foreign businessmen, but it is actually there to provide air support in case of insurrection.'

'Also there was Ramiro Valdés,' said Mama Oya darkly. 'A devil, truly.'

'Minister of Informatics and Communications, also minister of the Interior – the Secret Police, also the minister of Agriculture. He is Adolf Hitler, this man. He went to a conference in Venezuela, and the joke in Havana was that he'd gone there to fix their *silla eléctrica*, their electric chair. He is a sadist and a murderer, amigo, and very dangerous.'

'Were you here on the night when Eddie's brother disappeared?' Holliday asked.

'Buy something from Mama Oya and perhaps I'll tell you.'

Holliday took a twenty-dollar bill out of his wallet, laid it on the card table and picked up a freezing-cold Coca-Cola from the cooler. He used the metal bottle opener hanging from a string threaded through a hole high on the side of the container and took a sip.

He was surprised. It tasted exactly like the five-cent bottles he'd bought as a child from Pop Mercier's grocery store down the street from Uncle Henry's house in Fredonia, New York. You'd drop a nickel into the slot and it would allow you to drag your drink through a maze of metal tubes until it was free, dripping water and wonderfully chilled on a hot summer's day.

'It is the same as you remember, isn't it, gringo?' Mama Oya said. 'The Mexicans use sugar instead of corn syrup.'

'Is that so?' Holliday said, trying to be calm in the face of a tiny old woman who seemed to be able to read his mind and then some. He took another long pull on the Coke. She was right; the taste was lighter and sweeter than the heavy goop they sold in cans now. It was like stepping into the past.

'That is so, gringo.' The old woman smiled. 'And yes, I was here on the night that Eddie disappeared.'

'Did he speak with you?' Eddie asked.

'Yes.'

'You were still here so late at night?'

'The Plaza des Armas is my home, gringo. I have no other. Domingo knew where I go to dream.'

'What did he tell you, Mama Oya?'

The old woman turned over the top card in her large deck and laid it out on the table. It was a tarot card, but unlike any Holliday had ever seen. It showed a dancing man, his belt hung with skulls, a machete in one hand, a severed head in the other and the face of the devil. The colors of the card were green and black, and the number 7 was printed above the image, as was the name Ogun printed in heavy, dark ink.

'*Ogún oko dara obaniché aguanile ichegún iré*,' the old woman hissed. 'He told me that if Eddie came, to tell him that he had gone to the Valle del Muerte. The Valley of Death.'

Other than looking a little silly, like Mr Spock in the old *Star Trek* series, having a Bluetooth screwed into your earhole had a great number of advantages for the average intelligence agent – you no longer looked like a complete idiot talking to yourself in virtually any situation or environment and you could keep in touch with anyone else on your surveillance team. William Copeland Black sat on a stool in the Insomnia Coffee Shop on Grafton Street and kept an eye on Fusilier's Gate, the main entrance to St Stephen's Green. It was a gray day, threatening rain, but there were still lots of people on the pedestrian mall just outside the big picture window of the coffee shop.

Dr Eugenio Selman-Housein, Fidel's personal physician, was in play. After an afternoon of shopping on Grafton Street, he was supposed to enter the Green through the Fusilier's Gate on his way back to the Shelburne. So far he was almost twenty minutes late. Black wasn't worried – yet – but he was beginning to get that familiar stiffness in the back of his neck that meant something was going wrong.

'Anything?' he said. There was a series of responding clicks in his ear. One click for no, two for yes. Where was the doctor?

And suddenly there he was, walking right by the Insomnia's window and stopping for the light at Grafton and King streets, a shopping bag in each hand, his expression clearly nervous. He was wearing a hideous Marks & Spencer green cardigan, gray trousers and brown shoes. He looked like a thin, badly dressed owl behind his wire-rimmed spectacles. The doctor crossed King Street to the shopping center on the corner, then crossed again to Fusilier's Gate and walked into the park.

'Got him. Target is in the park.' Two shopping bags. A black-and-gold one from Zara and a red-on-white one from H and M.'

There was a voice in Black's ear. 'Three. I see him.'

Black started silently counting to himself. At twenty-five, there was nothing; at forty-five, a man in his thirties wearing sunglasses, a leather jacket and a pale green Gucci T-shirt crossed to Fusilier's Gate from the far side of Grafton Street. He had slicked-back black hair, tanned skin and a single earbud line running down to his T-shirt and then under it.

'Three, he's got a shadow. Black leather jacket, green T-shirt, cream-colored linen pants.'

'Three. Got him.'

'Three, give him a ten-second lead and then follow him. I'm coming in now. You know what to do,' Black said.

'Yes, sir. Three out.'

'The rest of you keep your eyes open. He's got ears on. There's going to be others around.' Once again there was a series of clicks.

Black swallowed the last of his cold coffee, left the store and walked across Grafton Street, thick with tourists even this early in the season, especially with everything in the country being on sale these days. He crossed over to Fusilier's Gate and quickened his pace. He spotted Major a hundred feet behind Leather Jacket. Major was wearing a London Fog belted raincoat and a gray fedora, looking like something out of a Humphrey Bogart movie. Black spoke quietly. 'Three, start the ball rolling.'

Major began walking faster and so did Black. By the time Major had drawn even with the man in the leather jacket, Black was only twenty feet behind them both. Major drew ahead of the man and Black saw the shadow's shoulders visibly relax. The man slowed his pace, letting Major get even farther ahead. Black put his hand into the right-hand pocket of his suit jacket and popped the top off the fountain-pen-like device he was carrying. In fact, it was a modified version of an insulin pen filled with a light dose of dihydroetorphine.

In high concentrations the Chinese drug is used by zoos to tranquilize rhinoceroses. He laid his thumb across the CO_2 delivery button and lengthened his stride. Ahead of the man in the leather jacket, Major veered slightly and kept walking. He was now directly ahead of the shadow. The shadow dropped back a little, which in turn brought Black almost beside him to the left. Sensing someone behind him, the shadow turned. Black smiled and nodded pleasantly.

The shadow turned again just as Major dropped to one knee and began fiddling with a shoelace. The man in the leather jacket stumbled, trying to get out of Major's way, and barged into Black, who already had the CO_2 pen in his hand. As the shadow bumped into him, Black jabbed the end of the pen into the man's thigh and hit the button. The timing was perfect. In the five seconds it took for the drug to take effect, Black and Major managed to get the shadow to a bench and get him seated. Oddly, in the distance he could hear a brass band playing the theme song to *SpongeBob SquarePants*.

Black took a few extra seconds to go through his jacket pockets. He came up with a billfold and a blue Cuban passport with the words *Pasaporte Dimplomatico* in gold across the bottom. According to the passport the shadow's name was Rudolfo Suarez and he was an assistant attaché at the Cuban embassy on Adelaide

Court. Not likely. Black put the passport back into the unconscious man's pocket.

'This is Four. I've got a Hispanic couple at the run from the Shelburne entrance to the Green. Something's up.'

'Fucking hell,' said Black softly. The doctor had been told to wait at the fountain in the center of the park. If he saw two Secret Police coming after him, he was bound to panic. He was pretty shaky as it was. 'Stop them, Four.'

'How?'

'How the bloody hell should I know? Arrest them, shout fire, tackle them. Shout out Viva Fidel! Just stop them!' Black turned to Major. 'Come on, double time.'

The two men began to stride quickly down the wide paved pathway. A hundred yards ahead of them, they could see the fountain and the bewildered-looking figure of the doctor. Suddenly the skies overhead opened and it began to pour. People in the park began to run for cover. Dr Eugenio Selman-Housein vanished behind a silvery curtain of rain.

'Goddamn bloody Ireland and its bloody weather,' said Black. He and Major began to run. The brass band was playing 'Tonight's the Night' from the *Bugs Bunny/ Road Runner Hour*.

They reached the fountain and at first Black thought the doctor had rabbited, but then he saw him slouched on a bench a few yards away getting whatever slight protection he could from the large oak tree spreading its branches above him.

'Give him your coat and hat,' Black said to Major.

'But . . . ,' said Major.

'Do it!'

Major did as he was told. Gripping the doctor by the arm, Black led the frightened man down the narrower southern path away from the fountain. Behind them Black could hear raised voices, at least one of then in Spanish.

'*Lo que está pasando?*' The doctor asked, getting more upset with each passing second.

'Everything's going to be fine,' soothed Black. He jerked his head and Major peeled off and headed back toward the fountain.

Hunched over against the pounding rain, Black and Selman-Housein moved quickly down the pathway. It was the Garda Band playing under cover of the bandstand's conical Victorian roof, the brass buttons on their policemen's uniforms as shiny as their instruments.

They were playing 'Teddy Bear's Picnic' now, much to the delight of their audience, a giggling flock of young children all dressed in yellow slickers, boots and rain hats, just like the children in the *Madeleine* books his mother had read to Black as a child.

Far behind them now Black heard the frantic wailing of a police car on the far side of the Green.

'I have changed my mind!' Selman-Housein moaned. 'Let me go!' The doctor tried to pull away from him, struggling against Black's grip, but Black held on ever harder, almost lifting the older man off his feet.

'Too late, amigo,' said Black harshly. 'You made your bed and now you're damn well going to lie in it.'

Four was waiting at the open gate exiting onto the street. Four was a man in his fifties named Tommy Thompson, an ex-SAS Special Forces master sergeant with a face like granite and biceps like steel.

'The doctor's having pangs of homesickness, Tommy,' said Black.

'Not a problem, sir,' replied the hard-faced sergeant. He gripped Selman-Housein by his other arm and together he and Black propelled the smaller man through the gate and across the rain-soaked road to the opposite side. They piloted the Cuban fifty feet south to the front door of Staunton's on the Green, two Georgian houses joined to make a small boutique hotel.

They lifted him up the single step, pulled open the door, then marched him straight down the main hall-way and out the rear patio exit. They stepped back out into the sheeting rain and followed the narrow brick pathway to a small gate. Holding the doctor firmly, Tommy Thompson lifted the latch and the three men stepped out into Iveagh Gardens.

The Gardens, a smaller version of St Stephen's Green, was hidden from sight on three sides by build-ings and on the fourth by a high brick wall and a screening stand of trees. The gardens had been a gift from Benjamin Guinness of the beer dynasty and named for his son, Edward, the first Earl of Iveagh.

Empty now because of the downpour, the Gardens

had a sinister, brooding look like something from an Alfred Hitchcock movie. Ignoring the feeling of imminent doom creeping down his neck along with the rain, Black pointed the doctor down the path to the only public entrance to the Gardens on Clonmel Street, halfway down the park.

'Listen to me! Listen to me!' Selman-Housein screamed. 'I must go back to the hotel! I have left important documents there!'

'Come along, then, Doctor – there's a good fellow,' said Tommy Thompson. 'I wouldn't like to hurt you, now, would I, sir?'

'*Me cago en tus muertos!*' Selman-Housein screeched. He turned his head and spat in the sergeant's face.

'Whatever you say, sir,' Thompson said quietly. He wiped the spit and rain from his face, then slapped the Cuban hard across the back of the head.

Clonmel was less a street than a broad alley between two buildings on Harcourt Street. Reaching the open gates of the park, Black saw that the yellow and red fire brigade ambulance was already in place.

'What is this!' the Cuban said, balking, eyes widening at the sight of the ambulance, its rear doors already open and waiting.

'It's a fucking trolley bus,' said Tommy Thompson. 'What did you expect, an embassy limousine, mate?'

'I will not get in this thing.'

'Oh yes, you bloody will,' said Tommy. He grabbed the little man under the armpits and heaved him head-first into the rear of the ambulance, following close behind. Black stepped up into the ambulance as well, and together he and the sergeant managed to get the Cuban strapped down onto the gurney inside.

'Why are you doing this to me?' Selman-Housein moaned beseechingly, his eyes filling with tears.

'Verisimilitude,' said Black.

'*Qué?*'

'To make it look real,' explained Black, slapping a slab of sticking plaster over the man's mouth, followed by an oxygen mask. That done, Black rapped on the driver's partition wall with his knuckles. The siren started and they hurtled up Clonmel to Harcourt Street and began to weave through the streets of Dublin at rush hour in the pouring rain. Twenty minutes later, siren still wailing, they reached the N4 and headed west toward the Lujan Bypass and the countryside beyond. Five minutes later, the siren silent, they turned in at Weston Executive Airport and the waiting, unmarked white Gulfstream 5.

Without removing either the mask or the tape, they got Selman-Housein down off the ambulance and up into the sleek white jet. One of the leather couches had been removed from the rear of the aircraft and the gurney fitted perfectly, clipping solidly onto the two U-shaped bolts in the fuselage wall. The door closed with a hiss and the pilot and the copilot began to spool up the Gulfstream's twin Rolls-Royce engines. A few moments later they taxied out to the runway and then hurtled down it, finally leaping into the air and heading southwest, climbing steadily, finally getting out of the rain and into the fading blue sky beyond. Far to the west the sun was already heading downward into the night.

Black finally took off the mask and ripped off the tape from Selman-Housein's mouth. 'Get me down from here,' snapped the Cuban doctor angrily.

'Not a chance,' answered Black. The thought of listening to the man's complaints for the next six hours was intolerable. He took out his CO_2-powered syringe and recocked the arming lever. He pushed the syringe tip against the bulge of the older man's fatty love handles and hit the fire button. The doctor was unconscious almost instantly. The shot would keep Selman-Housein deep under all the way to Washington. Black smiled. 'Render unto Caesar that which is Caesar's. Render unto Joseph Patchin's that which is Joseph Patchin's.'

9

Back at the hotel, Holliday took his *National Geographic* map of Cuba out of his suitcase and spread it out on one of the beds.

'Show me,' he said quietly. Eddie shook his head.

'Not here,' said the Cuban. He pointed to the French doors leading out to the balcony. Holliday nodded. Eddie opened the doors and Holliday stepped out into the cool evening air.

A table and chairs sat facing out toward the sea and the Malecon far below. The tide was in and people were promenading along the famous seawall, half of them tourists and the rest predatory prostitutes. A breeze was blowing. From the balcony it was a vision of paradise, but Eddie ignored it. He was too busy checking the table and chairs and even the candle lamp in the middle of the table for bugs. He found what he was looking for under the third chair, an old-fashioned radio microphone that belonged in a Cold War museum. Eddie pointed to it, carefully carried the chair back into the sitting room of the suite and then came back out onto the balcony again, closing the French doors behind him.

'I turned on the radio so the microphone will not be

lonely. They are playing an old speech of Fidel's – it will go on for hours.'

'They really bug hotel rooms?'

'Certainly.' Eddie smiled. 'They must give the last few Chinese at Bejucal *something* to listen to.'

Holliday spread out the map again, anchoring it with the candle lamp. There was enough light from the French doors to see the map clearly. 'Show me,' he said again.

Eddie ran a large black forefinger through a gently curving arc in the center of the island. 'These are the mountains of Escambray. They run like a spine down the middle of Cuba, not high, but mostly covered with jungle. The roads are still dirt and the only way in or out is in military trucks. This is where the War of the Bandits was fought.'

'War of the Bandits?' Holliday asked.

'It is an old story in Cuba, once taught to schoolchildren, but heard of very little in the United States.'

'So tell me,' said Holliday.

Eddie lit a cigar with his old Zippo, something that Holliday hadn't seen him do in a very long time. Being back in Cuba and the loss of his brother were clearly taking their toll.

'There are two versions – the bedtime story CIA agents tell their grandchildren and the one Fidel tells. The only one that I know to be true is the one from 1962 in which my brother at fifteen years old fought in the Sierra del Escambray with an old Springfield rifle and almost died.'

'Who was he fighting?'

'The remains of Batista's army – the truly corrupt one who had so much to lose – control of drugs, prostitution, gambling, other criminals, some right-wing anticommunists and of course the CIA. Fidel spent three years trying to get them out with the regular army, but his losses were too high; fighting in the Sierra del Escambray is like fighting your own shadows, and the Batistanados were better armed – by the CIA.

'Eventually Fidel had a better idea; he gathered together everyone and anyone he could think of – young people especially. He soon had fifteen thousand volunteers. They walked, almost arm in arm, through the jungle like when you search for a lost child, a *cordón?*'

'Cordon.' Holliday nodded.

'Anyway, like this they enclosed the banditos like fish in a net and then they killed them all. My brother was wounded badly in the leg. He almost lost it and walks with a limp still, and Fidel lost many people, but eventually all the banditos were gone. It took almost three years. By the second year the CIA saw there was no hope, so they withdrew their support.'

'And the Valley of Death?'

'The Sierra del Escambray is divided into two parts, the Sierra Guamuhaya and the Sierra de Sancti Spiritus. Between them flows the Agabama River. This is the Valley of Death.'

'You think this is where he has gone to hide himself?'

'No,' said Eddie. 'I don't think he is hiding; to hide, all you have to do is lose yourself in the favelas of Havana. There are places in those slums and *baracoas* even the Secret Police will not go. I think perhaps he knows something, maybe too much. I think perhaps he has gone there to find something.'

'So, how do we get there?'

'To go by the motorcycle or even a rented car would attract too much attention.'

'We're tourists. We can go anywhere.'

'This is Cuba, *mi colonel*. You cannot go anywhere without a reason, even a tourist. And this is not a place where tourists go.' For a moment Eddie's eyes settled on the tourists and prostitutes lingering by the sea wall. Then his focus shifted farther out.

'By sea,' said Eddie finally. 'We must find a boat.'

'One of my people in Cardinal Ortega's office in Havana has been in contact,' said Father Thomas Brennan, head of Soladitum Pianum, the Vatican Secret Service. Brennan was in the office of his master, Cardinal secretary of state Antonio Niccolo Spada. The cardinal, every day of his seventy-nine years etched into the lines on his face and every glass of Bardolino he'd ever sipped visible in the blown veins of his hooked and shiny nose, looked up at the disheveled Irish priest and frowned.

'His Eminence Jaime Cardinal Ortega is an unrepentant *finocchio* and even the pope knows it,' said Spada. 'What does his bum boy have to tell us – that

Fidel has finally confessed his sins?' He coughed dramatically and waved his hand at the cloud of smoke from Brennan's fuming cigarette, the ashes of which were all over the front of the priest's wrinkled black *collarino* shirt. Brennan was standing at the ornate Italian Renaissance-style oak carved console table that served as Cardinal Spada's bar.

'No, but someone else did.'

'Don't keep me in suspense, Brennan. The longer our conversation goes on, the longer I have to endure the foul stench of your cigarette.'

'A sin that has haunted me since I was eight and my da gave me enough money to buy a five-pack of Gallaghers. We all have our burdens, I'm afraid.' The priest toyed with the cut-crystal stopper of a decanter of sherry on the bar for a moment.

'Get on with it,' snapped the cardinal. If the *testa di merda* wasn't so valuable, he would have had the little Irish *bastardo* snuffed out like a votive candle in the Sistine Chapel.

'It was some time ago in the cathedral. According to the priest, the man had been drinking and was clearly very upset. He was incoherent about most things, but the priest was able to pick up one or two things of interest. The words *Valle des Muertes*, the Valley of Death, and *Operación de Venganza*. The priest eventually reported it to me.'

'Why in the name of all that is holy would we be interested in the ravings of a drunk Cuban in his cups muttering tales of death and revenge? It sounds like one of those dreadful *romanzos* His Holiness likes to read before he goes to sleep.'

'The priest knew the man. His name was Domingo Cabrera and he works for the Cuban Department of the Interior – their DGI, the Secret Police.'

'Cabrera,' said Spada, frowning. He took off his glasses and pinched the bridge of his nose with a thumb and forefinger. 'Why do I know that name?'

Brennan whisked some ash off the front of his shirt and down onto the seventeenth-century Anatolian Lotto rug that covered the cardinal's floor. 'Because he is a close companion of Colonel John Holliday, whose path has crossed ours on several occasions. He cost us Pesek, the assassin, last winter and we lost any chance of ever finding the Book because of his antics in the Kremlin. He cost us Harris in Africa the year before that and he also knows far too much about the death of the present Holy Father's predecessor and our possible involvement in that "arrangement."'

Spada laid his hands flat on the table. The liver-colored age spots were everywhere now and the veins stood out like thick wormlike cables. The skin was so thin it looked like parchment, and unless he concentrated he could no longer stop the faint, tremulous shaking. It was the very earliest stage of Parkinson's disease, but according to the doctors, at his age the symptoms, especially the cognitive ones, would progress rapidly. He sometimes wondered why he cared so much about living and had finally concluded that it was because he was so terrified of what faced him, or did not face him, after death. He frowned. Best not to think of such things.

Carrie Pilkington had done the *New York Times* crossword puzzle that morning in six minutes and fifteen seconds. Forty-five seconds longer than the all-time world's record but pretty good all the same, especially for a twenty-seven-year-old, fresh out of Harvard with a postgraduate degree in ethnomusicology, making her the youngest doctor of anything in the Central Intelligence Agency.

She still wasn't sure quite how or why she'd been recruited by the Company except that a mysterious man smoking a pipe had approached her at the American Crossword Puzzle Tournament two years ago shortly after she'd taken second place. He'd asked her if the Harvard sweatshirt was real and when she said yes he'd given her his card and wandered away into the crowd, never to be seen again.

Initially she'd gone to the recruiting seminar simply out of curiosity, but after she'd listened to the speech and gotten the booklet describing pay grades and benefits, it occurred to her that her doctorate in ethnomusicology wouldn't give her that kind of package in a university for years and it was also beginning to look as though her best bet for employment these days was probably going to be more on the level of high school band teacher somewhere in Missouri.

She applied, was accepted and went through an orientation course that did not involve guns, knives or twenty different ways to kill someone with a soup-spoon. Now here she was, manning the Netherlands desk after Bert Coptic's unfortunate and unforeseen massive coronary 'event' that left his wife to collect his pension and about three dozen hidden Snickers bar wrappers in his bottom drawer.

The Netherlands desk was hardly the beating heart of intelligence in the agency and was just about as low as you could get on the hierarchical bureaucratic ladder, but Carrie didn't mind; over her six months on the desk she'd noticed that Holland, and Amsterdam-Rotterdam in particular, was something of a minor crossroads in the game, like the intersection of a 'Down' and an 'Across' clue in a puzzle. And there was nothing Carrie Pilkington liked better than a puzzle except for that singular moment when all the pieces fit together to form a complete picture.

As intelligence analysis went, the young Miss Pilkington's methods were seen as a little odd by most of her colleagues in the Western European Section on the third floor of the aging building in MacLean, Virginia. Carrie's clues were gathered one by one and written cryptically on yellow Post-its in her own personal code and then stuck up on the gray metal wall of her cubicle. While other analysts pored over computers, flipped through dossiers and clipped newspapers, Carrie gathered Post-its and stared until she had enough of the little yellow squares to give her the picture on the cover of the box.

Like now.

An NSA intercept from Ramstein Air Force Base.

A car rental from Kaiserslautern, the closest town to Ramstein AFB.

A Dutch employee of the Canadian consulate in Amsterdam accused of selling passport blanks to a known document forger.

A tap on the phone line of a Dutch lawyer who was under suspicion of being a double agent.

The murder of the same known document forger as the one implicated in the case of the consulate employee.

The name and telephone number of the owner of a well-known expatriate bar found in the iPhone directory of the forger.

The resultant still photo from the expatriate bar's security cameras after the rousting of the bar owner by the Militaire Inlichtingen en Veiligheidsdienst, the Dutch Military Intelligence and Security Service commonly known as the MIVD.

After she'd compared it to the computer dossier, the still photo was the icing on the cake. Carrie plucked all the Post-its off her cubicle wall, rearranged them in order just to make sure, then put them into her personal shredder one by one. Then she turned to the telephone.

'Tell him what you told me,' said Rufus Kingman, deputy director of operations. Kingman was the replacement for Mike Harris after that man's defection to the dark side and his consequent dark and violent end in the bowels of central Africa. Kingman was a young man trying to be old school: dark suits, white shirts, ties with small knots and razor-cut hair. Joseph Patchin, director of operations, really was old school and he didn't like Rufus Kingman one tiny little bit. On the other hand, Kingman's father was a onetime White House chief of staff and a big stick in the Pallas Group and it never hurt to have a soft place to land when you finally pulled the rip cord on the civil service parachute. Pensions weren't what they used to be, and his divorce was eating him alive.

The young woman standing in front of him was young, pretty and dark-haired. She had the Irish good looks and long legs he'd found so attractive in his wife once upon a time, but he'd been married too long and was getting too old to care very much, which was a depressing thought all on its own.

Apparently the young lady was an analyst out of the Western European Section, an area of the Company he rarely thought about and almost never visited. Her name, according to Kingman's quick and dirty briefing over the telephone, was Carrie Pilkington.

'Yes, Miss Pilkington?'

The girl was very straightforward and spoke without hesitation. 'Colonel John Holliday and his friend Eddie Cabrera are in Cuba. Cabrera's older brother, Domingo, has disappeared under suspicious circumstances. Domingo Cabrera is a member of the Dirección de Inteligencia, or DI, and the bodyguard and driver for Deborah Castro Espin, Raul Castro's eldest daughter.'

Carrie Pilkington paused. 'Both Holliday and Cabrera are traveling on forged passports.'

'How sure are you of this information?'

'One hundred percent.'

'What makes you so sure?'

'We know Cabrera phoned from Ramstein and discovered that his brother had disappeared. We know Holliday was in Amsterdam at Darby's expatriate bar and that he inquired after fresh documents. We know a document forger named Dirk Hartog was killed in his own workshop with his own nine-millimeter Walther PPK. Presumably he'd tried to cheat or otherwise betray Holliday and his friend.' The girl paused again. 'Just before coming up here, I received confirmation from the RCMP's Canadian Security Intelligence Service that two men answering the descriptions of Cabrera and Holliday boarded an Air Canada direct flight to Havana.'

'Is that it?' Patchin asked.

'Yes, sir.'

'Thank you for your input, Miss Pilkington.' It was a dismissal. The young woman smiled and turned with one of those pleasant little skirt flips some women's hips can manage so easily and then she was gone. 'Who's head of analysis for the European Section?'

'His name is Compton, sir,' said Kingman, as though the question was beneath him.

'Well, tell Compton to either fire her or transfer her because she'll have his job in a few years.'

'Yes, sir,' said Kingman.

'That was a joke.'

'Yes, sir, very amusing.'

'Find out if the Cuban has settled in, would you?'

'Yes, sir.'

'And tell Black I'd like to see him at his convenience.'

'Yes, sir.' This time it was Kingman's cue to depart and he did, leaving Patchin alone with his very unpleasant thoughts.

10

The Chullima Shipyards were located at the mouth of the Almendares River on the western side of Havana just past the swing bridge and close to where the Malecon breakwater and promenade ended.

Eddie piloted the old Russian motorcycle across the swing bridge, then turned down the dirt track that led to the sheds and wharves of the shipyards. He pulled to a stop in front of a tumbledown shed and switched off the key. It was noon and brutally hot and Holliday could feel the sweat trickling down his spine as he climbed out of the sidecar. The waterfront here was bustling and the snap of welding torches and the drone of industrial belt sanders filled the dusty air. There seemed to be a lot of laughter as men called back and forth to the tinny sound of Lady Gaga's 'Paparazzi' coming from a radio somewhere.

'So, tell me about this man Arango,' said Holliday as they made their way down the boardwalk by the riverbank.

'Montalvo Arango is a disgusting pig and a criminal,' answered Eddie, smiling broadly. 'He stinks like an old fish – he drinks too much *ron* and smokes very cheap cigars. He is the true *viejo hombre del mar,* this man.' The Cuban paused and winked. 'But he has a boat.'

They found both the man and the boat at the far end of the shipyard, closest to the mouth of the river. In the distance Holliday could see half a dozen men fishing from the stony beach with hand lines and rods. According to Eddie, under Cuban law what they were doing was a crime for which they could be sent to prison, the arrest and imprisonment deferred if they handed over half their catch to the policeman who caught them.

'*Buenas tardes, Montalvo,*' said Eddie. The man looked up from what he was doing. He could have been anything from seventy to a hundred and seventy. His eyelids drooped in folds over watery brown eyes and his mahogany-tanned narrow face was seamed and cut by wrinkles as deep as scars. The skin of his cheeks drooped over a bristly chin, and his neck had as many wattles as a turkey. The parts of his face not cracked and slashed by wrinkles were sprinkled with dark moles and warts from being in the bright sun for most of his life. The butt of a cigar hung wetly from his thin pursed lips. From what Holliday could see of his sideburns and the foliage sprouting from his flat, saucerlike ears, his hair was white. The top of his head was covered by a stained and ragged fedora that looked as if it came out of a thirties gangster movie.

'*Buenas tardes, Capitaine Cabrera,*' said Arango. He took the cigar stub out of his mouth and hawked a dark, mucousy mass off the side of the wharf and into the water. It was the first time Holliday had ever heard Eddie being called by his military rank.

'*Qué pasa?*' Eddie asked, although it was obvious what the old man was doing. Kneeling on the concrete boardwalk with a worn blade in his gnarled hand, he was gutting a fish that had to be five feet long, thick tendrils as long as eels hanging from its wide, rubbery mouth. Holliday had seen a documentary about this kind of creature – it was a wels catfish, probably introduced by some well-meaning Russian aquaculturist as a food source years before. At thirty pounds, they were a good source of protein, but let them get into the food chain and they could live for thirty years and reach lengths of nine feet and weights of over three hundred pounds. They were cannibals, happy to eat their own kind and also the occasional fisherman or swimmer who got too close.

'*Estoy limpieza de las tripas de este grande barbo repugnante ahora,*' said the old man. His sun-bleached cotton pants and ancient, laceless sneakers were covered with blood and bits of flesh and his wifebeater undershirt was streaked like a butcher's apron.

He glanced at Holliday, his eyes squinting upward. 'I catch at the river mouth this morning, when I am coming in from the sea,' he said in English. His voice was as rough as his cigar and his mouth was missing a few teeth here and there. He turned to Eddie. '*Su amigo pirata hablaba nada de español?*'

'His pirate friend speaks enough Spanish to get by,' said Holliday.

'Then we get along okay,' said the old man, and spat into the water again. As he gutted the fish he tossed the already flyblown trails of slimy offal into the water and then began cutting the giant fish into large fist-sized pieces and throwing them into a pair of old foam coolers beside him. '*Cebo,*' he grunted. 'Bait.' He nodded toward the boat clewed to the wharf a few yards behind him.

The boat looked almost as old as Arango. Once upon a time the hull had been white with a light blue superstructure, but sometime in its life it had been painted deep blue fading up to gray. On the horizon she would disappear against the sea and the sky, and Holliday had a fairly good idea why.

She was filthy, paint peeling everywhere. The stem was battered with its varnish worn off down to the bare wood from decades of turbulent passages, and the canvas sunshade on the flybridge above the cabin was gray and torn. To Holliday's eye she looked to be about thirty-five or forty feet long and lay squat in the water as though she was bottom heavy. For a wooden boat of that weight, it was odd that the whole side of the hull for two feet above the waterline was so beaten up and scratched. That kind of wear and tear usually meant the boat was used to traveling at brutally high speeds. The name on her transom was in red picked out in black:

TIBURON BLANCO

Even his basic Spanish was good enough to translate that: *White Shark.*

Arango sucked on his cigar, gave Eddie a look and picked up the first of the foam containers, the sinews on his wiry sun-blackened arms leaping out like stretched cables. He hauled the cooler back to the boat and heaved it over the gunwale and into the cockpit at the stern. Taking the hint, Eddie picked up the second bait box and followed suit.

The old man straightened, arching his back. He took a long puff on the cigar, the pull making a dry, crackling sound. He looked up at the sky and blew the smoke upward. Lady Gaga had been replaced by Pittbull doing 'Ay Chico.' Arango looked down at Eddie again. He hawked and this time the blob of nicotine-colored phlegm landed within an inch of Eddie's feet.

'*Qué quieres, cabron?* What you want with a poor old man like me?'

Eddie took out a Romeo y Julieta Short Churchill he'd purchased at the hotel tobacconist's and lit it with his old Zippo.

'Because I want your boat, *cabron – quiero alquilar su barco maldito, maldito el hombre de cerdo.*'

'How much you pay me? Dollars.'

'How much do you want?' Holliday asked.

'Two hundred a day.'

'Fine.'

'Three hundred?'

'A hundred and fifty,' answered Holliday.

'No, no, two hundred,' said Arango hastily.

'*Sí,*' said Eddie.

'Plus diesel.'

'*Sí.*'

'And food.'

'*Sí.*'

'*Ron.*'

'One bottle a day.'

'*Cerveza, así.*'

'*Fijado.*'

'And cigars like those?' Arango said, pointing a bony finger at the Short Churchill Eddie had just fired up.

Eddie grinned, turned to Holliday and winked again. He turned back to Arango and handed him the already lit cigar. The old man carefully took the juicy stub of the cigar from his mouth, stuck a fat tongue on the end to make sure it was dead and stuck the thing behind his ear. He put the Churchill into his mouth, chewed happily and wiped his hand on his undershirt before extending it to Holliday. A little apprehensively Holliday shook the man's hand, surprised at its strength.

'We got a deal, American. You drive a hard bargain.'

'*Vete a la mierda, viejo.* Let's get aboard.'

Oak Lawn Farm is a two-hundred-acre secluded estate at the foot of the Blue Ridge Mountains near Covesville, Virginia, and about a two-hour drive south of Washington, D.C. The home sits on a gentle knoll, surrounded by elegant hardwoods and ancient boxwoods overlooking pastoral and mountain views in every direction. The main house was constructed in 1780 and added onto throughout the 1800s. It has four bedrooms, two full bathrooms, a powder room, five working fireplaces, a country kitchen, an upstairs sun porch and greenhouse, a wraparound porch and a pergola on the main floor, a three-bedroom guest cottage and a smaller two-bedroom studio. The whole thing had been picked up by the CIA for $3.2 million. At most it is used three times a year, usually for high-level management conferences with allied agencies and the occasional off-the-books Fourth of July picnic or barbecue.

William Black sat on the wooden bench under the two-hundred-year-old oak tree that had given the estate its name, and smoked a cigarette. He remembered his father telling him about the old OSS training school he'd gone to just before the Americans fell pell-mell into World War Two. He was with some woman other than his mother then, and not for the first time Will Black found himself thinking about the fact that children never really knew their parents, nor the parents their children. It was one of those timeless conundrums, like why is there war.

He'd been in the States for five days now, all of them spent with dear Dr Eugenio Selman-Housein here at Oak Lawn. So far there hadn't been any time to see his son, Gabriel, or even spend an hour with him at the school. Selman-Housein had to be encouraged for taking every small step closer to revealing what he knew, like an infant child being potty-trained. Not only was the task frustrating and time-consuming, but it was also boring.

The MI6 officer sighed. Maybe Dick Cheney, bless his evil, black heart, had the best idea – pour water down the irritating bastard's throat until he coughed up what you wanted him to tell you.

So far the skittish and extremely irritating little Cuban had told Black, Kingman and the Pilkington girl they'd been lumbered with very little. According to Selman-Housein, Fidel was on his deathbed, but Castro had been on his deathbed ever since Juan Orta, a corrupt government official who often had lunch with El Comandante and his cronies, tried on six occasions to poison the Bearded One's favorite midday meal, his *perrito caliente* – hot dogs. Black shook his head – hot dogs! The useless twaddle you learned working for MI6. Military intelligence indeed. Spying reduced to bureaucratic folderol and nitpicking.

Black heard footsteps behind him and turned, expecting to see Kingman. It was Pilkington.

'Oh,' she said. 'I didn't see you there. I came out for a smoke, as well.'

'Feel free,' said Black, shifting down the bench. The young woman took out a packet of Marlboros and shook one out. Black lit it with his father's old World War One Imco foxhole lighter.

She took a deep lungful of smoke and then blew it out gratefully. 'Very politically incorrect of me, I know,' she said. 'Drinking makes me dizzy, smoking pot is kind of boring after a while and I get sleepy reading Nicholas Sparks. I have no other vices.'

'What about sex?' Black asked pleasantly.

'I thought the Brits didn't have sex,' she said.

'Only members of the royal family,' answered Black. 'Answer the question; I'm a professional interrogator. I'll wheedle it out of you eventually.'

'To be honest,' said the Pilkington girl, 'I can't remember.'

'First rule of interrogation – when a person begins a sentence with the phrase "to be honest," it's odds on she's lying.'

The Pilkington girl gave him a long look, took another drag on her cigarette and let it spin out of her nostrils. 'He's stalling,' she said finally, changing the subject abruptly.

'Pardon?'

'Selman-Housein. He's stalling.'

'Why?'

'He's no dummy. He's been Castro's doctor since the first stroke in 1989. You manage to stay on Fidel's A team for twenty years, you've got to know how to shuck and jive if you want to survive. Know too many of *El Comandante's* secrets and you usually wind up in a car accident, a plane crash or having a massive heart attack for no good reason. Get real close like Che did and you wind up with the boss sending you on a hopeless mission to Bolivia and then siccing the CIA on you.'

'You know your history,' said Black.

The pretty young woman shrugged. 'I read a lot and I do my homework.'

'So, why did he defect?'

'I don't think he did,' she said quietly.

'Then what's he doing in a Virginia farmhouse eating chicken pot pie and apple brown Betty or whatever it is you Americans call bread pudding?'

'I think he's a messenger.'

'I don't understand,' said Black.

'Think about it. The good doctor goes to conferences all over the world, all the time. Why now and why Ireland of all places? He was in Montreal a month and a half ago – it would have been a lot easier for him to defect from Canada, but he didn't.'

'All right, why now and why Ireland?'

'The Dirección de Inteligencia has one of the best foreign intelligence operations in the world. They know who the CIA chiefs of station and the MI controllers are for each and every U.S. embassy and British embassy, as well. I think he defected in Ireland because of you, Mr Black.'

'Why on earth would he do a thing like that?'

'Because I think it's true. The DI in Havana probably has a file on you six inches thick. They know your mother was American, they know you have a special relationship with the agency and they knew if the doctor defected in Dublin you'd almost certainly rendition him to us, but he'd have MI6 as the middleman and he wouldn't be "disappeared" to some black site in Lithuania, pardon the pun.'

'You really have done your homework,' said Black, impressed. 'But it's all a bit fanciful, don't you think?'

'Not really,' she said. She finished her cigarette and

stubbed it out in the small glass ashtray between them on the bench. She took out another Marlboro and Black lit it for her.

'Go on,' he said.

'Well, we knew that Holliday and Cabrera left Toronto for Havana – we have them on surveillance video from Pearson International. Backtracking from there, I found out they'd been staying at the Park Hyatt in downtown Toronto. Holliday made one telephone call of consequence while he was there setting up an appointment with a man named Steven Braintree, a professor of medieval studies at the University of Toronto. Braintree's office is a hundred yards from the Park Hyatt, by the way.'

'Fascinating,' said Black. 'But hardly relevant.'

'I'll get to that,' said the Pilkington woman. 'At any rate, Braintree is an expat American who came up to Canada as a matter of conscience during the first Bush war in Iraq. I reminded Professor Braintree that despite now paying Canadian income tax he still has to file U.S. income tax each and every year, which of course he hadn't been doing. I then asked him what he and Holliday had discussed during their meeting.'

'Do tell,' urged Black.

'Apparently there was a secret offshoot of the Templars in Cuba dating back to the sixteenth century called La Hermandad dos Cavaleiros de Cristo. The Brotherhood of the Knights of Christ, most often shortened to simply La Hermandad, the Brotherhood.'

'Once again, fascinating but hardly relevant.'

'There have been persistent rumors that La Hermandad still exists. A secret cabal of ten families that have been the real power in Cuba for five hundred years.'

'Persistent rumors,' murmured Black. 'Not hard evidence.'

'Apparently the lineage of this cabal is matriarchal. One of the families is named Ruz, Castro's mother's maiden name. Another is Rodriguez, as in General Eduardo Delgado Rodriguez, head of Cuban intelligence. Do you known Selman-Housein's full name?'

'Enlighten me.'

'Selman-Housein Sosa. Inside El Templete, a Templar chapel in Havana that is officially used only once a year, there is a painting by French painter Jean Baptiste Vermay showing the first town meeting held in Havana. First and foremost in the painting is a man in knight's armor, a conquistador named Juan Ortega *Sosa*.

'Fidel Castro Ruz, General Eduardo Delgado Rodriguez and Selman-Housein Sosa – all members of La Hermandad. It has to mean something. We just don't have enough letters.'

'Letters?' Black asked, confused.

'As in a crossword puzzle. We find the missing letters to fill in the blank squares and we'll have our answer.'

'You really are an impressive woman, Miss Pilkington.' Black smiled.

'Call me Carrie.'

'Like the Stephen King story?'

'That's me.' She stubbed out her cigarette and stood up. 'Shall we go back and start waterboarding the doctor so we can fill in the blanks?'

'My thoughts exactly,' said Black, standing as well. 'But alas, that world has gone the way of the dodo.'

'Darn,' said Carrie.

11

The man in the tropical camouflage battle dress adjusted his headset and stared at the portable control-panel-in-a-suitcase on the ground in front of him. He was surrounded by banks of ferns and undergrowth, the shadows of the tall pines and eucalyptus trees turning the rain forest floor into a complex pattern of contrasting light and shadow that swallowed up the man in battle dress and made him close to invisible.

The air was full of the soft, gentle scent of butterfly lilies and the sweeter odors of jasmine and ginger mixed with the rotting smell of overripe bananas and plantains that had fallen from the trees above to lie on the dark, rich earth below. Everywhere around the man the elegant song of the *tocororo* could be heard and the harsher telegraphing of the ivory-billed woodpecker.

Before he'd slipped the headset on, the man had even heard the furious whisper of hummingbird wings nearby and the twittering of the tiny green and red *cartacuba*. This was the Topes de Collantes, the highest point in the Sierra del Escambray, a mountain twenty-six hundred feet above sea level, its flanks covered in a smothering blanket of almost impenetrable jungle foliage. What few roads existed were unpaved and dangerous for anything but high-wheeled military vehicles and sturdy four-by-fours. This place had come close to defeating Fidel more than fifty years ago, and it was no place for casual visitors now.

The man in the tropical battle dress saw none of this beauty now, nor did he hear anything beyond the empty cycling hum in his headset. He reached down with his right hand and picked up the Vectronix laser range finder. He put the small device up to his eye and looked out through the stand of trees in front of him to the brightly sunlit meadow beyond. It was empty, sloping downward gently, the tall yellow rattle grass shivering in the gentle breeze. By autumn the seed pods of the grass would be mature and the field would sound as if it were home to a million rattlesnakes as the pods shook in the wind.

'Go, One,' he said softly into the microphone.

A figure rose out of the grass fifty yards ahead. He looked as if he was carrying a large foam children's glider. Lifting the model airplane high, he took a few running steps and launched it downhill. As he did so the man with the control panel pushed a toggle switch and the almost invisible propeller behind the wings of the aircraft began to spin. The man with the portable unit picked up the handheld game controller and began to work the controls with both thumbs. The glider, with its silent electrical motor, began to climb into the sky until it was invisible. On the screen of the portable control unit, the surveillance package began sending video and data.

The device was a Desert Hawk III mini-drone. It was thirty-six inches long with a fifty-four-inch wingspan and an interchangeable payload package of up to 2.2 pounds – one kilogram. The Hawk could fly at altitudes that ranged from nap of the earth to eleven hundred feet. It even had an infrared package for night sorties. It had a hundred-minute endurance time and could be controlled portably or by a remote operator thousands of miles away. The images could also be satellite-linked to anywhere in the world, and the man with the portable unit lying in the jungle was well aware that what he was seeing on the screen was also being watched at the Blackhawk Security Systems headquarters at the Compound in Mount Carroll, Illinois. Screw up and he'd be dead meat or at the very least unemployed. Thank God and the people for all those hours he'd spent playing *Call of Duty: Modern Warfare 2*.

'What's he supposed to be looking at?' Major General Atwood Swann asked, seated in the Big Chair in Blackhawk Security Systems Compound War Room. He was watching the giant flat-screen monitor showing the Desert Hawk Display from Topes de Collantes seventeen hundred miles away.

'Nothing in particular,' replied his second in command, Colonel Paul Axeworthy. 'This is the afternoon recon run. The Hawk's got a range of about ten miles or so; in that kind of terrain that's at least half a day's march. Put up the Hawk for an hour or so and you can make sure nobody's sneaking up on you. Not likely, but it's a prudent precaution under the circumstances.'

'It's going well?'

'The men and equipment are deployed. Nobody's made any mistakes and the only contact with the locals has been with Ruiz,' said Axeworthy.

'Our man in the hotel?'

'Yes, sir.' The colonel paused. 'Any word yet, sir?'

'They picked up the doctor. It's just a matter of time now.'

Dr Eugenio Selman-Housein sat in his chair at the head of the George Wythe Jeffersonian table in Oak Lawn's dining room. He was enjoying a second helping of prime rib, roasted potatoes and asparagus along with a vintage Laboure-Roi Côte de Nuits Villages burgundy that he was drinking at an alarming rate for a man of his slight build, not to mention his age.

Will Black watched him from the other side of the table and wondered if the good doctor had a tapeworm. One way or another, a man who drank that much without showing the slightest effect had to have a liver the size of a Volkswagen.

The doctor put down his knife and fork, took a sip of wine and smiled pleasantly at Black and Carrie Pilkington. 'In truth, *mi amigo y mi amiga*, I must say, the Central Intelligence Agency feeds its defectors well, and in such a delightful environment.' He paused. 'I do miss Senor Kingman, though; he was *muy divertido . . .* entertaining?'

Kingman had returned to Washington after the first three days of the doctor's filibustering. His excuse for leaving was to make a personal report on the situation to Joseph Patchin, but all the telephones at Oak Farm were secure and encrypted and there was also a video link.

Black was reasonably sure the real reason the deputy director had left was that he thought the Cuban's constant beating around the bush was because he had nothing of value to disclose and was simply looking for a free ride. Consequently the doctor wasn't worth his valuable time. Both Black and Carrie had tried to convince him about Carrie's theory that Selman-Housein was stalling because he was on some sort of prearranged schedule, but Kingman dismissed the whole idea out of hand.

'This isn't some fanciful story about Masonic treasures buried under the streets of New York, Miss Pilkington,' he'd chided. 'This is serious business.' Kingman had laughed, jeering. 'If there was a secret society of ancient knights running Cuba, don't you think the CIA would know about it?'

Black had to stop himself from reminding Kingman that, among other things, the CIA hadn't seen the collapse of the entire Soviet Union coming, had backed the nascent groups that became al Qaeda in Afghanistan, and that both the CIA and MI6 consistently ignored the Iraqi threat to Kuwait going back to the 1960s, despite all the James Bond films or Tom Clancy's Jack Ryan. In the final analysis, neither agency was very good at winkling out the secrets of other countries.

In the Oak Farm dining room, Selman-Housein picked up his knife and fork again and began slicing up a roast potato. He speared a morsel with his fork, popped it into his mouth and chewed happily for a moment.

'Wonderful,' he murmured.

'In the United States we have a saying, "to sing for your supper,"' said Carrie.

'*Qué?*' Selman-Housein said, frowning.

'*Ganarse el pan,*' explained Black.

'You speak Spanish?'

'Fluently, Doctor. I took a dual honors degree in political science and Spanish at Oxford. I also spent two years at the embassy in Madrid. *Así que no me jodas, Doctore, ahora mismo!*'

Selman-Housein looked shocked at the profanity, then shrugged. He offered a brief smile, put down his knife and fork again and repeated the ritual of the wine and the linen napkin. He stared down the table at Black and wagged a disapproving index finger back and forth.

'I am offended,' he said primly. 'In Cuba no man or woman would treat their guest this way.'

'This isn't Cuba, Doctor. It's North Carolina, and you're not a guest – you are a defector and a traitor to your country.'

'How you talk is not hospitable anywhere, Senor Black.'

'Hospitality is over. It's been a week and you've told us nothing. If you're playing some sort of game, it ends now.'

'There is no game, Senor Black. Of this I assure you, and I am no traitor. I am a refugee and that is the status I will claim if you continue to speak to me so rudely.'

'A status you'll never get, you arrogant little shit,' said Carrie pleasantly. 'I'll make sure of that, believe me.'

'This is America,' protested Selman-Housein. 'You cannot do that. There are laws.'

'You're wrong about that,' said Black. 'This isn't America. This isn't even Guantánamo. This is nowhere and nobody knows you're here. This is *un agujero negro*, Doctor, a black hole. You don't exist and there are no laws. Carrie and I could snap our fingers and you'd disappear. Poof! If that's what you want, then consider that plate in front of you your own personal Last Supper.'

There was a long silence. Finally the doctor reached out and picked up the bottle of burgundy. He examined the label briefly, then poured the remainder of the bottle into his glass.

'Mr Black, Miss Pilkington, do either of you or the agencies you represent have the slightest idea of what will happen when our great leader, *que Dios tenga en su Gloria*, finally dies?'

Carrie shrugged. 'The presumption within the CIA is that his brother, Raul, will take over the reins but that the country will be run as a military oligarchy. Which is exactly how it is run now. My personal theory is that it will be ruled by La Hermandad dos Cavaleiros de Cristo. The Brotherhood.'

'You know of La Hermandad?'

'I do. My superiors think they're a fantasy.'

'They are no fantasy, senora. They are quite real. We who are not members of their *sociedad secreta* call them something else: Los Diablos.'

'The Devils,' said Black.

'Yes, but the Devils have become frightened because they know the truth.'

'What truth?'

'That when Fidel dies they will not have the power to stop what is coming.'

'And what would that be?' Carrie sighed. Black smiled. The good doctor really was long-winded, but after a week of inane conversations about everything *but* Cuban politics, he was willing to let the man talk all he wanted.

'There are eleven million people in Cuba. Of those, at least two million live in Havana – the real figure may be closer to three million, but no census taker has dared set foot in the *baracoas*, the slums, for more than a decade.' The doctor gave a hollow laugh. 'Fidel says there are no slums in Havana, so that is that, I suppose.' He shook his head and took a long swallow of wine. 'The birthrate in Cuba is almost nonexistent. The whole population grows older each year.

'The health care system is a bad joke. State-of-the-art hospitals and excellent doctors for those who can pay – tourists and members of the Central Committee of the Communist Party, but for the rest, verminous bedding and black market drugs. Food is running out, but to fish in the rivers or the sea invites jail. Farmers without shoes or electricity eat, but the people of Havana and the other towns and cities starve. With Venezuela in an uproar, Cuba's only supply of fuel is now in jeopardy. It is all coming to an end.'

'So, what are you saying?'

'When Fidel dies, there will be a demonstration by many dissidents. I could not tell you which groups, but there will be such a demonstration and someone will die at the hands of the Secret Police. That death will lead to anger and more demonstrations. Those demonstrations will lead to riots. All this will happen in one day or perhaps two at most and they will be riots the like of which you have never seen before.

'There are fewer than twenty thousand men and women in the Cuban armed forces. A few helicopters, perhaps a dozen. If called upon, at least half of those men and women in the Cuban armed forces will refuse to fire on their fellow Cubans.' The doctor laughed again and drank the last of his wine. 'Especially with guns that have no bullets and tanks that have no fuel or lubricating oil.'

Selman-Housein smiled gently, his eyes behind his spectacles softening for a moment. Black even thought he saw tears welling up. 'On New Year's Eve in 1959, there were riots in Havana as Batista fled the city, but they were good riots, riots to cut the rot from the country's core like a tumor in the brain.

'I know. I was seventeen years old then, and like everyone else we rioted with joy.' He took off his glasses and pinched the bridge of his nose, then looked up, blinking. 'There will be no joy in the riots that will come. There will only be madness. It is the motto of our country come to pass – *Patria o Muerte*, Homeland or Death – and the people will choose death when Fidel dies and the revolution collapses. Everything will end in the *Valle de la Muerte.*'

Carrie shrugged. 'It all sounds very dramatic, Doctor, but when you get right down to it, what are you telling us? More nothing. Fidel Castro could live for years.'

'Fidel Castro will be dead in thirteen days,' the doctor answered. 'And I have given the Brotherhood the means of killing him without leaving any trace. When the deed is done, they will begin their *Operación de Venganza* and Cuba's freedom shall be gone forever.'

'Operation Vengeance? What exactly is that?' Black asked.

'On the twelfth of April 1962, President John F. Kennedy promised that the United States would never intervene militarily in Cuba's affairs. It is a promise that has been kept by every American president since that day. That promise is about to be broken.'

'How?' Carrie Pilkington queried, an urgent note in her voice.

'The Brotherhood is planning a terrorist attack on the United States that will make your nine-eleven pale into insignificance. Hundreds of thousands will die and there is no way to stop it.'

PART TWO

Ignition

The *Tiburon Blanco* made her way slowly down the Caribbean coast of Cuba, every inch the hired sport-fishing boat taking two well-heeled tourists onto the ocean waves in search of black marlin, tuna and mahi-mahi. The outriggers were extended, bait was cut and sometimes Holliday or Eddie would troll an empty line from the fighting chair just in case someone was paying too much attention.

Holliday was well aware that the U.S. intelligence community had a Broad Area Space-Based Imagery Collector – a polite euphemism for spy satellite – dedicated to the Caribbean, and Cuba in particular. He also knew, despite public denials, that the Pentagon still carried on weekly U2 flights over Cuba in an upgraded version of the venerable old spy plane that had first uncovered the Cuban Missile Crisis.

The BASIC satellites were so good they could read the time on your wristwatch from fifty miles up, so Holliday wasn't taking any chances; to keep his face from view he wore a long-billed New York Yankees ball cap whenever he went out on deck.

It was almost five hundred miles from Havana to La Boca at the mouth of the Rio Agabama, and it took them a week to get there. According to Montalvo

Arango, to travel at night was dangerous. If there was any chance of being spotted by *la guardia costera*, it was after dark. The old fisherman told them it was more a matter of the coast guard being seen than the coast guard seeing them; a *guardia costera* ship – usually nothing more than a harbor patrol boat – spent more time ferrying people to Mexico for a price than guarding the sovereignty of the Cuban coast. When they weren't smuggling people, they were usually smuggling drugs either in or out of the country, so as a rule it was best to keep out of their way.

At sunset the *Tiburon Blanco* would head into the shallows and find a small bay or cove where they could anchor for the night. Arango would use a hand line to catch enough fish for their dinner, open a jar of his own pickled mangoes for dessert and that and a few glasses of Ron Mulata would end their day. Holliday and Eddie occupied the two bunks in the forward cabin and Arango spread a blanket and slept under the worn canvas of the flying bridge. The whole cycle would begin again the following morning at dawn.

On the evening of the seventh day, they reached La Boca, the mouth of the Rio Agabama. Like most rivers in Cuba that ran down to the sea, the Agabama's delta was a mangrove swamp that extended for more than three miles before they actually reached the river itself. The swamp smelled terrible.

'*Ay! Este sitio huele a huevos podridos!*' Eddie said.

'The rotten egg smell comes from the sulfur dioxide in the silt,' said Holliday.

'Sometimes you are like an encyclopedia, *mi colonel*. You know everything.'

'Blame my uncle Henry. He had a full set of Encyclopedia Britannica, Fourteenth Edition. Twenty-four volumes. He made me read one whole volume every summer. I reached the volume with mangrove swamp in it just after I got back from Vietnam.'

'Lotta good crab in there,' grunted Arango. The evening before, the old man had managed to catch them half a dozen spiny lobsters and they'd feasted on lobster tails and garlic butter as a change from their fish diet. According to Arango, catching one of the creatures illegally was good for five years in El Condesa. Six of the creatures would probably get you life.

The old man eased the boat carefully up the river, watching the color of the water and moving the wheel in tiny increments to avoid the thin gray lines of mud that lay like long, dangerous fingers out into the main stream. Go aground in the mud and you'd have to wait for the next high tide, and that wasn't good at all; the mouth of the Rio Agabama wasn't the safest place to be.

'Why?' Holliday asked, standing beside Arango in the wheelhouse. 'What's the problem?'

The old man lit the stub of his cigar with a kitchen match and pointed a bony brown finger. '*Por ahí*,' he said. 'That is the problem.'

A football field away, hidden by the mangroves, a pair of eighteen-foot flatboats appeared, each equipped with some sort of long-shaft mud motor. There were three men in each of the two boats and they were coming fast. The engines of the boats had a familiar growl and it only took a few seconds for Holliday to identify the noise. It was the same roar made by the Ural motorcycle Maximenko had lent to them back in the *baracoas* of Havana.

The men at the throttles of the boats were both standing; their passengers were seated, weapons across their laps. From where Holliday stood they looked depressingly like AK-47s.

'Can we outrun them?' Eddie asked, coming forward from the cockpit.

'We can try,' said Arango. He reached out and pushed the twin throttles as far as they would go. The *Tiburon Blanco* shivered like a Thoroughbred coming out of the starting gate, and the bow lifted upward, hard.

Holliday looked back as they left both boats behind. The man in the bow of the lead boat put down the AK-47 in his lap, then picked up something equally familiar.

'Oh, shit,' said Holliday. The man in the boat stood up, the RPG tank killer mounted on his right shoulder. There was no time for explanations. Holliday pushed the old man out of the way and spun the *Tiburon Blanco*'s wheel hard to starboard. There was an echoing boom from the lead boat and a trail of smoke as the warhead roared across their stern within a foot of hitting them. The warhead hit the river behind them and exploded, sending up a fifty-foot geyser of stinking mud and water.

'*Esos cabrones intentó matar a mi barco!*' Arango roared furiously. Cigar fuming, he went down into the forward cabin, muttering under his breath and leaving Holliday at the wheel without another word.

'Where are they?' Holliday yelled, looking back over his shoulder.

'Getting closer!' Eddie responded, raising his voice above the roar of the engines and the pounding of the hull as they hammered up the river.

'Tell me if you see the guy with the RPG again!'

'*Sí, mi colonel!*'

Ahead of him Holliday saw the river widening. The mangroves were gone and he could have been back in the jungles of Vietnam along the Mekong. Huge ferns bowed over the banks, and the water was thick with the flat green pads of water lilies. Behind them crowds of cedars, ebony, kapok, giant figs, mahogany, oaks, pine and royal palm trees made a dense jungle.

Suddenly Arango appeared carrying something across his narrow shoulder. Holliday couldn't quite believe his eyes; it was an ancient-looking Browning .50-caliber machine gun. Across the old man's other spindly shoulder hung a long, trailing belt of gleaming ammunition. The old man paused, squinting at Holliday.

'You know how to use this *puta madre*, American?'

'Yes.'

'Then help me.' The old man turned. 'Cabrera! *Tomar el volante!*'

Eddie nodded and came forward, taking over the

wheel from Holliday. Holliday then took the heavy machine gun off Arango's shoulder. The old man went nimbly up the ladder to the flybridge. 'Follow me!'

Holliday did as he was instructed, shouldering the big gun and climbing up the ladder. He heaved the gun onto the deck of the flybridge and clambered after it. Arango stood under the flapping canvas, digging into an old wooden toolbox. He hauled out three lengths of tapped steel pipe and screwed them together into one long piece. He then took the completed pipe and dropped it into a socket on the deck. Then he added an old pintle mount he took from the pocket of his ragged cotton pants and screwed that into the top of the pipe.

'The gun,' he instructed.

Holliday nodded and staggered across the bouncing, heaving deck with the Browning in his arms. Together the two of them manhandled the machine gun onto the pintle and Arango locked it in place.

'You shoot,' said Arango. 'My eyes, they not so good anymore.'

'All right.' Holliday nodded, taking his place behind the gun. He slid the bolt forward and flipped open the top of the weapon. Arango fed the first shell of the belt into the receiver and Holliday reversed his previous actions, closing the top and pulling the bolt all the way back. There was a double click announcing that the belt was locked into place. 'What now?' Holliday asked.

Arango gave him a gap-toothed grin. 'We attack!'

*

Will Black, Carrie Pilkington and Rufus Kingman sat in the seventh-floor office of the CIA director of operations and waited for Joseph Patchin to speak. Patchin was staring at his ego wall. He allowed himself a nostalgic smile. There were pictures of him with agency directors from Bill Casey to Leon Pinetta and presidents from Carter to Baby Bush, and he'd outrun them all. He'd had a career to be proud of in the intelligence business, and now he could feel it coming down around his ears. He turned back to face the other people in his office.

'He didn't say anything else?' Patchin asked, looking at Will Black, the MI6 liaison.

'No, sir, nary a word,' said Black.

'Did we threaten him, Miss Pilkington?'

'Yes, sir. Guantánamo and letting him go in Little Havana in Miami with a sign around his neck. We even threatened to send him back to Havana.'

'Didn't work?' Patchin asked glumly.

'No, sir. He clammed up entirely.'

'What about Guantánamo, Kingman?'

'The president would have our balls, I'm afraid, sir.'

'Never been a fan of bowdlerizing,' murmured Black. Carrie smiled.

'What?' Kingman asked.

'Nothing,' said Black. 'Just thinking out loud.'

'What about a black house – somewhere really unpleasant?'

'There's still one in operation in Albania, sir.'

'What do you think, Black? A little boarding, sensory deprivation, that kind of thing?'

'I seriously doubt that it would do any good, Mr Patchin.'

'And why is that?'

'Because I don't think he has anything more to say.'

'You believe Miss Pilkington's "messenger" theory, too?' Kingman sneered.

'I do. I also believe that Selman-Housein was given just enough information by the Brotherhood to get you to react exactly the way you are now. You've got half the threat analysts at Counterintelligence wetting their pants and looking for exactly what sort of terrorist threat from Cuba could cause the death of hundreds of thousands of people, and you've got everyone at Homeland Security running around defenestrating themselves.'

'De what?' Kingman asked.

'Defenestration,' said Carrie, 'a fourteen-letter word meaning to be thrown out of a window. It's what happened to Jezebel, the false prophet from the Old Testament who used too much makeup. You see it every now and again in the *New York Times* crossword puzzle.'

Black smiled. Kingman was silent, staring. Patchin raised an eyebrow.

'The president isn't about to throw himself out of an Oval Office window, even if he could, which he can't, but he *would* like some suggestions about the direction we should take.'

'Holliday and Cabrera, his Cuban friend, are the key to all this. They're looking for Cabrera's brother,

Domingo. Domingo fled because he knew too much. Find Holliday and we find Domingo Cabrera.'

Patchin thought for a moment. 'It'll do until we think of something better. How's your Spanish, Black?'

'Fluent,' he answered.

'Yours, Miss Pilkington?'

'High school and a course in conversational Spanish at university.'

'We can't send either one of them!' Kingman protested. 'He's not one of ours and she's just an ... analyst.' Kingman looked shocked at the very thought.

'Mr Black is as American as you or me. His mother spent most of her working life at the agency.'

'But ...'

'Done a lot of fieldwork, have we, Rufus?' Patchin said.

'No, sir, none.'

'Speak any Spanish?'

'Not much, sir. I've been to Cancún two or three times.'

Patchin turned to Black. 'You'll be a journalist for the *London Times*. Miss Pilkington, as well. She's an expat Canadian. Can your people in London arrange a backstory?'

'Not a problem,' said Black.

'Fly to the Bahamas tonight and catch a flight from Nassau to Havana as soon as you can. We need answers, and we need them fast.'

13

The bow of the *Tiburon Blanco* pounded up and down on the wind-ruffled water of the Rio Agabama as Eddie threw the wheel around, guiding the old cruiser downriver toward the oncoming pirate flatboats. They were firing again, but either the range was too long or they simply had bad aim.

Above him on the flybridge, Holliday squinted into the bright sun reflecting off the river in almost blinding shards of light. He held on to the old wooden traversing handles, both thumbs resting on the long 'wishbone' trigger. The Browning M2 had a range of better than a mile, but Holliday wasn't taking any chances. At a hundred and fifty yards he saw the man with the RPG on his shoulder stand in the bow of one of the oncoming flatboats. Holliday traversed slightly to the left, then pressed on the spoon-shaped ends of the trigger.

The effect was almost instantaneous. In the first five seconds, sixty-five rounds chattered loudly out of the old gun. Shell casings flew while the massive bullets chewed through the bow of the starboard flatboat like a monstrous invisible buzz saw. The man standing with the RPG vanished in a puree of blenderized blood, flesh and bone, the rocket in his now nonexistent hands firing wildly, leaving a smoking trail into the jungle, where it exploded in a furious geyser of plant growth and rich, dark soil.

With his thumbs still on the trigger Holliday put forty rounds along the length of the flatboat, killing the man in the middle seat. The third man flung himself overboard an instant before the last of the rounds hit the gas tank and blew the remains of the boat into splinters. The man who'd jumped overboard swam quickly toward shore doing a frantic Australian crawl to get out of the line of fire. Unfortunately the flatboat's engine, an old, hundred-and-twenty-pound Shovelhead Harley engine, as well as the twelve-foot driveshaft and the still-whirring prop, fell out of the fireball and the mushrooming cloud of black smoke, striking the base of the swimmer's back. His spine was shattered and he drowned simultaneously.

'*Coño!*' Arango said, staring. 'You shoot pretty good for a *yuma*.'

Holliday took his thumbs off the trigger, and the chattering death from the ancient machine gun stopped. The second flatboat had turned away long before and was hiding somewhere in the heavy screening foliage that overhung both banks of the river. Holliday released the grips of the machine gun and checked the belt. There was still more than half of it left.

'You have more ammunition belts?'

'*Sí.*' Arango nodded, still staring at the remains of the flatboat as they swirled downriver in the current. 'Six or seven.'

'You'd better bring them up here,' suggested Holliday. 'Those guys will be back.'

'*Bastardos,*' said Arango. He took the fuming cigar stub out of his mouth and spat a throatful of tobacco-colored phlegm over the side.

'I'm afraid we might have gotten ourselves in over our heads,' said Will Black as they left Joseph Patchin's seventh-floor office. 'I'm not sure where we should start.'

'That's where I come in,' said Carrie. 'Remember I said it was like looking for clues in a crossword puzzle? Well, I think I just remembered one.'

'What is it?' Black asked. They pushed the elevator button, and the doors slid open.

'It's not what – it's where,' said Carrie as they stepped into the elevator.

'All right, I'll play along,' said Black. 'Where?'

'Just down the road in Fairfax County,' she answered. 'Fort Belvoir, to be precise.'

The National Geospatial-Intelligence Agency's main mission is collecting, analysing and distributing visual intelligence gathered from surveillance satellites operated by all of the U.S. armed forces, as well as surveillance material from the hundred or more daily sorties of spy planes, drones and high-altitude electronic-intelligence-gathering aircraft. The agency can also determine, from quite a distance, what an object or a building is made of, or conduct sophisticated pattern analysis of human characteristics, like gait and body size. It also possesses some of the most sophisticated facial recognition software on earth.

The NGA was also responsible for the data gathered and the real-time video for Operation Neptune's Spear, which led to the death of Osama bin Laden in Abbottabad, Pakistan. It was the NGA that provided the video link watched so intently by the president, the secretary of state and various other guests invited to the show in the famous photograph released by the White House. It also has mastered 'all weather' imagery analysis, and the sensors on its satellites, and drones can see through heavy overcast and thick clouds.

Although it has a number of facilities spread around the country, NGA's main 'campus' is a two-million-square-foot building just outside Fort Belvoir, Virginia. The structure is both large enough and high enough to hold the Statue of Liberty in its atrium.

Black and Carrie sat in one of the agency's theaters on some unnumbered, underground level of the top-secret complex. From the time they'd rolled through the first security gate outside the building, they'd been under escort by a blank-faced man who looked as though he could put Black across his knee and crack his spine in a single movement. He was dressed in a dark, well-cut suit that wasn't quite tailored enough to hide the lump under his left arm. He never introduced himself, smiled or made any pretense of interest in either one of them. He belonged in Disney World's Hall of Presidents as an Animatronics Secret Service Agent.

The theater was built like a studio screening room. Thirty comfortable leather armchairs were arranged around a fourteen-by-eight-foot plasma screen hanging on the far wall. A riser behind the seats contained a podium and control console. The tall, thin man with receding dark hair and a beak nose standing at the console was Paul Smith, senior analyst and interpreter for the Central American Division, which included Cuba and the rest of the Caribbean. As well as the nose and the thinning hair, he had a thin, perfectly trimmed mustache only very vain men consider growing. Except for Animatronics Andy standing silently by the door Smith, Black and Carrie Pilkington were the only people in the room.

'Apparently you have some sort of clout,' said Smith, his voice adenoidal as though he suffered constant sinus congestion. 'The request came directly from the White House.' The thin man sniffed. 'This is very short notice.'

'Can't be helped,' said Black. 'This is new information and we're on a very strict timeline.'

Smith sniffed again. 'What precisely are you looking for?'

Carrie answered, 'Some topographical feature in Cuba known as La Valle del Muerte, the Valley of Death.' Smith's mustache twitched in annoyance and he began tapping keys on his console. Carrie leaned over and whispered into Will Black's ear, 'The doctor mentioned it just before he clammed up.'

'I remember,' Black replied with a nod. 'But it's a bit thin, don't you think?'

'It's all we've got.'

'There are two and they are one and the same,' said Smith. 'The Agabama River divides two ranges of the Escambray Mountains. It flows from a place called La Boca on the Caribbean side and after a series of divisions exits into the Atlantic at a small village called San Francisco. A conquistador named Diego Velázquez de Cuéllar landed in Cuba near the mouth of the river on the Atlantic side. He'd been sent by Columbus with specific orders to conquer the island and find places where people could settle. He was also told to keep his eye out for any loose gold or treasure he found lying around since his relationship with Queen Isabella was becoming somewhat strained financially.'

Black wanted to tell the nasal little twit to get on with it, but Carrie was right. To go to Cuba blind was to invite failure. Smith continued with his pedantic little lecture. 'At first Velázquez de Cuéllar wanted to take some of his small boats up the river, perhaps with an eye to seeing if it was a navigable way to reach the opposite shore, but his local Indio guides said that much of the river was occupied by evil spirits that brought on sickness and sometimes death. The symptoms the Indios displayed were close to what the Spaniards knew as vómito negro, black vomit, which we now know was –'

'Yellow fever,' supplied Black, staring at the blank

screen in front of him, waiting for something to appear on it.

'Indeed,' said Smith with another sniff. 'Yellow fever. At any rate, the Indios called the whole place the Valley of Death.'

'And this was when?' Carrie asked.

'The early sixteenth century.'

'Anything more current?' Black said.

'During the War of the Bandits between 1959 and 1965, the Agabama River Valley was also known as the Valley of Death. Probably because of the number of bodies floating down it as Castro's teenage army wiped out the last of the Batistinados.'

'Show us the river ... whatever you called it,' said Black.

'The Ag-A-Bam-A,' said Smith, enunciating with painful, condescending care. Suddenly an image appeared on the screen of a topographical map and a river running through it, winding like some enormous twisting worm. From what Black could see, there was a narrow plain, foothills and then the mountains themselves. The topographical map was now overlaid with a satellite shot of the same area. The mountains were covered in dense jungle foliage and there were virtually no population centers beyond a scattering of small villages.

'Anything else?' Black asked.

'This was flagged for interest about two weeks ago,' said Smith. The images were overlain again, this time by an infrared night shot. There were several bright blobs of color high in the mountains. 'It was interesting enough for an RQ-170 Flying Wing to be deployed from Creech in Nevada to take a look.'

'And what did it see?' Black asked.

'This,' said Smith. The image changed again. This time it was a daylight shot. While the huge ninety-foot-wingspan stealth drone flew at fifty thousand feet, it could give imagery close enough to see the dirt under a man's fingernails. It was video data from an RQ-170 that gave the president and his friends the overall shots of the late and unlamented Osama bin Laden's Pakistani pied-à-terre.

The image on the screen showed a collection of large camouflaged tents, what appeared to be a line of four-wheeled ATVs under more camouflage material and a number of men walking back and forth across a compound that had obviously been cleared from the jungle slopes around it. The image then tightened in on a single figure. He was wearing the black beret and camo gear of the Cuban Tropas Especiales, their version of Delta Force.

'Company strength,' said Smith. 'We found a few others like it scattered through the area.'

'Who are they?' Black asked.

'They look like Cuban Special Forces on exercise. That's the general consensus here.'

'They could be something else,' said Carrie, her voice hesitant and thoughtful.

'Who?' Smith asked, obviously irritated. 'The army of Haiti invading Cuba?'

'I'm fairly sure I've seen those uniforms before.' She paused. 'You can't get any more detail, can you?'

'A great many countries use black berets and that elm leaf camouflage. And no, I cannot get any more detail,' snapped Smith. 'The image is at maximum resolution. Is there anything else I can do for you?'

Black was about to say no when Carrie spoke up again. 'Has there been any recent activity on the Agabama River?'

Smith sighed and began to enter the query on his keyboard. He had the answer a few seconds later. 'River pirates operating close to the mouth of the river. Apparently they go after tourists on sportfishing boats.'

'Can we get real-time coverage on that area?' Carrie asked.

'River pirates?' Smith said. 'Hardly a matter of national security, Miss Pilkington. You're trying my patience.'

'And you're trying mine,' snapped Black in response. 'Bear in mind where the request for your cooperation came from.'

Smith's small mouth opened for a moment as though he was about to speak, then snapped shut, the thin mustache above his upper lip quivering like a frightened caterpillar. He bent over his console and began tapping keys.

'This is from a low-orbit NROL-49 satellite in geostationary orbit over the Caribbean.' Smith hit a key and an image appeared on the screen. It was a high-angle view of a broad river. 'From twenty miles up.'

'Can it look for anomalies?' Black asked. MI6 had its own version of the NROL, so he knew a little about the satellite's performance.

'Yes.'

'Is it picking anything up?'

'There's a large oil slick about eight miles upriver.'

'Can we see that?'

'It's four in the afternoon, Mr Black. Shadows might present some difficulty.'

'Try.'

'As you wish.'

The image fogged out, shifted and then resolved itself.

'One thousand feet,' said Smith. There was definitely a rainbow-hued slick of oil fanning out on the water trailing off as the current pulled it toward the sea.

'Follow it to the apex of the slick,' Black ordered, any pretense of politeness stripped from his voice. Smith did as he was told. The apex of the slick was two miles upriver.

'There,' said Smith. 'Two hundred feet.'

'What could have caused that?' Carrie asked.

'I have no idea,' said Smith primly.

'Either someone spilled a large can of outboard motor fuel or a boat sank,' said Black. 'Take us upriver please.' Smith zoomed out and the image angled upriver. The man was right; long shadows fell across the river now. 'Check for anomalies,' ordered Black.

'Here,' Smith answered shortly after fingering his console. 'Five hundred feet.'

'It looks like a boat,' said Carrie, squinting.

'It is a boat,' said Black. 'It looks as though it's tied up to a tree.' He turned back to Smith. 'Closer, please.'

'Fifty feet.'

'There's someone sitting in the stern,' said Carrie. 'And there's something in front of him on the transom.'

'Closer,' said Black.

The image refocused and resolved again. 'Twenty-five feet,' said Smith.

'What is that thing in front of him and what is he doing?' Carrie asked.

'That thing, as you call it, is a Browning fifty-caliber machine gun and he's cleaning it.' He paused. 'Closer please, Mr Smith.'

The image zoomed in. 'Ten feet,' said Smith.

'Are we close enough to use that facial recognition program of yours?'

'No need,' said Carrie, staring at the enormous image on the screen. 'I recognize him from his file. That's Lieutenant Colonel John "Doc" Holliday.'

After dropping off Animatronics Andy back at the security gate, they headed out onto the highway, Carrie at the wheel of the agency Ford. She hadn't said a word after identifying Holliday.

'That place gives me the willies,' she said as they moved north against the evening traffic. 'So does Mr Smith.'

'He's a bureaucrat, Carrie.'

'He's also a liar.'

'I beg your pardon?'

'I'm no military expert, but I know enough about the state of the Cuban army to know that they don't waste time sending their Special Forces into the jungle for exercises. The Tropas Especiales are almost completely an urban force used to put down dissident demonstrations. Not to mention the fact that their weapon of choice is the AK-47. The men in those images were carrying MK-17 SCAR assault rifles; that's U.S. Special Forces and most of the private armies like Blackhawk, KBR, Obelisk, Dyncor in the States and Control Risk and Blue Hackle in the U.K. I also know I saw more stacks of ammunition boxes than probably exist in the entire Cuban army inventory. The worst of it is that Smith lied.'

'Why?'

'I don't have the slightest idea, but I know it means one thing – something's going on and we don't know a damn thing about it.'

14

The papal nunciate in Havana is located on a wide treelined boulevard in the Miramar District of Havana a short walk from the beach. It is a large two-story brick mansion with a turret on one side and a green tile roof. The entire front of the building is surrounded by a piazza-style porch.

The office of the papal nuncio himself, Bruno, Cardinal Musaro, was in a large bright room on the main floor that looked out onto a small orchard of orange and lemon trees. The office was lavishly furnished with Persian carpets, a seventeenth-century Spanish lacquered and gold-inlaid desk, several armchairs and floor-to-ceiling bookcases on two walls. The third wall behind the desk was taken up by a huge bow window and the fourth wall was hung with a number of priceless icons on the left and held a floral-patterned vestments cupboard on the right. The room was finished off with a nineteenth-century antique floor globe by W. & A. K. Johnston of Edinburgh to the right of the desk.

Cardinal Musaro, a gray-haired man with a broad, handsome face, took off his reading glasses as the semi-retired archbishop of Havana entered the room, escorted by one of the nuncio's priest attendants. The priest withdrew and Musaro gestured toward a chair in front of his desk. Both men were dressed in ordinary priestly garb that made no reference to their status.

Jaime Cardinal Lucas Ortega y Alamino, a slightly pudgy man with gold-rimmed glasses and thinning hair he regularly dyed black, sat down with a heartfelt sigh. Although Ortega was seventy-five years old – Musaro's senior by almost ten years – both men had been elevated to Cardinal Pius II and both men wore identical solid gold Crucifixion rings on the third fingers of their right hands. They were of equal status in the eyes of the Church, so there was very little small talk between them.

'You have just returned from the Holy See?' Ortega asked.

'Yes, a few meetings.'

'How are the politics there, Bruno, as complicated as ever?'

'As complicated as ever, Jaime.'

'You spoke with Spada and his imp?'

'Brennan, you mean? Yes, I met with both of them, as we discussed earlier.'

'And?'

In answer Musaro opened his desk drawer and took out a small purple velvet box. On the top of the box, in gold, were the crossed keys and mitre that was the symbol of the pope. Musaro opened the box and put it down on the desk, facing Ortega. The former archbishop of Havana looked at it the same way he would look at a venomous snake. Inside the box was a ring identical to the one both he and Musaro wore – the Cardinal's Ring.

'It is an exact duplicate, Jaime; no one will know the difference. I took the venom supplied by Selman-Housein to Rome and Brennan's people did the rest. The ring contains the full venom load of eight Brazilian wandering spiders. The ring is made like a jet injector for diabetes. All it takes to fire is the pressure required to shake hands. That much venom will induce death within a few hours. There will be shortness of breath, paralysis and eventually asphyxiation.'

'Dear God,' whispered Ortega.

'God has nothing to do with it, Jaime; it is simple pragmatism. With Castro dead, the strongest independent body in Cuba will be the Catholic Church. We can control the country's future, guide it down the appropriate path.'

'You know how many times this has been attempted before?'

'According to *El Jefe*, six hundred and thirty-eight, although I doubt the number is accurate.'

'Whatever the number, Fidel is still here and the assassins who made attempts on his life are not,' said Ortega.

'Most of the attempts were by the CIA or their proxies. This is not the same.'

'Why?'

'Because we have God on our side, of course,' said Musaro, folding his hands across his chest.

'You wouldn't be the first to think that,' said Ortega,

a note of bitterness in his voice. 'The German soldiers in World War Two had it stamped on their belt buckles: *Gott mit uns*.'

'In this case, however, Jaime, it is true.'

'You'll have to explain that.'

'We are men of the world, Jaime. I am aware of your sexual proclivities, as is the Vatican. To us it is irrelevant.'

Ortega flushed crimson. 'Then why do you mention these spurious allegations of my "proclivities," as you refer to them?'

'Because Castro knows about them, too. The disappearance of the gold chalice, censer and pyx from the Cathedral of the Virgin Mary of the Immaculate Conception of Havana, for instance.'

Ortega's flush darkened even more. 'That was a common thief; he broke into the cathedral at night. He was never caught.'

'All thieves in Cuba are caught, Jaime; that's why Cuba has so many prisons. No, it was a "special friend" of yours, Jaime, one of the assistant priests. I believe his name was Domenico Montera. You had him transferred to your alma mater in Quebec.'

'That's a lie!'

'True or false, Fidel knows about it, too. He holds it over your head like a Damocles sword.'

'For the love of Christ, Musaro! You're giving me a *motive* to assassinate the man, not an alibi!'

'On the contrary, Ortega, it is the perfect alibi.'

'How so?'

'Fidel hates you, you hate Fidel, but you spread his theories of the people's revolution with almost as much fervor as he does. You are his creature, Jaime, and everyone knows it from the highest to the lowest, and everyone knows something else, as well.'

'What is that, Cardinal Musaro?' Ortega asked sullenly.

Musaro answered, something close to pity in his voice, '*Que no tienen el coraje de matarlo.* You would not have the courage to kill him, Jaime.' Musaro paused. 'And that makes you the perfect candidate.'

'Because no one would believe such a coward would do such a thing?'

'Your words, not mine, Jaime.'

Ortega eyed the box on the table and the heavy, solid gold rectangular ring inside it. 'Will he feel pain?'

'Not initially. As you know, Castro has suffered from diabetes for a number of years and has peripheral neuropathy in both his hands and feet and has considerable nerve damage as well. He will feel nothing as you shake his hand.'

'He will feel pain eventually, though?'

'Excruciating,' answered Musaro. 'It will look very much like a stroke. He will be unable to talk, but essentially his entire body will be suffering from severe inflammation. His lungs will fill with fluid, and he will suffer extreme pain in all his joints. Eventually he will be unable to draw breath and he will die of asphyxiation.'

Ortega reached out and snapped the box shut, then slipped it into the pocket. 'Good. I will do it.'

'You know when it is to be done?'

'The feast of St Lazarus. It has been his favorite saint's day since his diverticulitis. I am always invited to give the blessing. The older he gets, the more Catholic he becomes.'

'A common trait among old men,' said Musaro. He sat forward in his chair, placing his hands flat upon the polished inlaid desk. 'The Feast Day of St Lazarus is on the twenty-first day of the month. The deed *must* be done on that day. A great many people are counting on it, Jaime. A great many people are counting on *you*, Jaime.'

'And my reward for committing murder?'

'On the night of his death, you and I will be flown to Rome on an Air Canada 777. On the day after your arrival, the cardinal electors will meet to select a new dean since the ever-controversial Cardinal Soldano is over eighty and no longer eligible to vote in any future conclaves. You will become the next dean of the College of Cardinals.'

'It is an elected position. How can you guarantee such a thing?'

'There are currently ninety-four cardinal electors. I am owed favors of one kind or another by seventy-six of them, more than enough to obtain a two-thirds majority of sixty-two.'

'You've taken care of everything,' said Ortega.

'I am the apostolic nuncio, the envoy of the pope and therefore the envoy of God to this country.' Musaro lifted his shoulders and smiled, the light from the big bow window behind him turning his hair into a halo with a tropical Garden of Gethsemane at his back. His voice was soft but filled with the power of a man saying Mass in a cathedral. '"*Deos enim religuos accepimus, Caesares dedimus*": The gods were handed down to us, but we created this terrible Caesar ourselves, Jaime, and having created him, we have the responsibility of removing him from this world. *Alea iacta est,* Jaime. For Fidel the die has been cast and you have been chosen to be his Brutus. *Deus animae tuae misereatur.* May God have mercy on your soul.'

It took another three days for the *Tiburon Blanco* to make its way up the broad valley of the Agabama to the small town of Condado, once a rail center for agricultural goods from the small surrounding farms. The rail line that had once served the town had died with the revolution, the tracks overgrown with weeds, an ancient steam engine enduring a humiliating and rusting demise, the single glass eye of its enormous headlamp pointing the way down a track that was no longer there. Mountains rose on three sides, and only a few miles ahead the valley narrowed to its end. Ahead lay the much narrower Valley of Death, the river winding and curling deep into the heart of the Sierra del Escambray.

In the time that had passed since his arrival in Cuba, Holliday had developed a deep mahogany tan. In a pair of grease-covered cotton pants, rubber tire sandals and an old Bruce Springsteen Darkness Tour

T-shirt, he almost looked like a local. It was Eddie who suggested that he wear a bandanna low over his fresh scar and his ruined eye. The bandanna looked a little odd, but the scar was too terrible to miss and too easy to describe. If they didn't need supplies for the boat, the prudent thing would have been for him to stay behind. They had filled the boat's huge hidden tanks at the little harbor in Tunas de Zaza just before reaching La Boca and the mouth of the river, so at least fuel was no problem.

Arango guided the boat upriver toward the town with special care. Even with the shallow five-foot draft, the *Tiburon Blanco* had almost grounded several times as they approached Condado. As the summer progressed, the water would become even shallower, making passage up or downriver impossible. The old man eventually found a short stretch of stony beach and Eddie threw out a concrete block anchor to make sure the boat didn't drift away downriver if Arango decided to take a nap.

Both men said good-bye to Arango, dropped off the side of the boat and down onto the beach. They began the half-mile walk into town, empty knapsacks carried over their shoulders. They found a narrow dirt road between fields of early wheat and tobacco and followed it, dust rising in puffs from their sandaled feet. The sun was relentless in a hot blue sky and Holliday no longer wondered why the average Cuban walked so slowly; to go any faster was to invite a heart attack.

'You trust him?' Holliday asked.

'Arango? Of course,' said Eddie.

'He was plenty upset by those pirates,' said Holliday. 'What's to stop him from heading back downstream and abandoning us?'

'Four things,' answered Eddie with a grin. '*Uno* – he only has half his money. *Dos* – it takes at least two people to fire that machine gun. *Tres* – he knows I would find him and cut out his heart. *Quatro* – I have the glow plug relay fuses from both engines in my pack. He is not going anywhere.'

The town was small and almost deserted and its largest industry appeared to be a trucking company using old military vehicles to transport produce grown in a number of large greenhouses. The town square was almost empty as though the people had left on the last train out of town decades before. Doors were closed, windows were shuttered and the only movement came from little spirals of dust whirling in the hot breeze.

They found a *carnicería* that had some relatively fresh meat to sell, and the butcher gave them directions to a farm stand on the other side of town where they managed to find what they needed in the way of fruits, vegetables and even a clutch of fresh eggs. The old lady running the little stand was careful to pack the precious cargo in a paper bag lined with straw.

Their errands done, the two men headed back to the boat. '*Hola!* Arango! We've found the *huevos* you wanted,' called out Eddie as they eased themselves over the gunwales. Both men froze as a figure stepped

156

up out of the well leading down to the cabin. His skin was the color of teak, his hair snow-white. He was as tall as Eddie but not even close to being as muscular. He had dark, deep-set, suspicious eyes beneath heavy black eyebrows that were starkly at odds with the whiteness of his hair. He carried a big Makarov pistol in his right hand.

'Where is Arango?' Eddie asked harshly. Holliday was acutely aware that he was unarmed.

'*Él está abajo, dormido. Borracho,*' answered the white-haired man.

'Prove it,' Eddie said.

Without taking his eyes off them, the man with the white hair used his left hand to slide back the cabin door. Arango's snores were loud and regular. '*Está usted satisfecho . . . mi hermano?*'

'Speak English,' said Eddie.

'Why should I speak your Yucca friend's language? It is the language of the enemy.' The white-haired man sneered. His English was at least as good as Eddie's.

'Because it is polite,' said Eddie. 'Or have you forgotten simple manners along with everything else our parents taught us?'

'Your parents?' Holliday said.

'Yes, *mi colonel*,' said Eddie, his voice brittle with anger. 'May I present you to Domingo Romano Cabrera Alphonso? My brother.'

15

'Why this place in particular?' Will Black said, paying the driver of the pristine 1953 Oldsmobile taxi, then climbing out into the superheated air.

'Because there aren't that many places in Cuba that rent private airplanes,' said Carrie Pilkington. 'In fact, this guy is the only one I could find.'

The faded sign on the rusted old corrugated hangar said SERVICIOS DE AVIACIÓN P. LAFRAMBUESA. The hangar was located on what looked like an old, cracked, concrete hardstand at the northwestern perimeter of Playa Baracoa Airfield. Playa Baracoa was twelve miles west of Havana, its single runway within sight of the sea.

Once upon a time Playa Baracoa had been an important airbase, but it had been inactive for years, old MiGs rusting away on overgrown hardstands, a few old Russian MiL 18 helicopters and some short-range Yak 40 VIP transports in case some bigwig in the military took it into his head to visit friends at the other end of the island or fly to Cancún for the weekend.

There was a man working on an airplane in front of *Servicios de Aviación*. P. Laframbuesa. He was in his early sixties, tall and gangly, his bib overalls and his old straw hat making him look more like old MacDonald on his farm than an airplane mechanic.

The plane itself looked almost as out of place as the man. It was canary yellow with tricycle landing gear, the front two wheels on high pylons that tilted the nose upward like some sort of curious insect. Both the upward-hinged doors were open and Black could see that there was room for a pilot and copilot and Spartan seating for two more in the cramped little cockpit.

The man turned as they approached. He smiled and doffed his straw hat. Underneath it was a shock of curly salt-and-pepper hair. Carrie almost laughed. It was the first time she'd actually seen a man's eyes 'twinkle.' She smiled back at him. He looked like a six-foot-two version of the Lucky Charms leprechaun.

'*Puedo estar de servicio?*' the leprechaun asked, the Spanish formal with a strangely flat accent.

'*Nos gustaría alquilar su avión,*' answered Black. '*Hace que lo realmente volar?*'

'Of course she flies, and lower your voice or *Miroslava* will hear you,' said the man. His English had the same flat drawl as his Spanish.

'Who's Miroslava?' Carrie asked.

'She is,' said the man, stroking the aircraft's rounded snout, '*Miroslava* the Golden Oriole. She's a PZL-104 Wilga and proud of it. A hundred and twenty miles per hour, range of four hundred and twenty miles; take you anywhere in Cuba you want to go.'

'You're not Cuban.'

'Name's Pete Laframboise,' said the man. He held out a hand and they both shook it. The grip was strong and firm and the hand felt as though it had done its fair share of hard labor. 'I'm a political exile,' he added pleasantly.

'Laframboise, *laframbuesa*, very cute,' said Carrie.

'I thought so,' he replied.

'What kind of political exile?' Carrie asked.

'You're way too young,' said Laframboise. 'FLQ, *Federation de Liberation du Quebec*.'

'The Cross–LaPorte kidnappings in Montreal, October 1970,' said Carrie promptly. 'LaPorte was murdered and the prime minister invoked the War Measures Act, same thing as martial law in the States. First real case of terrorism in North America. The FLQ went around planting bombs in mailboxes.'

'Not bad,' Laframboise said, turning to Black. 'Who in hell does *she* work for?'

'If I told you I'd have to kill you.' Black smiled. He paused. 'You don't sound very French-Canadian.'

'I'm not. I'm all Anglo. But I was young. I was going to McGill University. I fell in with the "wrong bunch," as the saying goes. Her name was Paulette and she was very passionate about . . . politics. We were part of the team that kidnapped James Cross, the British trade commissioner. In return for letting him go, we were all exiled to Cuba. The rest went back years ago. I was the only one who stayed. I like it down here. No winters, no snow to shovel. No hockey, either, but what the hey, you can't have everything, even in the Socialist Paradise.'

'And you wound up flying airplanes?'

Laframboise shrugged and smiled. 'I already had my license by the time I got to Montreal. Back then they needed crop dusters, so there was a ready-made job.'

'You're very forthcoming about yourself,' said Black.

'Some people couldn't give a crap. Just get them to the fishing and pick them up again without any chatter. You two are different. I could tell that right off. You're no fishermen. You're not even tourists, so I thought I'd be up front. Now it's your turn; you be up front with me and maybe I'll let you hire *Miroslava*.'

'Fair enough,' said Black. 'We're looking for someone in the Sierra del Escambray. If we don't find him, a lot of people are going to die.'

'You're a Brit. Who do *you* work for?'

'MI6.'

Laframboise glanced at Carrie. 'Which means she works for . . .'

'That's right.' Black nodded.

'You've got big brass ones to play spy games in this country – I'll give you that,' said Laframboise. 'In Cuba they drop you in jail for five years for not handing over your ID fast enough.'

'This is no game, Mr Laframboise. This is the real thing. I wasn't kidding that people are going to die unless we find this man, and very soon.'

'Who is he?'

'His name is John Holliday. He's traveling with a Cuban mercenary named Eddie Cabrera. They're looking for Cabrera's brother, Domingo.'

'Who's this Domingo character?'

'An ex-agent of MININT,' answered Carrie. 'The Ministerio del Interior.'

Laframboise lifted a bushy eyebrow. 'Believe me, dear, I know what MININT stands for. I've had my own run-ins with them every once in a while.' He shook his head. 'You really like to pick exciting friends, don't you?'

'He's hardly a friend,' said Black. 'But we really do need to find him.'

'And this stuff about a lot of people dying is true?'

'I'm afraid so.' Black nodded.

Laframboise shrugged. 'Okay, me and *Miroslava* are in.'

'It may well be dangerous,' warned Black.

'What the hell?' said the tall, gangly man. 'What's life without a little danger?' He grinned. 'Besides, if things get really bad, we'll just fly to the Caymans so I can spend all that money I've been squirreling away for a snowy day.'

'All right.' Black nodded again. 'We need to go back to our hotel and pack a few things. Can you be ready in an hour?'

'*No problemo.*' The pilot nodded.

After twenty-two years of military service, fighting in three wars for his country and receiving two Purple Hearts, the Distinguished Service Medal, a Bronze Star and divorce papers and losing any sort of custody for his two kids, Major Frank Turturro was making the princely sum of six thousand six hundred and thirty-three dollars a month. Of that, twenty-four hundred dollars went to alimony, twelve hundred to child support and seven hundred on car payments. He'd maxed out all his credit cards, his overdraft protection had been revoked and he was still on the hook for his ex-wife's student loans for the degree she'd gone after and failed to obtain while in search of her 'inner woman.' When all was said and done, he barely had enough left over for beer and pretzels.

He'd been in the U.S. Army for twenty-two years and had post-traumatic stress disorder stretched wire thin from Baghdad to Kabul and back again. More than once while lying on his back on some stony piece of ground in the middle of goat-butt nowhere staring up at constellations that were nothing like the ones he'd grown up with, he'd seriously considered putting his Browning .45 between his teeth and giving it the old heave-ho.

Instead he went home after his last tour, took his pension in a lump sum and paid all his debts, then took a contract with Blackhawk Security and went straight back to Helmand Province, this time at six thousand a week. That was four years ago, and now he was a light colonel commanding his own small battalion of top-notch men, all of them combat veterans like himself and making a hell of a lot more than six grand. Mind you, commanding an elite unit about to start a revolution in Cuba was no ordinary ride in a Humvee down the dangerous streets of Sadr City in Baghdad.

Lieutenant Colonel Frank J. Turturro stared through the olive drab Steiner binoculars. In the clearing below he could see a low, concrete block building with a shed roof made of corrugated iron. A narrow dirt road wound up the steep slope of the mountain, passing directly in front of the building. A Soviet GAZ-67 jeep knockoff from the good old days sat in a dirt parking lot beside the building, and a couple of rusty bicycles were leaned on the wall beneath the overhanging porch. A Cuban flag hung limply on a pole to the right of the old school, and a roughly made pole barrier blocked the road.

According to his intel, the building had once been a school, but the birthrate had fallen to nothing in the area years before and now the structure was a barracks and checkpoint for the Policía Nacional Revolucionaria, or the PNR, Cuban National Police Force. His intel had also told him that the barracks held an eight-man squad, two men on patrol, two men at the checkpoint barrier and a second shift asleep or simply off duty within the barracks.

Turturro shifted the binoculars slightly. Two blue-uniformed men in baseball caps were seated in white plastic garden chairs on the open verandah of the building. Both men had their chairs tilted back, both were smoking cigarettes and the one closest to the parking lot had a beer bottle nestled between his legs.

'Time,' said Turturro, his voice barely a whisper.

'Fifteen fifty-eight hours,' said Anthony Veccione, the man on his left with the LAW rocket tube cradled in his arms. According to Veccione, his friends called him 'The Therapist' because he got rid of people's anxieties – permanently.

The M72 already had the tube extended, the sights up and the spring-loaded safety pulled out into the 'Armed' position. All Tony had to do now was to sit up on his knees, put the tube on his shoulder and squeeze his fingers on the big button-style trigger mechanism on the topside of the tube. The M72 was slow and old, dating back to the Vietnam War, but it could blow through eight inches of tank armor and it would turn the inside of the old school building into a meat grinder. Veccione had a second tube strapped to his back in a special pack.

'Two minutes until the shift change,' said Turturro. He turned to his right. Lying beside him was Nick Cavan, the best of the four senior snipers in Turturro's company. 'You ready, Nick?'

'Yes, sir,' said Cavan. He was using an XM2010 Enhanced Sniper Rifle, which had only been in operational use for a year. This particular version was fitted with a suppressor, a muzzle brake and a Leupold Mark 4 variable-strength telescopic sight that could do virtually anything except iron your laundry. The weapon used Sierra Match King Hollow Point Boat Tail ammunition that could take out a butterfly's eye at fifteen hundred yards.

'Time?' Turturro asked again.

'Fifteen fifty-nine,' Veccione said.

'Any second now,' said Turturro. He felt the familiar ache in his jaw that came just before an operation began, like grinding your teeth while you were awake. 'Remember, Nick first, then Tony.' Turturro pressed his headset button. 'Everyone else set?' There was a series of electronic clicks in his ear. In the distance he could hear the grind and rattle as the two-man patrol vehicle struggled up the mountain road. The old Gaz 67 appeared around the corner and the lieutenant colonel held his breath. Showtime, he thought.

And then it all went to hell.

As the Soviet-style jeeps pulled into the parking lot, Turturro heard another engine sound. This one was a struggling whine and then a grinding noise as someone tried to downshift. A few seconds later a white, mud-spattered Gaz minibus appeared around the corner. The lieutenant colonel adjusted the focus on the binoculars, trying to make out who was in the van.

'Shit,' said Turturro.

'What?' Nick Cavan asked, his cheek pressed to the stock of the vicious-looking sniper rifle.

'A bus full of cops. They must be servicing all the checkpoints in the area.'

'What do we do?' Cavan asked. 'Abort?'

Turturro thought for a split second. 'No,' he said. 'Change of plan.' He turned to Veccione. 'How long to get the second LAW out and ready to fire?'

'Never timed it,' said Veccione. 'Under ten seconds. Seven, eight maybe.'

'Okay, switch targets. As soon as the minibus stops, take it out. We can't let any of those cops set up or get into the bush. This whole thing depends on wiping them all out. Once you hit the bus, get the second shot ready and hit the building. Tony picks off any strays.' He pressed the button on his earpiece. 'Follow my lead. We've got company.'

The minibus pulled to a stop in front of the building and the two guards seated on the shaded porch tipped their chairs forward and stood up. The driver's-side door of the minibus opened and as the driver put one leg out Turturro distinctly heard the sharp clicking sound as Veccione squeezed the trigger mechanism on top of the M72. A sound like a door slamming right beside Turturro's ear registered and even before the first round hit, Veccione was hauling the second round out of his pack. Simultaneously he fired the virtually soundless sniper rifle, pulled back the bolt and fired a second time.

The first LAW round went through the windshield of the minibus as the two guards on the porch went down, each with a single round through the chest. The LAW round detonated in the minibus, blowing out all the windows and peeling off the roof like a tin of beans exploding in a campfire. As the first men stumbled out of the barracks doorway, Cavan began dropping them with the big boat-tail bullets, managing two center-mass shots and one head shot before the second LAW rocket went smoking through the dark doorway of the barracks, making Cavan and his single shots redundant.

The rocket exploded, lifting the corrugated metal roof a foot off the rafters and enveloping the entire scene in a roiling cloud of dust and smoke. One man, probably the driver of the minibus, staggered out of the choking cloud, his right arm in tatters to the elbow and most of his scalp and face an open, bloody wound. Turturro gripped the binoculars and forced himself to keep on watching. Beside the lieutenant colonel the bolt on Cavan's rifle gave its lethal, heel-clicking *snick*. The minibus driver's head disappeared in a blossoming pinkish cloud and the rest of him sank to the ground.

Turturro waited. The smoke began to dissipate in the wind as the last echoes from the LAWS rockets faded away against the hills. The gas tank on the minibus exploded briefly, bucking the back end of the vehicle into the air. All four tires were burning furiously and Turturro began to smell the raw stink of the melting rubber.

He pressed his finger to his earbud. 'Go,' he said. From behind him a dozen men in camo gear with an M-4 carbine in one hand and a cane-cutting machete in the other rose out of the jungle and headed down the hillside to the clearing. Each man had a brown jute sack tucked into his belt.

Turturro stood and followed them, taking a can of red Krylon spray paint from the satchel hanging from his belt. Veccione and Cavan stayed behind, their jobs done. Turturro touched the switch on his earbud and spoke into his throat microphone again. 'Get me hands and heads, gentlemen, as many as you can. Remember, we are the wrath and hammer of God come down on Fidel and his devil boys today. Let's scare the shit out of these bastards!'

Turturro reached the bottom of the hill and crossed the parking lot to the side wall of the barracks. The smell of hot metal and burning rubber fumed like a choking pall. He shook the can of Krylon to mix the paint, then quickly drew a circle with a large Z. Beneath the design he spray-painted the slogan:

VIVA ORLANDO ZAPATA!

Orlando Zapata Tamayo being a martyr who died in a Cuban jail after an eighty-five-day hunger strike and whose ashes were now buried beside the veterans of the Bay of Pigs invasion of 1961. Turturro smiled as he put the dot beneath the exclamation mark. Nothing like having a dead man to lead your insurrection. That was the problem with people like Adolf, Fidel or Stalin – eventually all their warts began to show; a martyr stayed dead and pure forever. He looked at his watch. Seven minutes. He switched on his throat mike again.

'Okay, people, time to make like old soldiers and fade away. Somebody's going to get curious about all the smoke and bangs.' Turturro turned around and headed back up the hill. A few seconds later his men followed, their jute bags bouncing heavily against their hips. Nine minutes and the clearing was quiet again except for the crackling of flames as the rafters in the barracks burned. Birds began to sing in the trees again and a long, curling trail of black smoke rose into the clear blue sky of a peaceful afternoon.

16

Capitaine Julio Ortega Montez kept the ancient Air Cubana Antonov 24 cargo plane headed roughly in the direction of Mexico. The instruments were working, keeping a steady altitude of twenty-five thousand feet over the Gulf of Mexico, and the two old turboprops were spinning with no more than their usual thundering roar.

The right seat was empty, not unusual for this sort of short-hop flight; the Brotherhood liked to keep their movements and activities as private as possible. He was not flying alone, of course; as usual the man with the cases was strapped in to the bucket jump seat in the cargo hold with strict instructions not to let his precious cargo out of his sight. As well as the man with the cases, the hold held two tons of live rock lobster, five tons of pineapples and four tons of avocados, none of which any Cuban citizen would ever see, much less eat.

Knowing that, Capitaine Julio Ortega Montez reached into the breast pocket of his uniform shirt and pulled out a packet of Rothman's cigarettes, a carton of which one of his fellow pilots had picked up for him on his last Canadian flight. Smoking on any flight was strictly forbidden, but what were they going to do, fire him? There weren't that many experienced pilots left in Cuba.

At fifty-five years of age, Julio had been flying his entire adult life. He soloed at the National Flight Academy at the age of eighteen in a Czech-made L-29 Delfín jet trainer, then worked his way up through a variety of MiGs until his body couldn't take the g-forces anymore.

He spent some time behind a desk, but after less than six months they had him flying Air Cuba passenger flights. When he turned fifty they switched him to short-hop cargo runs to Mexico and occasionally to Venezuela. He only made fifty dollars a week when he was working, and eighty dollars a month when he was off, but that much money could go a long way in Havana these days and he augmented his government pay with a variety of black market 'imports' and 'exports.'

A hundred *cohibas* he got from a contact at Habanos for five U.S. dollars, he sold *wholesale* to a smuggler in Mexico for ten dollars apiece. There were ways around the revolution if you were smart enough.

His father had worked in the Havana Engineering Office during the Batista years, and from the stories he'd told Julio, everything had come full circle again. Under Batista, Cuba had been oppressed under a vicious, corrupt dictator who used the police and the army to punish his enemies while he consorted with gangsters.

After a few years of idyllic solidarity in the early

days under the *Comandante*, Cuba was now once again ruled by a dictator who used the police and the army to punish anyone he even *thought* was his enemy and was surrounded with corrupt officials and gangsters in uniform who spirited millions out of the country every month on flights just like this one. Fidel had promised the country a socialist paradise and had given them a thug's cesspool instead.

Ortega laughed. What could you expect from a senile old fool who'd supported Gaddafi right up until they'd pulled the bald, sociopathic mass murderer out of a drainage ditch and filled him full of holes?

Ortega snuffed out his cigarette in a small glass jar with a screw top he kept in the cockpit for just that purpose. He laughed again. He supposed that crazy old dictators had to stick together. The pilot checked his watch; the ninety-minute flight was almost over; he could already see the green line of the mainland coming up ahead of him.

The pilot began to sing an old Mercedes Sosa song his mother had taught him – 'Alfonsina Y El Mar': '*Por la blanda arena, que lame el mar, su pequeña huella, no vuelve más*' – 'On the soft sand that is licked by the sea, her small footprint will never return.' Sad songs for sad times. Ortega sighed and began his final approach to Cancún International Airport.

The four-seater Polish Wilga cruised at five hundred feet over the rugged, jungle-covered hills. 'Are you sure about this?' Black asked, putting his hand on Montalvo

Arango's scrawny shoulder from the rear seat of the little plane.

'The caves near Aserradero is what the man said, senor,' said Arango, raising his voice over the rattling tumble of the unmuffled engine. 'I only know what he tell me.' For five hundred dollars they had convinced a reluctant Arango to come with them, but only with the promise that if the *Tiburon Blanco* was stolen the British government would replace it. Without batting an eye, Will Black solemnly agreed.

'You know what he's talking about?' Black said to Laframboise. 'It all looks like Cambodia down there to me.'

'Sure,' said the pilot, his right hand gently tweaking the stick in front of him. 'This whole area is full of sinkholes and caves.'

'Any of them particularly well known?' Carrie asked.

Laframboise laughed. 'If this guy's on the run, dearie, I doubt he's going to hide out anywhere famous.'

'True enough,' said Carrie, 'but is there anyplace local that's got some kind of story attached to it?'

'What kind of story?' Laframboise asked.

'A ghost story maybe, a kid getting lost. Some old legend.'

'*La caverna de los asesinados,*' said Arango, crossing himself. 'In the time of the bandito war.'

'They murdered men there?' Black said, doing the translation in his head: *the cavern of the murdered ones.*

'The militiamen trapped them there. The militia were only boys, fourteen, fifteen years old. Edito's brother, Domingo, was one of them. Their leader made them throw gasoline bombs into the cave. Those who were not burned to death were killed as they tried to escape, then thrown back into the flames. No one will go there for fear of *los fantasmas inquietos*.'

'The restless ghosts,' said Black.

'*Sí.*' Arango nodded.

'Well, Domingo Cabrera would certainly remember it,' said Carrie, seated beside Black. She glanced down at the rolling landscape below. 'The question is, how do we find it?'

'It is sixteen miles east of Aserradero,' said Arango.

'Are you sure?' Black asked the aging man.

'Yes, I am sure,' said Arango.

'Why?' Carrie asked. 'I thought you told us Domingo Cabrera didn't tell you where they were going when they left with his brother and Holliday.'

'There was no need for him to tell me,' said Arango darkly. 'I was the militia leader who ordered those young boys to burn the Batistardos out of the cave. I was the one who threw the first *cóctel Molotova* into the cave to show the boys how it was done.'

There was a long silence in the cabin of the little aircraft, the roaring of the engine filling the air. Finally Black leaned forward and spoke to Laframboise. 'You know where he's talking about?'

'Near enough.' The pilot nodded.

'Any place to land?'

'There's a river but it's too wild and narrow to put down.'

'Anywhere else?'

'I heard stories about a guy with a hunting lodge and a private airstrip in that area. He was a doctor and a friend of Batista. His name was Martinez, I think.'

'Dr Enrique Gomez Martinez,' said Arango. 'He died in *la guerra de los bandidos*. He got rich giving the rich women of Habana abortions they did not want their husbands to know about.'

'Can you find the airfield?' Black asked Laframboise.

'No sweat,' said the pilot. 'Easy-peasy.' He laughed.

'They still say easy-peasy?'

'Not that I'm aware of,' said Carrie.

'Okay. Just sit back and enjoy the view and I'll see what I can do.'

Four hours after the Air Cubana flight piloted by Capitaine Julio Ortega Montez landed at Cancún International Airport, a silver-sided truck bearing the familiar blue-and-white starburst logo of the Meade Optical Corporation went through the Matamoros-Brownsville border crossing. After a brief Level II inspection of the driver and his assistant's documentation, the truck was passed through, then traveled its regular route to the cargo terminal at Brownsville-San Pedro Island Airport.

With the exception of one large box, the shipment of Glacier binoculars and Condor spotting scopes was loaded onto an Amerijet 747 heading for New York. The last box was opened by the driver's assistant, who then took the two large Halliburton cases from the Air

Cubana flight to the domestic passenger terminal, where he rented a dark blue Chrysler 300 from Avis, placed the two cases in the trunk and began the forty-eight-hour drive to Orlando, Florida, and the Contemporary Resort at Walt Disney World.

'You have to be kidding,' said Carrie Pilkington. 'There's a tree growing out of the runway!' She stared down at what was left of the old airstrip.

'Not to mention the burnt-out DC-3 and the fact that what's left of the airstrip runs along an exceedingly narrow ridge, Mr Laframboise,' added Black. The hulk of an old airliner, propellers bent, the portside wing ripped off at the root and the entire tail section torn off, lay at the far end of the landing strip, most of it overgrown with jungle foliage. A quarter mile to the west, perched on a rocky outcropping, Black could also see what looked like the stone foundations of a building, the roof and walls collapsed into the interior.

'The building was Dr Gomez's hunting lodge. The story is that at the last minute he got cold feet and tried to fly the plane out loaded with as much loot as he could hump down from the lodge. Him and about thirty or forty of his Batista buddies got roasted by a lucky shot from an old RPG2 before the plane could go wheels up. Great plane, the DC-3. You still see them around sometimes.'

'You can't land there,' said Carrie firmly. 'There's not enough room. We'll hit something, either that tree or the wreck. There just isn't enough room.'

Laframboise sighed. 'At a guess, dear, how high would you say that big shrub you call a tree is?'

'It looks to be about fifteen or twenty feet high,' said Carrie, staring down as Laframboise banked the little airplane, turning it into the wind.

'And how far is the tree from the wreck?'

'Eight or nine hundred feet?'

'You agree, Mr Black?'

'I'd say you're just about right.' Black nodded.

'*Ya está todo jodido loco,*' muttered Arango, shaking his head and staring down through the big side window at what he knew was certain death. '*Jodido loco.*'

'The stall speed for *Miroslava* is about twenty-five miles per hour. If I come in over the tree at forty miles per and kill the engine, she'll glide in over about fifty feet before she touches down like a feather. Landing she needs about five hundred feet, takeoff less than four hundred. Easy-peasy.'

'What about potholes?' Carrie said.

'Missy, now you're just splitting hairs.'

Laframboise brought the aircraft fully into the wind, then twisted the throttle on the stick to slow them down, simultaneously pushing the stick forward to lower the nose. The Wilga dropped slowly and by the time they reached the far end of the ridge, they were less than a hundred feet above it. Out of the corner of his eye, Black saw the ruins of the house on the knoll flash by and then he was looking down the airstrip at the vision of a young pine tree directly in their path.

I'm about to die because a pinecone blew onto an

abandoned dirt airstrip in Cuba in 1996, thought Black. He couldn't think of a more irrelevant way to end his life. 'Killed by a pinecone' was no fitting epitaph for the James Bond of his time.

The Wilga dropped even lower in Laframboise's remarkably steady hand and the pine tree loomed even larger in the wraparound windshield. Black felt his stomach knot, his bowels loosen and bile rise in his throat as they hurtled toward the tree. He closed his eyes for a second or two, then for some mad reason, opened them again as though his brain was forcing him to witness what was about to tear his body into tiny pieces mixed with chunks of Polish-fabricated metal.

Some small thing managed to intrude into the farthest point of his peripheral vision. Camouflage. The impossibility of seeing the nose and propeller of an old British Spitfire and then the tree was twenty feet in front of them, and then somehow it was below them.

Black was sure he felt the top boughs of the tree scratching the bottom of the fuselage and then they hit the dirt, bounced slightly and slowed as Laframboise waggled the tail to lose even more speed. They finally came to a stop about four hundred feet from the remains of the bullet-ridden wreckage of the DC-3. Off to his right and the edge of the landing strip, Black saw what had caught his eye just before they didn't hit the pine tree: an Embraer Super Tucano turboprop fighter plane under a cleverly designed fly tent of camouflage netting interwoven with enough pine boughs to make it blend in with the trees that covered the ridge.

That was crazy enough, but what he *really* couldn't figure out was how they'd managed to land it with the tree in the way. Laframboise had obviously been thinking the same thing. He glanced into the rearview mirror set just above the center of the windscreen.

'Tree's a phony,' the pilot said. Black followed his glance. The fifteen-foot tree was lying on its side in the middle of the runway. 'They stick it into a hole to make the strip look unusable.'

'Senors?' Arango said, his voice nervous as he stared out through the windscreen. Laframboise looked forward.

'Oh dear,' he said.

'Who the hell are they?' Carrie said, frowning.

A dozen men in camouflage fatigues, combat boots and black berets stepped out of the trees behind the DC-3 and were approaching the Wilga. Each of them was carrying a stubby little H&K MP5 submachine gun.

'This is not good,' said Will Black. 'This is not good at all.'

17

Holliday, Eddie and Domingo Cabrera stood on the dirt road between the slope of the hill and the wildly rushing river behind them. The river was one of the small tributaries of the Agabama, and for much of their time they had followed its course into the mountains.

Holliday squatted down, examining the deep tread marks in the dirt. 'They were big,' he said. 'Either two or three of them. I'm not quite sure. Two huge wheels in the front and two sets of double wheels in the rear.'

'There were three vehicles,' said Domingo Cabrera.

'How can you be so sure?'

'Because I am sure,' said the white-haired man, his voice tense. He turned away from the road and began to climb the scrub-covered hill toward the mouth of a cave high above the river. Following, Holliday noted that it looked as though there had been recent activity on the slope, as well; a few scattered concrete railway ties, a short length of slightly rusty track – some kind of narrow-gauge rail line like the kind you might find in an old gold or silver mine, of which there were quite a number in Cuba.

They reached a small shelf of rock outside the mouth of the cave. Except for the floor of the entrance, it was rough and natural, about forty feet wide and thirty feet high at the peak. The rails and ties were intact as they ran into the dark recesses of the cavern.

'A mine?' Holliday asked, slightly out of breath after making the steep climb. He looked up at the roof of the cave and saw a series of heavy-duty lag bolts deeply rooted in the stone.

The lag bolts held huge U-bolts, and the U-bolts were threaded with the remains of wire cable that had been run through a complicated series of high-tension pulleys. 'Not a mine, something else,' he said, answering his own question.

Holliday stepped into the cave and followed the rails into the interior. It was dark, but there was still enough light coming from the entrance to let him see. He was at least two hundred feet along the track when the cave opened up enormously.

Not quite Carlsbad but large enough – at least five hundred feet long, six hundred wide and a hundred and fifty feet high, the ceiling lost in permanent darkness. In a limestone cave of any size, there are usually stalactites hanging from the ceilings and their twin stalagmites rising from the floor. Both were caused by water seepage taking excessive minerals from the stone over a period of thousands of years, accreting them into the spiky formations. Here there was nothing except the sawn-off remains of where stalagmites had once been, the work clearly done by some sort of circular concrete saw.

Off to his left Holliday saw an air mattress raised on a bed of pine boughs, the remains of a campfire, a stockpile of dry wood and kindling, a knapsack, a very old-looking kerosene lantern, a pair of Soviet-era KOMZ binoculars in their leather case, a military-style collapsible canvas bucket for water, a machete and all the other necessities of survival in the wild, including a Russian Saiga .308-caliber hunting rifle. Domingo Cabrera had clearly been living in the cave ever since his disappearance.

A large skeletal structure appeared out of the gloom. It looked like the underpinnings of a set of bleachers from a baseball stadium minus the seats and the floor. It went up in three tiers, each tier twenty feet above its neighbor, angled back in a zigzag and covered with the ubiquitous Cuban corrugated iron roof sixty feet above the floor of the cave.

The roof was sloped toward the back of the bleachers and was beginning to develop its own sets of small stalactites and stalagmites, gluing it firmly to the curved sidewall of the cavern. Give it five thousand years and the bleachers would have turned into a cave within a cave – an enormous mound of accreted minerals.

As Holliday approached he saw that the bleachers were a set of curved metal cradles, eight for each level, and that there were even more U-bolts and turnbuckle-pulley arrangements in the iron roof of the three-tiered unit and that there was also some sort of chain mechanism.

He also saw that the rail line ran the length of the bleacher unit and then dead-ended at a wedge of concrete with a steel bumper bolted to it. Holliday stared for a long time, then finally shook his head.

'All right,' he said, turning to Domingo and Eddie, who had followed him down the tracks. 'I give up. What the hell is it?'

'It is a very long story, Colonel Holliday. It goes back many, many years; more than five hundred years if you want to hear all of it.'

'I know about the Brotherhood, *Los Hermanos*. Start from after that.'

Domingo Cabrera looked around the cave, his eyes taking on the appearance of someone remembering the past and not enjoying it at all. He shook his head, then closed his eyes for a moment, his lips moving silently as though he was praying. Holliday looked over at Eddie. Holliday's friend made the sign of the cross over his chest and nodded toward his older brother. Finally Domingo opened his eyes again and spoke.

'Do you know about the War of the Bandits?'

'Batista supporters in the hills, CIA weapons drops. Sort of a counterrevolution after Fidel.'

'The hills, Colonel Holliday. It went on from just after the *Comandante* took power until 1963 or 1964, but really it was over before the *Bahía de Cochinos*.'

'The Bay of Pigs.'

Domingo Cabrera nodded slowly, gathering his thoughts. 'The *Comandante* was fighting people who fought like he had fought in the Sierra Maestre – guerrillas, fighting, running, fighting, running. In the end he had to use Batista's own tactics against these guerrilla fighters. He used numbers, mostly young militia like me. Thousands of us to fight perhaps six or seven hundred of them. We knew very little about real fighting then. Almost none of us had ever fired a weapon except in practice, and many of us died. Many of my childhood friends died.'

'What does this all have to do with *that*?' said Holliday, pointing toward the metal framework beside them.

'Let him speak,' said Eddie softly. It was the first time Holliday had heard Eddie speak about his brother with any sort of kindness or compassion.

Domingo made a sweeping gesture with his right arm. 'On May the seventeenth, 1961, just after the invasion at the *Bahía de Cochinos,* one hundred and eighty-seven died in this cave. They were burned to death, most of them.'

'You seem very sure about the numbers.'

'I am.' Domingo nodded back over his shoulder. 'I helped take out the remains and throw them into the river down there. Your friend on the boat, Capitaine Montalvo Arango, was our leader and taught us how to throw *los cócteles Molotov.* At first we thought it was *muy divertido*, very funny, but then they started running from the cave covered in fire and screaming and then it was not so funny anymore.

'After that the local people began calling this place *la Caverna de los Asesinados*, the Cave of the Murdered Ones. The people of the Escambray are very religious – Santeria of the very old kind. They said the cave was the home of Eshu, the *orisha* of *el Infierno.* Hell. From then on the cave was *tabú.* You know this word?'

'Yes.' Holliday nodded.

'Because of this, *El Comandante* and the other members of the Brotherhood thought it would be an excellent place, especially since Eshu's number is three.'

'Three what?' Holliday asked. The tracks of three vehicles in the dirt road outside, three tiers to the massive metal structure in the cave. He looked at the structure again, then down at the tracks at his feet. He suddenly had a very bad feeling about the whole thing.

'By October of 1962 our Soviet comrades had delivered thirty-two Dvina missiles to Cuba. What you call SS-4 or Sandal type. They were supposed to send forty more of the larger SS-5 missiles at a later time.

'Your U-2 overflights detected the missiles at San Cristóbal and that was the beginning of what became known as the Cuban Missile Crisis. The crisis ended when Khrushchev and Kennedy came to an agreement and the SS-4 Sandal missiles were removed. This is when the Brotherhood's idea was born.'

'I don't think I'm going to like this,' sighed Holliday.

Domingo continued. 'What Kennedy and the rest of the people involved *did not* know was that several dummy SS-4 missiles without warheads had been sent to Cuba months before so that the Cuban technical crews could practise on them. These dummy missiles were sent back to the Soviet Union in place of a number of the real ones.'

'Three of them,' said Holliday, seeing it all with a sudden, terrible clarity.

'Three of them.' Domingo Cabrera nodded. 'The three nuclear missiles which were brought here, away from the prying eyes of your U-2s and later your spy satellites. The missiles are very simple, almost laughably so compared to the missiles of today. Their guidance systems are no more than gyroscopes. They have been here for fifty years, the warheads in mothballs at a hidden location close to Havana.'

'And now the missiles have gone.'

'Do you know where?'

'If this is part of the Brotherhood's *Operación de Venganza,* I would think that they have been returned to their original sites in Pinar Del Rios, San Cristóbal to be exact. The hidden silos were built in a place well away from the mobile sites – a small area known as the Valle del Templete; it marked the route of the first explorers who discovered Havana. When the deal was struck between Khrushchev and Kennedy, nobody mentioned the silos, so they are probably still there.'

'What exactly is *Operación de Venganza?*' Holliday asked.

'On the day following Fidel Castro's death, three nuclear missiles will be launched at the United States, one aimed at what is now Orlando International Airport, but which in 1962 was McCoy Air Force Base. McCoy is where the U-2 that discovered the missiles landed and where all further U-2 flights over Cuba originated. The other two missiles will be aimed at Miami. The warheads are one megaton each.'

'How could the Brotherhood know when Fidel was going to die? You can't keep missiles like that ready to launch indefinitely.'

'They know because one of their number is going to assassinate him, Jaime Cardinal Lucas Ortega y Alamino, the archbishop of Cuba. He always celebrates the Feast of St Lazarus with *El Comandante*. His death will look natural, a stroke or seizure of some kind.'

'How did you discover all this?' Holliday quizzed.

'I worked for the ministry all of my adult life, always in low-level positions. I never was given even a bicycle for transportation to the ministry from my home, let alone an automobile.' The white-haired man shook his head. 'My last job was as a driver and part of the security detail for Deborah Espin.' Domingo Cabrera smiled sadly. 'In Cuba the one thing more invisible than a chauffeur is a black chauffeur; people speak of things they should not, as though you were not even there. And Deborah Espin is a very heavy drinker, as well. Her tongue gets very loose when she has been drinking. My mistake was to listen.' He shrugged. 'In the end someone discovered that I knew too much and I had to disappear. My only other choice would have been to die peacefully in my bed with a bullet in my brain like many others at the ministry before me.'

'I still don't understand the purpose of it all,' Holliday said after a moment's thought. 'Wiping out Orlando and Miami is going to kill a lot of people, but for what? It's a horrible, meaningless gesture.'

'The Brotherhood knows that on the death of Fidel, Raul and his family will flee the country. Raul keeps *una jet ejecutivo* at Ciudad Libertad Airport in the Atabay District of Havana for just this purpose. It is only ten minutes away from his home. With Raul gone, the country will descend into chaos.

'Eventually a military dictator will rise above the rest, but it is unlikely to be one of the Brotherhood's choosing, and between the death of Fidel and the rise of this new strongman a great deal of damage will be done. The only way to stop this, at least according to the Brotherhood, is to enact *Operación de Venganza* and force the United States to invade Cuba.

'The embargo would disappear overnight, the old Cuban families would take back what was theirs fifty years ago and so will the American companies that Fidel nationalized. It will begin a new era of prosperity for our country without bloodshed. Cuban bloodshed at least.'

Holliday stared at Eddie's white-haired older brother. The plan made a terrible, mad kind of sense. Under any other circumstances an American invasion of Cuba would have seen the United States vilified and ostracized around the world, but with a million or two dead by nuclear fire in a sneak attack worse than Pearl Harbor, an invasion would not only have just cause, but it would be politically correct, as well. Swift retribution. With that scenario in play, *any* president would be guaranteed four more years, no matter how low his polling numbers were.

'Dear God,' whispered Holliday.

Domingo Cabrera smiled sadly. 'I am afraid God has not visited Cuba in many years, Colonel Holliday.'

'When is the Feast of Lazarus?'

'The twenty-first day of this month. Seven days from now.'

'So there's nothing we can do to stop this thing.'

'No, Colonel, I am afraid there is nothing we can do at all.'

The man who had carried the two oversized Halliburton suitcases on the Air Cubana flight booked into the Disney Contemporary Resort and used his Amex card to prepay his two-week reservation. With that done, he gave the single dark blue Samsonite case he'd purchased in Houston to a bellboy, picked up his room key and went back outside.

He turned down the offer of one of the half dozen or so valet parkers, then took the Chrysler out into the enormous complex of parking lot that served the Contemporary Resort as well as several other Disney facilities. After he ensured that no one was watching, he removed two local New Orleans plates from the trunk, removed the rental Texas plates and screwed on the ones from Louisiana.

He'd spent an hour in New Orleans looking for the same model of Chrysler just to confuse things if it came to that. Finally he put the fourteen-day permit on the dashboard, locked the car and walked back to the hotel. He asked the concierge to get him a cab, tipped the man and rode to Orlando International Airport in time to catch a one-ten JetBlue flight to Nassau, which arrived an hour later.

In Nassau he switched from his authentic but bogus

American passport to his Cuban diplomatic passport and caught the three-fifteen Compañía Panameña de Aviación Airlines flight to Havana via Panama City. The flight took a little less than five hours all told and he arrived back in Havana in time for a late dinner in the Comedor de Aguiar dining room at the Hotel Nacional.

With his dinner completed, he took out the pocket-sized Inmarsat satellite phone, pulled out the blade antenna and dialed the suitcases in Orlando. The suitcases immediately demanded his authorization code, which he sent. Following that, he ran a series of test numbers to the suitcases, which then informed him that everything was in order.

He ended the data communication function, folded away the blade antenna and then had a look at the dessert menu. He chose the Copa Lolita crème caramel with two scoops of vanilla ice cream and a rum and raisin sauce. He ate his dessert slowly, savoring each bite, then had the waiter fetch him a Bolívar Petit Belicosos and a Havana club on the rocks. He lit the cigar and blew a swirl of the rich aromatic smoke into the air. He took a sip of his drink and leaned back against the banquette. He smiled happily. All in all, it had been an excellent day.

PART THREE

Liftoff

18

Vatican secretary of state Cardinal Antonio Niccolo Spada contemplated the remains of his breakfast on the lap table lying over his thighs and wondered how it was that Thomas Brennan, a lowly parish priest, always found some way to disturb his digestion.

At his age the cardinal's breakfast was not what it used to be – which had once been asparagus spears topped with two fried eggs, crumbled pancetta and bread crumbs seasoned with Parmesan, followed by sfogliatelli stuffed with ricotta and/or cannoli along with several cups of strong espresso.

Now it was what lay before him: a single soft-boiled egg, a piece of dry, whole-grain toast and tea with lemon. On occasion when he felt like living danger-ously, he would add a small glass of freshly squeezed orange juice, more for the irony of the fact that the Vatican kitchen's oranges were inevitably Jaffas imported from Israel than for the flavor. In fact, he'd developed a taste for powdered Tang in the Sixties and still much preferred it.

Spada picked up his glasses from the night table and put them on. He looked around the bedroom and wondered if all the struggle had been worth it. He imagined that one day in the near future he would die here, hopefully in an undisturbed sleep.

The room was large, the tall French doors that looked out onto the Vatican Gardens covered by tasseled silk drapes in dark blue. The furniture consisted of a tall, freestanding armoire for clothing, a desk, a small table and several chairs. The bed was a four-poster fifteenth-century oak monstrosity carved and worked as ornately as a Botticelli masterpiece in gold. The walls were bare white plaster, the ceiling high and crisscrossed with heavy wooden beams as old as the bed.

Except for a simple wooden crucifix on the wall behind him, the only decoration in the room was a large painting by the Renaissance artist Benozzo Gozzoli. The name of the painting was *Casting Devils out of Arezzo,* which depicted Saint Francis doing an exorcism outside the walls of an Italian city – fitting under the present circumstances, although in this case the city was Havana and the exorcist was certainly no saint.

Spada sighed. A man of his years should be dozing in his country garden listening to the bees hard at work and smelling the ripening grapes on his vines, not contemplating his own descent into Hades for planning the assassination of a foreign head of state while trying to digest his mean and simple breakfast. He rang the small silver bell on his lap table and waited.

A few seconds later his steward, Mario, appeared, a dour-looking man in his sixties wearing a dark suit, a white shirt and a dark tie. The steward approached

Spada, nodded briefly and removed the table from Spada's lap. Spada pulled the lapels of his jade green silk dressing gown a little more tightly across his chest and pulled the light duvet a little higher above his waist. Mario waited patiently while the cardinal adjusted his bedclothes.

'Send him in,' said Spada. Mario nodded and turned away. Like most of the Holy Father's servants, Mario was a member of Memores Domini, a lay brotherhood dedicated to a life of obedience, celibacy, silence and contemplative prayer. It wasn't common knowledge but members of Memores Domini who served in the Vatican were chosen for their below-average IQs, their illiteracy and their unwavering loyalty. It was the same qualities that convents looked for in their acolytes. You didn't want nuns who gossiped and thought for themselves; you wanted nuns who would work and do what they were told.

Brennan entered the room. 'Your Eminence,' he said, after closing the heavy door behind him.

'Sit,' said the cardinal.

Brennan pulled a chair away from the desk and brought it closer to the bed. He sat. Spada smiled. Brennan was a boor but he wasn't a complete idiot; he knew better than to light one of his foul-smelling cigarettes in Spada's private apartments.

'You wish to make a report at this abominably early hour?' Spada asked.

'It's your friend Musaro,' said the priest.

Spada groaned inwardly; he'd known Musaro since

the little upstart from nowhere had been ordained at the cathedral in Otranto and had kept his eyes on the man ever since. Even then he knew that Musaro was dangerous and he'd done what he could over the years to keep the man out of any key positions in the Holy See.

Somehow Musaro had managed to turn what amounted to exile from the halls of power into a career, becoming nuncio, or ambassador, to any number of countries experiencing problems within the Church. Long before anyone else had seen it, Musaro had recognized that Italy wouldn't rule the Vatican forever and had gathered favors from outside the Vatican for years. Eventually, as both the Polish pope and Ratzinger had proven, the young priest from nowhere was proved to be correct in his judgment.

'Tell me,' said Spada.

'There's been a lot of back chatter about him in the halls these days. It's getting louder by the day.'

'Back chatter?'

'Spy talk for gossip, Your Eminence. Cries and whispers, you might say.'

'What kind of gossip?'

'Nothing specific at this point. It's merely that he's the subject of a lot of conversations. I've had this from a number of sources. He's like a squirrel gathering nuts for the winter. Calling in favors. In politics it would be called maneuvering for position. In military terms he's enlisted his forces.'

'Against who?'

'Not quite sure,' mused Brennan. 'But a lot of the talk appears to be originating in the college. Your colleagues.'

Spada nodded to himself. It made sense. There was no doubt that the most powerful man in the Vatican after the Holy Father was the secretary of state, but the position of dean of the College of Cardinals was a very close third. It was the dean, after all, who presided over the conclave to elect a new pope, and on a number of occasions – most recently Pope Benedict – the dean was elected to the position himself.

'He wouldn't be campaigning on his own behalf,' said Spada thoughtfully.

Brennan nodded his agreement. 'Not Musaro's style. He much prefers to be the power behind the throne, not the power sitting on it.'

'Quite so,' said Spada. 'Is there any idea who is most favored?'

'Not yet,' said Brennan. 'But I wouldn't be surprised if it was Ortega.'

Spada stared at the rumpled Irish priest seated beside the bed. He felt a chill run down his spine. 'That would be insane! There's far too much scandal attached to him, not to mention our present situation. The Church has enough troubles without a . . .'

'A poof electing the Holy Father?' Brennan smiled.

'Indeed,' replied Spada, gathering his dressing gown even more tightly around his sunken chest, suddenly embarrassed. The Cuban cardinal archbishop wore jeweled slippers in Havana Cathedral, used perfume, had no one over the age of twenty-five in his household or office and had posed for photo opportunities with Castro wearing a red velvet beret with a gold communist star on the front. Red velvet!

Personally Spada had nothing against gays, but to have such an openly and flamboyantly effeminate man as Ortega in a position of power could be terribly damaging to the Church's already tattered and battered image.

'On the surface it looks mad, of course,' said Brennan. 'But for Musaro it might be an excellent choice. Knowing what he knows would be enough to keep Ortega in line, and with Ortega as dean of the college it might provide Musaro with a way into the Vatican and into another seat of power for himself.'

'Mine,' said Spada, his voice flat. That *did* make sense. The Holy Father was the voice of God on Earth, but the secretary of state was the stick in His hand. 'Are you sure about this information?'

'As I said, it's only been gossip up to now, but if I was putting money on a pony to come in first at the sweepstakes, that'd be the one I'd choose.'

'If this is what Musaro's up to, it must be stopped.'

Brennan stood up and Spada smiled briefly; the poor man's desperate need for nicotine was almost palpable. 'If you want it stopped, it only leaves you with one choice, I'm afraid,' said the Irish priest.

'And what choice is that?'

'The choice of which piece you want to have removed from the board: the bishop or the queen.' Brennan smiled at his pun.

'Do you have someone who could complete the task on short notice?'

'Certainly,' said Brennan. A small but vital group within the Vatican intelligence apparatus had been in existence since the middle of the thirteenth century when a French Templar grand master named Guillaume de Sonnac had organized the first secret society of Vatican *assassini*.

'Let me think about this,' said Spada. 'We don't want to act precipitously.'

'Don't think too long,' warned Brennan, and with that he nodded, turned on his heel and left the cardinal's bedroom.

Joseph Patchin stood in the large living room of the house in Georgetown, D.C., and listened to the cocktail party chatter all around him. For a Georgetown soiree like this, it was surprisingly free of bureaucrats and politicians. Most of the guests were well-heeled supporters of the Athena Foundation, a philanthropic organization in the arcane and confusing business of supporting other, less connected and smaller charity groups around the world.

So, why on earth was he standing here in a tux with a glass of Midleton Very Rare Irish in his hand? He wasn't wealthy, he wasn't particularly well connected politically, at least by most of the guests' standards, and he was certainly no philanthropist. He was a divorced man in late middle age who'd taken a beating from his ex's lawyers as well as the markets and was one administration away from being unemployed.

The CIA operations director went through his mental address book and tried to remember the names of anyone he knew who was directly or indirectly involved with the Athena Foundation, but he came up empty. When he'd received the invitation, he'd asked Becky, his secretary, to discreetly find out if the invitation had been sent to him rather than to his ex-wife by some sort of oversight, but she'd struck out, as well. In the end he'd decided to attend the party just in case; turning down any social invitation in D.C. could be fatally dangerous to your career, while accepting cost nothing more than a wasted hour or two on a weekday evening and gave you the chance to drink someone else's expensive booze.

After an hour the only thing Patchin had discovered was that the house he was in was a Washington pied-à-terre belonging to the recently retired U.S. ambassador to Brazil and his wife, heiress to an old Florida sugar fortune as well as being on the board of directors for the Athena Foundation. From what Patchin had overheard at the party, the ambassador and his plump, dark-haired wife spent most of their time in Palm Beach or on their Mediterranean-based yacht in Monaco. None of it was ringing any bells in Patchin's mind, but he assumed that if he stayed long enough he'd find out why he'd been invited.

He was right; halfway through his second glass of the honey-smooth Irish whisky, he felt a light tap on his shoulder. He turned and found himself staring at the leonine, white-haired and statesmanlike figure of Max Kingman, CEO of the Pallas Group and father of Rufus Kingman, Patchin's own deputy director.

Max Kingman shook Patchin's hand warmly in a solid grip and simultaneously squeezed his left biceps with the other hand. Kingman looked like a shanty-Irish version of the Godfather: white hair swept back from a broad forehead, mustache neatly trimmed, cheeks and jowls freshly shaven and rosy with the unhealthy glow of a little too much alcohol and blood pressure sneaking up into the dangerous numbers. He was bucking the trend wearing a decades-out-of-date but perfectly tailored three-piece, dark blue pin-striped suit, a Valentine red bow tie and old-fashioned wing-tip brogues.

'The library is on your left at the end of the hall. Ten minutes,' said Kingman. He released Patchin's hand and his arm, then turned, making his way through the crowd, glad-handing men and giving the women courtly little bows as he maneuvered his way across the room like a shark swimming through a swimming flock of penguins.

Ten minutes later Patchin went down the hallway and stepped into the library of the ambassador's house. It was a large room with a huge mullioned window looking out on a very private, stone-walled rose garden. The ceiling was high with plaster moldings and there were three walls of floor-to-ceiling bookcases crammed with volumes that appeared to have been actually read rather than purchased by the yard by an expensive Washington decorator who gets to spend other people's money to give them good taste that his or her clients don't have. There were a number of old, well-worn leather club chairs gathered around a glass-topped, wood-strapped steamer trunk, a small but elegant wood fireplace and an eighteenth-century Chippendale desk that was doubling as a bar. Kingman poured himself a drink as Patchin entered the room and closed the door behind him.

'Get something for you?'

'No, thanks,' said Patchin. Two drinks was his limit when there was business in the offing; anything more than that and he'd probably wind up on the short end of any bargain.

'Sit,' said Kingman, gesturing to one of the leather armchairs. Patchin sat. The white-haired man dropped a trio of ice cubes into his amber-colored drink and sat down across from the CIA director. He sipped the drink, smacked his lips and set the glass down on the coffee table. He smiled at Patchin. 'Canadian rye,' said the older man. 'A weakness of my youth. Cheap duds, cheap broads, cheap booze.' Not likely. Kingman had been born with an oily Texas spoon in his mouth.

Patchin smiled and kept his mouth shut.

'How are things working out with Rufus?' Kingman asked. 'I knew your man, Mike Harris. Not well, but we'd met on occasion. Drank too much and a bit unstable, frankly. We all thought Rufus would be a perfect fit to replace him and he was being wasted at Justice.'

'He certainly knows what he's doing,' answered Patchin, keeping his tone neutral. He didn't ask who the 'we' was in Kingman's statement.

'Surprised at being invited to this boring little get-together?'

'More curious than surprised,' said Patchin.

'More than the walls have ears these days,' sighed Kingman. 'If we'd met in a civilized manner – in a restaurant, at your place of business or mine – it would be on everyone's damnable Blueberry in five minutes.'

Patchin smiled. He was reasonably sure that Kingman knew perfectly well that it was BlackBerry, not 'Blueberry,' and he was just as sure that the sly old bastard liked to keep up the sleepy, simple country-boy facade as a way of catching his adversaries off guard. Once again he made no response.

'But I do believe that old saw about there being safety in numbers.' The man who effectively managed the biggest private army in the United States paused for a moment and then continued. 'Which is why I have the ambassador throw these little booze cruises every once in a while.'

In other words, thought Patchin, you're telling me you've got an ambassador and his billionaire wife in your hip pocket; a big stick wielded softly.

It was time to wield his own stick.

'Your corporation does business with the Pentagon and the agency all the time,' he said quietly. 'Your son is my deputy director, which is certainly no secret. So, why the need for discretion? Your offices are closer to mine than this house is.'

Kingman picked up his drink, swallowed two fingers of rye whisky in a single gulp, then cracked an ice cube between his molars and chewed on the bits and pieces. 'Some meetings require more discretion than others,' said the old man. 'This is one of those meetings.' He rattled the remaining ice cubes in the glass. 'The man my son replaced was a fucking cowboy. Ernest goddamn Hemingway on steroids. He made his bed with the wrong whore and he paid for it with his life. We're hoping you don't make the same mistake.'

'I'm not sure what you mean,' answered Patchin.

'You don't know it yet, boy, but the whole world's about to blow up in your face. It's going to cost the man in the White House his second term unless he does exactly as he's told, and whether he does or not you're going to wind up being a sacrificial goat tied to a god-awful big stake. We're offering you a way out.'

That regal 'we' again. 'Do tell,' said Patchin mildly.

'Well,' began Kingman, 'we've got this little operation going on in Cuba . . .'

19

'The planes out there under the camouflage nets are Super Tucanos. I guarantee you they were provided by International Aviation Services, which is a subsidiary of Blackhawk Security,' said Carrie Pilkington, her voice firm with conviction. 'I knew they weren't Cuban Special Forces.'

'They're speaking Spanish,' said Laframboise, their pilot. 'And they sure as hell aren't Mexicans.'

'Maybe it's the Bay of Pigs again – Cuban exiles.'

'Not with that kind of equipment,' said Carrie. 'They're Americans.'

'We've been over this a hundred times since yesterday,' sighed the MI6 agent, Will Black. 'Let's give it a rest for a while, okay? I'm hungry, I'm thirsty and I am most definitely not in a good mood.'

Carrie, Will Black, Arango and Pete Laframboise were seated with their backs to the walls in the ruins of a single-story wooden structure that must have been what once had passed for a control tower or communications shack back in the days when the private airstrip had been in operation.

Over the years and decades since then, the jungle had grown up around the building, hiding it from the air. There was a walled outhouse-style toilet cubicle in one corner of the shack but no running water or any other kind of facility.

'From what I saw, there are at least a hundred men bivouacked here,' said Laframboise.

'There were enough crates of equipment stacked around under those camouflage nets for ten times that number of men,' murmured Carrie. 'They've got brand-new turboprop fighter planes armed with Hellfire missiles. Whatever this is, it's major league.'

The old wooden door of the hut opened and four uniformed men appeared, silhouetted by the sunlight outside. Like every one else they'd seen so far, the men all wore mirrored aviator-style sunglasses and had no rank insignia on their battle fatigues or their Special Forces-style berets.

The first two carried in a shaky-looking card table and the other two brought in five folding chairs. The men set up the table and chairs and then withdrew. Two more silent men brought four military-style covered trays and a carton of bottled water, then withdrew themselves. They left the door open.

Peering out, Will Black could see across the dirt strip to a small clearing carved out of the jungle and topped by yet another jungle-pattern camouflage net. Under the net was a large tent, flaps pulled open to reveal a sophisticated communications setup and manned by another half dozen soldiers, all of them wearing headsets and staring into computer screens and what appeared to be radar displays.

From what he could make out squinting through

the open door, they'd pulled the old Wilga off the end of the strip and halfway into the scrub brush beside the burnt-out DC3, then covered it with more of the jungle camouflage.

'I guess there's no point in making a run for it.' Laframboise grinned, getting to his feet and stretching. 'They've got poor old *Miroslava* bound up in a girdle.'

'No point at all,' agreed Black. He and Carrie stood up, as well. They went to the table and sat down. Arango joined them silently.

'Even if they didn't swat us down like flies, where would we go?' Carrie said sourly. 'It really is a jungle out there.'

They took the covers off the food trays. 'Roast beef, mashed potatoes with gravy, creamed corn, steamed spinach and green Jell-O,' said Laframboise, ripping open the little package of plastic utensils. 'Pretty good grub for a prison cell.'

They ate and drank and fifteen minutes later two men appeared and cleared away the trays, then disappeared. Two minutes after that a new figure appeared in the doorway. He turned away for a moment and barked an order in Spanish before he stepped into the old shack. He was tall, hawk-faced and visibly much older than any of the men Black had seen so far. Unlike any of those men, he also had a rank insignia on his beret – the single silver oak leaf of a bird colonel.

'*Su español es muy bueno,*' said Black. '*Pero usted no es Cubano.*'

'Your Spanish is pretty good, too, and you're not Cuban, either,' said the lieutenant colonel.

'Benefits of a classical education.' Black smiled.

'Brit.'

'Quite right.'

'I'm from Brooklyn.'

'Gee, I never would have guessed,' said Carrie.

'My name is Frank Turturro.' The lieutenant colonel smiled. 'Who are you?'

'My name is Carrie Pilkington. I'm an analyst in the Central Intelligence Agency.'

'I wouldn't say that too loudly, Miss Pilkington,' said Turturro. 'It's the kind of thing that'll get you in a lot of trouble in this country.'

'And being a lieutenant colonel in a foreign mercenary army doesn't?' Black snorted.

'What foreign mercenary army would that be?' Turturro asked.

'BSSI,' responded Carrie emphatically. 'Blackhawk Security Services International. The Super Tucanos with all the firepower out there were provided by International Aviation Services, Blackhawk's air force. Their headquarters is at the old Air Haven Airport in Alhambra, Arizona. You've even got half a dozen Lockheed Neptune bombers from the Sixties that Blackhawk uses to "pacif" natives in your South American operations.'

'You're very well informed, Miss Pilkington. I congratulate you,' said Turturro.

'It's my job,' said Carrie. 'What's yours?'

'I follow orders, Miss Pilkington, no more, no less.'

'Where have I heard that before? I wonder,' said Black.

'A Brit who speaks excellent Spanish in the company of a CIA analyst. You must be MI6.'

'Bond, James Bond,' said Black in a terrible Sean Connery brogue.

Turturro smiled and leaned back in his chair. He stared at Pete Laframboise, then reached into the breast pocket of his fatigues and tossed over a package of unfiltered Camels with a matchbook tucked into the cellophane. Laframboise tapped one out of the pack and lit it, taking a deep drag, and then let it roll out from his nostrils and his mouth with a contented sigh.

'So, who are you?' Turturro asked.

'Nobody,' said the pilot. 'Just along for the ride.' He took another drag on the cigarette and smiled. 'Actually, I *am* the ride.'

'You own the Wilga?' Turturro asked.

'"Owned" isn't a real word in Cuba, Mr Colonel, sir,' said Laframboise. 'You only own something here until the government or some bigwig gets it into his head that he doesn't like it or he wants it himself and then, poof, it's gone. It's like power, Colonel. It's an ephemeral thing; it only exists if you can hang on to it and for as long as you can hold on to it.'

'Deep thinking for a crop duster,' said Turturro.

'Before I left the country in a hurry, I was finishing up a postgraduate degree in political science at McGill

University in Montreal.' He picked up the Camels from the table. 'Mind if I keep these?'

Turturro nodded. 'Go ahead.'

Laframboise slipped the matches back under the cellophane, then put the packet of cigarettes into his pocket.

'And you?' Turturro asked, staring at Arango. The Cuban turned his head and spat onto the floor.

'I am the man who cut off your compadres' *cojones* fifty years ago. I was also the man who loaded the rocket into the RPG that brought down that airplane out there.'

'A CIA analyst, an MI6 agent, an old *Fidelista* and a gray-haired grad student from Montreal fly into an armed camp in a piece-of-crap crop-dusting plane. Why?'

'Sounds like the opening to a bad joke,' said Carrie. 'We know why we're here, but what about you?'

'This is the part when the bad guy tells the hero his evil plans for world domination?' Turturro said. 'I don't think so.' He stood up. 'You'll be held here until things are . . . under way. After that you'll be released and you'll be on your own.'

'Not much of an interrogation,' said Black. 'Where are the lasers and the pools full of sharks? Snakes maybe?'

'There are no poisonous snakes in Cuba,' said Turturro. 'And I don't need to interrogate you. For the moment I just need to keep you out of the way. Try to escape and my men will shoot you. Survive that and there's thirty miles of jungle between here and the next best thing to civilization. So just stay put.' Turturro walked to the doorway, then turned. 'Don't piss me off,' he said, and then he was gone. A guard stepped halfway into the room and shut the door.

'That was a bit weird,' said Carrie. 'It wasn't much of an interrogation, was it?'

'You believe any of that bull-puckie?' Laframboise drawled, still smoking the Camel.

'I don't think he has the slightest idea of what to do,' said Will Black. 'We weren't part of whatever game plan he's got in mind. Flies in the ointment, so to speak.'

'So, what does he do with us?' Carrie said.

'He goes up the chain of command until he gets someone who can make a decision.'

'What chain of command?' Carrie asked. 'Who is Blackhawk working for? The Pentagon wouldn't sanction an invasion of Cuba; they wouldn't dare and neither would the president.'

'I don't know who his ultimate employers are, but the colonel is in the middle of something very big here. Those men and that equipment aren't here as some sort of resistance army in the mountains. They're an assault force.'

'You think this is part of Selman-Housein's *Operación de Venganza*?' Carrie asked.

'I think it has to be.' Black nodded.

'Okay, I'm lost,' said Laframboise. He wet his fingers and pinched out the butt of his Camel. 'What the hell is Operation Vengeance and what does *El Comandante's* doctor have to do with it?'

'It's a long story.'

'I'm not going anywhere,' said Laframboise. 'And neither are you, boss.'

'We'd better be,' said Black, staring at the closed door, his tone ominous.

'Why's that?'

Carrie answered, 'Because pretty soon the colonel's going to get his orders from on high and he's going to kill us.'

20

The old man sat in the shade of the avocado tree growing beside the main house and watched his great-grandchildren splashing and playing at the far end of the large swimming pool. Their laughter seemed very far away, almost as if they were living in a different world from his own. In his world the voices were clear and the images were sharp and brightly colored and there was no need for the hearing aids he wore or the bifocal spectacles that pinched his nose.

He let his head fall forward a little and glanced at his hand on the arm of the old wicker chair. The chair came from the old family finca in Oriente where he and his nine brothers and sisters had spent their early childhood.

Cords of sinew and veins ran like creeping worms beneath parchment, liver-spotted skin, and the nails were thick and ribbed like yellowing horn. The old man lifted the hand and placed the tips of his first and second fingers below his nostrils, hoping to catch some faint scent of the *cohibas* his man Eduardo Irizarri had rolled for him. There was nothing, not the slightest memory of an odor; not surprising, really. It had been a quarter of a century since he'd given them up, and he chuckled aloud as the thought drifted through his mind like smoke.

He'd had his first cigar with his old friend David de Jongh behind the gymnasium at the Dolores School in Santiago and they'd coughed their lungs out on one of Father Alvarez's Montecristos. They'd called him *Bola de Churre* then – 'Greaseball.' Not anymore, and he smiled at that thought as well.

All so long ago, and that long life, a life without great love or change or real happiness, had been haunting him for some time now. What had he missed except to outlive all his enemies and watch presidents of the United States come and go like the turning of their leaves in autumn? There was no fall or winter here; it was always summer, it was always the twenty-sixth of July and he and his brother and Camilo, Huber Matos and Che were young again and attacking the Moncada Barracks with nothing but hope and bursting hearts and a few old weapons. *Siempre Veintiséis!*

'Papa?'

It was his son Antonio, the handsome one who traveled with the baseball team.

'Yes, Antonio?'

'You looked very sad, Papa.'

'I was thinking about snow,' the old man said, remembering.

'Has it ever snowed here?' Antonio laughed at the idea of snow in this place.

But the old man remembered it clearly. It had been Christmas Eve, 1976, and a blizzard in Montreal diverted them to the old airport in Gander, New-foundland. He'd had Nitza and Margot prepare *papa rellena* and *lechon* in the airport kitchens for everyone, and then a reporter from the newspaper took him for a drive around the town. Behind the local hospital he'd seen some children with their *trineos*, their toboggans, sliding down a hill and he'd tried it for himself. He fell off, of course, and he and everyone had laughed except his bodyguards, but the children showed him how to make *los ángelas* in the snow and he'd lain there in the darkness, staring up into the night, the snowflakes falling on his beard and then his tongue.

'They were all different,' said the old man. 'They were all different and that was the problem.' The great constant that Marx had overlooked in his squalid Soho garret in London – that there are no constants and that every man was as individual as his fingerprints . . . or a snowflake.

'What was different, Papa?'

'The snowflakes . . . they were all different.' To bend eleven million minds to yours and hold them for fifty years was just like catching snowflakes on your tongue – impossible.

There was a long silence, broken only by the children in the pool and the wind spinning the leaves above his head.

'The doctor is here for your checkup, Papa.'

The old man blinked and came back to the present. He stared at his son, letting his mind put itself together like the pieces of a jigsaw puzzle. A jet lumbered overhead on its way toward the airport, its muted turbines like the rolling sound of distant thunder. A sound that didn't even exist in the world of the twenty-sixth of July.

'Eugenio has returned from *Irlanda*?'

'No, Papa, this is a new doctor for you.'

'I don't want a new doctor,' he said, his voice suddenly suspicious. 'Where is Eugenio?'

There was a long pause. Finally the old man's son spoke again. 'He may have . . . defected. He was last seen at his hotel in Dublin, but he disappeared in the big park they have there.'

'Perhaps he was abducted.'

'No, Papa, they do not think so.'

'They?'

'MININT, Papa.'

'Ibarra?' General Abelardo Colome Ibarra was minister of the interior, but Antonio Castro knew the seventy-three-year-old man had been showing clear signs of dementia for some time now. The only thing keeping him in his position was his longtime friendship with his *teo,* and even with that most of his responsibilities had been put onto other, younger shoulders.

'Yes, Papa.'

'Ibarra is insane, you know,' murmured the old man. 'An old American hand grenade exploded too soon and he had a sliver of shrapnel in his brain. At Cuevo, near the old house in Biran.'

'Papa,' said Antonio gently. 'You must let the doctor

218

examine you. We want to make sure you are well enough for the festivities next week.'

'Festivities?'

'The feast of St Lazarus, Papa. Everyone will be here for you. You must see the doctor to see if you are well enough.'

'*No doctor!*'

The sound of the old man's voice rang out like a pealing bell. It was enough to startle the yellow-breasted *zapatas* in the avocado tree into hurried, noisy flight. It was the voice of a man who had ruled a generation. Even the children stopped playing in the pool for a moment. The young man sighed. He knew that tone. 'Yes, Papa,' said this son meekly. He placed his hand on his father's shoulder and together they silently watched the children playing in the swimming pool. There were some things that you just didn't argue with Fidel Castro about, and this was obviously one of them. The doctor could wait.

Holliday sat with Eddie in the shadows of the cave entrance. Through the Russian binoculars, Holliday watched as two men climbed up the hill toward them. The man in the lead was Domingo Cabrera, but the withered old man behind him was a stranger.

The old man was wearing an old straw cowboy hat, an old-fashioned wifebeater undershirt, a pair of jeans and worn-out high-laced combat boots. He had a weapon in his hands, a canvas bag on his hip and something that looked like a bowie knife in a leather sheath hanging from his belt. From where Holliday sat, the old man's weapon looked like an old Remington 1912 shotgun with a homemade leather sling, but the man was clearly no threat to Eddie's brother. Domingo strode on ahead, his own Saiga .308 carelessly slung over one shoulder, his knapsack over the other.

According to Domingo, there was a tiny farming village six or seven miles from the cave where he sometimes went for supplies, but he never mentioned bringing one of the villagers back with him. The runaway MININT officer had told the villagers he was a dissident hiding from the police, but how would he explain his brother and a man who was clearly a *yuma*?

The two men finally reached the cave and Holliday and Eddie stood and stepped out of the shadows. The old man with Domingo looked at them carefully, and Holliday saw his right index finger curl against the trigger of the old shotgun. The man was as black as tar, his face cut with lines and wrinkles so dense that it looked like darkly grained ebony. His eyes were a startling and very clear blue.

'*Está bien, Enrique,*' murmured Domingo. '*Ellos son amigos.*' Domingo slipped the rifle off his back as well as the bulging knapsack. '*No hay leña y el cubo es en la cueva.*'

Enrique nodded. He slung the shotgun over his shoulder on its homemade sling and went inside the cave, giving Holliday and Eddie a still-suspicious glance as he went past them. Domingo began gathering rocks and putting them in a circle. Some kind of fire pit. A few moments later Enrique reappeared with an armload of kindling as well as the canvas bucket. He dropped the firewood beside Domingo and then went back down the hillside with the bucket. Domingo began building a fire.

'We must leave here very quickly,' he said, arranging kindling.

'Why?' Holliday asked. 'Not that I have any objection.' What he really wanted was to get the hell away from Cuba as fast as he could and tell someone in authority what the hell was going on.

'There was a firefight at a checkpoint not too far from here. The guards were killed as well as a vanload of police. At least a dozen men altogether. No one survived. Whoever did it wrote the words "Viva Zapata" on the wall of the barracks in spray paint.'

'Emiliano Zapata from the Mexican War?' Holliday asked. 'That's nuts.'

'Presumably the message referred to Orlando Zapata, a dissident who died during a hunger strike several years ago,' said Domingo. He lit the fire with a kitchen match and it caught almost instantly.

'There's a bunch of dissident guerrillas running around in the mountains?'

'I do not think so,' said Domingo. 'Enrique has a mule. He was taking some eggs to the market when he heard the explosions at the checkpoint, and when everything was quiet he went down and checked. This is what he found.' Domingo turned away from the fire and opened his knapsack. He took out the expended tube of an M72 LAWS rocket, a dirt-stained black beret and a handful of brass shell casings. The shell casings were huge – at least two and a half inches long. Holliday recognized them instantly.

'Winchester .300 Magnums,' he said, picking one up and twisting it in his fingers. 'Sniper rifle ammunition. Definitely not for amateurs.'

'Or dissident guerrillas,' said Domingo. 'Look at the beret.'

Holliday picked it up. It was a standard military-style beret with a peak where a unit badge had been; he could even see the small, ragged stitching holes where it had been removed. He flipped it over and looked at the sweatband. Half worn off on the leather insert, stamped in gold, were the words MADE FOR BSSI, BY PARKHURST HAT CORPORATION.

'Oh, shit,' said Holliday. 'Not again.'

'Who is this BSSI?' Eddie asked.

'Blackhawk Security Systems International,' said Holliday.

'Ah.' Eddie nodded. 'The fools who blew up my *Pevensey* and attacked us in the jungle,' he said angrily. *Pevensey* was the battered old riverboat Eddie had piloted up the Kotto River into the Central African Republic. It was aboard *Pevensey* that Holliday had met Eddie for the first time.

Enrique came trudging back up the hill, the pail heavy in his hand. He reached the top of the hill and the cave entrance and gratefully lowered the pail.

Holliday had assumed he was going for water, but at first glance it looked as though the pail was full of mud.

'What's with mud?' Holliday asked.

'I know,' said Eddie, grinning from ear to ear. 'Watch.'

Enrique carefully unslung the old shotgun and put it down on the ground. He opened up the big canvas bag he had on his hip and took out a brace of three ring-tailed pheasants. He placed one of the game birds on the stone shelf outside the cave, stretched out the wings and carefully put a booted foot on each wing. He gathered the feet of the bird in one hand and pulled steadily. There was a wet tearing sound and the entire body of the bird came out of its skin, the entrails pulled out of the gut and still attached to the intact head and neck. He took a large knife from a sheath on his belt and sliced off the wings. The result was a perfectly boned, stripped and field-dressed pheasant.

He then proceeded to dress the other two pheasants in exactly the same way. With the three birds dressed, he scooped the muddy riverbank clay from the bucket and completely covered each bird. When all the birds were encased in the heavy clay, he pushed each one deep into the base of the small fire Domingo had built.

'*Que estará listo en treinta minutos,*' said Enrique. He squatted down on his heels, took a stick from the small pile of remaining kindling and used it to pile hot coals against the clay-covered birds.

'They will be done in half an hour,' translated Eddie.

'My mother used to call it *Faisán de Mendigo, Beggar's Pheasant*. It is a very old-country recipe.'

'I'm sure it will taste wonderful,' said Holliday, 'but what does it have to do with getting out of here?'

'Enrique is an *Italero*, a priest of the Santeria religion. Later he will use the entrails of the three birds to give us knowledge of our future.'

'You must be kidding,' said Holliday.

'Enrique is also the best guide and hunter in the mountains. If we want to get out of the Escambray, he must show us the way. Without him we are dead men.'

Holliday stared at the leathery old man squatting by the fire, poking at it with a stick. He was muttering to himself now, something that sounded like a prayer or incantation.

'Oshun ogoao mi inle oshun . . . igua iya mio . . . igua iko bo s . . . i iya mi guasi iya mi omo . . . y alorde oguo mi inl, ashe Oshun.'

'Go, Enrique,' muttered Holliday, wondering if Beggar's Pheasant would turn out to be his Last Supper.

21

Father Ronan Patrick Sheehan arrived in Nassau on the Eastern Airlines early-morning flight and he was dead tired. It had been a long trip, beginning in Rome's Fumincino Airport, then transferring to another aircraft at Heathrow and yet another in Miami. The things he did for God . . . and for Thomas Brennan.

Sheehan was a long-faced man in his fifties, jug-eared with grizzled, short gray hair and pale green eyes. He had a wide mouth and a long nose to suit his long face and a strong, square chin. He wore no collar; instead he was dressed in an open sport shirt, cream-colored chinos and worn-looking Nikes.

He traveled on a dark red Irish passport, and nowhere on the document was he identified as a priest. He was simply Nicholas Patrick Sheehan of Fethard-on-Sea, County Wexford, born there on November the sixteenth in the year of Our Lord nineteen hundred and fifty-three. There was no mention of the Jesuits getting him at twelve years old for the greater glory of God and beginning the journey that inevitably brought him to this place and on this day.

The priest in sheep's clothing picked up his single bag from the carousel, then stepped out into the over-heated and unconditioned air outside the Lynden

Pindling Terminal. He was immediately accosted by a man named Sidney who drove a beaten-up, rusted and off-white Toyota Corolla taxi.

'Good mornin', good mornin', how are you this mornin'?' said Sidney, opening the rear door of the old car with a flourish.

'To be honest I feel like hell,' answered Sheehan, handing the cabdriver his one small suitcase.

'You *do* look like somethin' unhappy the kitty cat put in the sandbox,' said Sidney. He shut the door, went around to the driver's side and slid behind the wheel, putting the suitcase on the seat beside him. The meter on the dashboard was an old Argo that must have weighed ten pounds. The last time Sheehan had seen one had been when he was on assignment in Bombay before they started calling it Mumbai.

In the front seat Sidney shook his gray head sorrowfully. 'This be what worl' travelin' does for you, then I want no part of it,' he said. 'Where we going today, boss?'

'Harbour Resort Paradise Island,' answered the incognito priest. Sidney cranked down the meter and it began to tick like a cartoon time bomb.

They drove away from the airport and around briny Lake Killarney, then turned onto West Bay Street with the beach on their left. They drove by the forest of hotels on Cable Beach, past Saunders Beach, which was open to the public, and past the fish shacks at the entrance to Arawak Key. Finally they reached Nassau itself, navigating through the jitney buses, past the banks and souvenir shops and restaurants until they reached the turnoff for Paradise Island, stopping to pay the dollar toll, then coming onto the island itself.

When they reached the resort, Sheehan paid the thirty-dollar fare with a fifty without taking change, took his one bag, then went inside and booked in. The Harbour Resort was on the channel side of the island, and his view was of a forest of masts from the marina on the opposite side. He pulled the curtains closed, turned off the lights and was asleep almost instantly.

Sheehan woke up just after eleven the following morning, showered, shaved and then went down to the main entrance. The concierge gave him directions and he walked around the Hurricane Hole Marina to the Green Parrot cabana-style restaurant beside the marina pool. He sat down at a barstool under the high-peaked canopy, looking across the bar and toward the pool. Beyond the pool was the arc of the marina.

The menu was enough to harden your arteries simply by looking at it, but he finally decided on a conch po'boy and a local Kalik beer. Twenty dollars for a sandwich and a beer. The Bahamas wasn't cheap.

He was halfway through the sandwich when the man sat down beside him. He was in his sixties, gaunt as a scarecrow with a long face, high cheekbones and a pointy chin. There were bags under his sad gray eyes.

Smith was either an insomniac or a drunk and, according to the file Sheehan had been given, hungover seemed the most likely. He took off his old blue captain's cap and set it on the bar. What was left of his thinning hair had once been surfer-boy blond but was now a dirty gray, and any visible skin was burned to a reddish brown from half a lifetime in the tropic sun. He was wearing a gaudy yellow black and green Hawaiian shirt, sun-bleached jeans and what looked suspiciously like Birkenstock sandals.

'Des Smith?' Sheehan asked.

'That's right,' said the man. 'How did you know?'

'Good guess,' said Sheehan. In point of fact, he'd seen Smith's photograph in the dossier Brennan had given him. The bartender came round and Smith ordered something called a Mudslide. 'Des short for Desmond?'

'Desperate,' answered Smith with a thin smile.

'Why's that?'

'No good with money, no good with business, no good with booze, no good with broads.'

'Bad combination.'

'What the hell?' said Smith. 'I've got no one to answer to. Won the boat in a poker game from some rich writer thirty years ago. Chartering ever since.'

'No objections to Cuba?'

'Good fishing in Cuban waters this time of year. Marlin, bluefin, mahimahi. *Sandpiper*'s registered in the Bahamas and I've got a Bahamian passport.'

'You sound like an American.'

'Nassau, born and bred. Went to school in Florida and had a family there, but that didn't work, so I came home.'

'Any family here?'

228

'Not anymore. All dead and buried.'

'Your ad said fifteen hundred a day, plus fuel and food.'

'That's right.'

'How about two weeks?'

'Twelve hundred a day plus any moorage fees.'

'Good enough. Twenty thousand cover it, all in?'

'Sure.' Smith nodded.

'How do you want it?'

'Certified cheque'll do. Any downtown bank.'

'Made out to?'

'Sandpiper Charters Limited.'

'Fine. I'll meet you at the boat in an hour.'

'Good enough. Slip thirty-four.'

Smith's Mudslide arrived – something dark brown in a martini glass with whipped cream on the top.

'What exactly is that?' Sheehan asked, climbing off his stool.

'Baileys, Kahlua and chocolate syrup over crushed ice. Good for a hangover.'

'Sounds revolting.'

'It is,' said Smith with that same thin smile. 'I'm doing penance for my sins.'

'You must have a lot of sins under your belt to drink something like that.'

'You have no idea,' said Smith, taking a sip of his drink.

'I think I do actually,' said Sheehan. 'See you in an hour.'

Sandpiper turned out to be a forty-three-foot Hatteras

Express – easily capable of making the trip to Cuba. Smith was loading groceries and supplies on board when Sheehan appeared, his single overnight bag in his hand. Smith gave Sheehan a hand up and then showed him around the boat.

There was a master cabin with a queen-sized bed, a salon, an ensuite head, crew bunks and a guest state-room forward. When they were done with the tour, Sheehan handed Smith a certified cheque for twenty thousand dollars drawn on the Bank of Nova Scotia on Bay Street.

Smith took the cheque, thanked Sheehan, then folded the slip of paper and put it into his shirt pocket. Sheehan went down to his stateroom to unpack. Des Smith cast off the lines and then went up to the flybridge to pilot *Sandpiper* out of the marina and into the channel. By the time Sheehan joined Smith, they were beyond the harbor, heading west along the length of the island.

They finally passed the stony beach at Clifton Point and turned south into New Providence Channel. Sheehan waited for an interminable hour after that listening to Smith prattle on about his life and his drunken escapades until he reached his limit. The water was a dark, almost sinister blue here and Smith was quick to tell him why.

'This is the Tongue of the Ocean. The water drops off from a hundred and fifty feet to more than a mile – six thousand feet in some places.'

'Really?' Sheehan answered. 'That's interesting. Any sharks in these waters?'

'Silkys, bulls, tigers, all kinds. Bulls especially out here in the deep water. Why? You looking to catch one?'

'Not really,' said Sheehan. 'I think you might, though.' He took the homemade four-inch trench knife out of his pocket, holding it between the knuckles of his left hand, and stabbed it hard between the sixth and seventh cervical vertebrae of Des Smith's spine. The man twisted once, the vertebrae separated and Des Smith died.

Sheehan withdrew the knife, wiped the small amount of blood onto Smith's jeans, then reached forward and eased the throttles for the two big engines into neutral. It wasn't all that different from his da's trawler *Pixie* back home. The *Sandpiper* began to slow.

Sheehan unceremoniously grabbed Smith by the collar and his belt, dragged him to the edge of the fly-bridge, then dumped him down onto the main deck. Sheehan came down the ladder, then rolled Smith over. He removed the certified cheque from the man's pocket and opened his shirt.

The Irish priest heaved the dead man up onto the transom, hanging the front half of his body over the gunwale. With one expert slice he opened up Smith's torso from waist to rib cage. Entrails slithered out in a slurping gush and hit the water with a splash. Grabbing Smith by the feet, Sheehan tipped the rest of the body over.

It sank immediately, pulling the sausage links of the intestines down with it. Sheehan doubted that the body would reach the seabed a mile below the *Sandpiper*'s hull before one or more hungry predators snacked on Desperate Smith's remains. Desperate no more.

'*Ave atque vale*, hail and farewell,' said Sheehan, staring down at the dark water and quoting his favorite Roman poet, Catullus.

Sheehan went back up to the flybridge, pushed the throttles forward and continued south down the deep water channel toward the Grand Bahamas Bank and then Cuba.

Standing at the helm, the sun bright in his eyes and his heart glad to be back on the sea as it was when he was a child, Sheehan began to hum and then sing the song his late mother had sung to him so many years ago. Somehow it seemed fitting considering what he'd done and what he was about to do.

> Over in Killarney
> Many years ago,
> Me mither sang a song to me
> In tones so sweet and low.
> Just a simple little ditty,
> In her good ould Irish way,
> And I'd give the world if she could sing
> That song to me this day.
> 'Too-ra-loo-ra-loo-ral, Too-ra-loo-ra-li,
> Too-ra-loo-ra-loo-ral, hush now, don't you cry!
> Too-ra-loo-ra-loo-ral, Too-ra-loo-ra-li,
> Too-ra-loo-ra-loo-ral, that's an Irish lullaby.

*

General Leopoldo Cintra Frias, the new Cuban minister of defense, did slow, methodical lengths of his sixty-by-twenty-foot pool in the Atabay District of Havana. At seventy-one, the husky, muscular Frias was determined to outlive a host of enemies, not the least of whom was a whole collection of Castros, Raul's children in particular and specifically Alejandro. He had too much power within the Ministry of the Interior, and like Shakespeare's Cassius, Colonel Alejandro Castro Espin had a lean and hungry look about him.

The swinging door to the pool enclosure squeaked open just as Frias reached the shallow end of the pool. It was Lieutenant Colonel Roberto Marquez Orozco, head of the Special Forces, the *Tropas Especiales*. He was clearly here on official business; he wore full uniform including red beret and black wasp – *avispa negras* – shoulder flash. He stood at the end of the pool like a stone statue. His expression was unreadable behind mirrored aviator sunglasses. If it wasn't for the red beret and the holstered Stechkin APS and a pair of twenty-round magazines on his belt, he would have looked like a California Highway patrolman.

Frias climbed out of the pool, took his white terry-cloth robe off the back of a lawn chair and then sat down. 'It is Sunday, Colonel Orozco. What brings you here dressed for war? Are they rioting on the streets of Havana? Is Mexico attacking us, Canada perhaps?' Frias knew perfectly well that Orozco had no sense of humor, but he liked sticking pins in the man from time to time. 'Perhaps they're just arguing about real-estate deals they're making with fat tourists with fatter wallets.' Since Comrade Raul's bread-and-circuses change in the law making it legal for Cubans to trade in their own properties, even with foreigners, the trade in run-down fincas in the countryside and even more run-down apartments in Havana had been fierce. Apparently brother Raul's idea of maintaining order was by buying it. 'Well,' he said. 'Is it any of those?'

Frias picked up a packet of Marlboros from the table beside his chair and lit one with a gold Dunhill lighter he'd picked up for himself the last time he was in Spain checking up on his properties there.

'No, sir,' Orozco said.

'Then what is it?'

'A checkpoint in the Escambray has been attacked. Twelve men killed, a barracks and a minibus destroyed. There was a message left on the barracks – Viva Zapata.'

'The idiot who starved himself to death?'

'Presumably.'

'Locals?'

'No, sir. The weaponry was far too sophisticated. A LAWS rocket, snipers, automatic weapons.'

'What are you thinking?'

'FAN softening us up?'

FAN was the Fuerza Armada Nacional, the combined armed forces of Venezuela. Since Chavez's cancer had first been announced, there had been rumors of an agreement with both Fidel and Raul that in the event of serious civil unrest in Cuba, FAN would be called in to quell it. There had also been more sinister rumors of a complete takeover of the nation at its weakest moment. A moment that clearly wasn't far off. Far-fetched, but not impossible.

'You believe that?'

'No, sir.'

'Then what?'

'The CIA?'

'The Americans?'

'Yes, sir.'

'Why do you think that?'

'The weaponry was American made. They have history in those hills.'

'It's good that you read your history, Orozco, but that was half a century ago. I know. I fought in the Bandit War when I was a young man.'

'Who else could it be?'

'Why don't you go and find out?'

'That is why I came, General.'

Frias's adjutant, Juan-Carlos, appeared, properly outfitted in a white steward's jacket. He carried a tray in his hand. On it was a bowl with half a large avocado, seasoned with lemon to keep it fresh, lightly salted the way Frias liked it, then filled with an ice cream scoop of shredded crab, shrimp and rock lobster meat mixed with finely chopped celery, crumbled bacon and mayonnaise.

Juan-Carlos set the tray down on the side table and then disappeared back into the main house. Frias crushed out the cigarette and picked up the bowl. He took a spoonful and slid it into his mouth. He chewed and swallowed.

'Exquisite,' said General Frias. 'Would you like Juan-Carlos to prepare some for you?'

'No, thank you, sir.'

'Then tell me what you want before my digestion is completely ruined, Orozco.'

'I need six MiL 8s and a dozen MRAPS.' MiL 8s were transport helicopters and an MRAP was a Mine Resistant Ambush Protected vehicle. The Black Wasps used a Polish-made AMZ Dzik.

'The entire air force only has ten MiL 8s, and you want six of them?'

'Yes, sir. I need transport for one hundred and eighty men. They'll rendezvous with the MRAPs in Aserradero and head into the jungle from there.'

'Have your troops take trucks to Aserradero.'

'The MiLs can have them there in an hour and a half. Trucks would take at least two days. We need a presence on the ground right now.'

It made sense. Frias took another spoonful of the avocado mixture and ate it, thinking. After a few moments he nodded. Orozco was smart, he was young and he was tough. And not someone you wanted in Havana when *el mierda golpeó el ventilador*.

'Good thinking, Colonel Orozco. Do it, and may you have great success.'

'Thank you, sir.' Orozco clicked his heels, saluted, then turned on his heels and left the pool enclosure. Frias went back to his avocado. He finished his snack, then took a cell phone out of the pocket of his robe and punched in a number. It only rang once before it was answered.

'Done,' said Frias. He hung up the phone and lit another cigarette. With a little bit of luck, Orozco and his men would be corpses rotting in the jungle by St Lazarus Day.

22

They moved along the faint jungle trail, Enrique in the lead followed by Domingo, then Eddie and Holliday in the rear. A point man throughout his military career, Holliday did not enjoy the position; militarily being the tail-end Charlie was vulnerable, poorly positioned to respond and able only to react to events farther up the line rather than initiate them.

It was usually the position given to the least valuable member of a team and the most expendable. He was also the most poorly armed; Enrique had his shotgun, Domingo had his rifle and even Eddie had Domingo's old machete. All Holliday had was Enrique's bowie knife and a wooden staff sharpened at one end to fend off the wild boars Enrique said lived in these overgrown woods.

'Where exactly are we going?' Holliday said quietly.

Eddie turned his head slightly. 'Enrique's village. Las Vegas Grandes. He says it is not far now, perhaps another mile.'

'I don't see any meadows around here – it's all jungle.' Ever since they'd left the winding river more than three hours ago, the terrain had become steeper and more difficult. The trail they were following looked more like an animal track than anything made by humans, and even at that it was no more than three feet wide, the jungle foliage crowding in claustrophobically. Above them a flock of Cuban solitaires scolded them with their earsplitting cries, then took nervous flight, wings beating the air loudly as they rose into the sky.

All of Holliday's senses were on high alert; it was too much like Vietnam where the jungles were killing grounds sown with trip wires, homemade land mines made of folded-over tin mess plates and even tiger traps filled with sharpened punji sticks covered in human excrement.

Villages full of old men and women could be booby-trapped, tunnel-riddled arsenals that could suddenly be full of suicidal enemies appearing out of nowhere and a ten-year-old kid behind the sights of an old Chinese-made RPD machine gun could wipe out a patrol in seconds.

On top of that, there was also a chance of being blown to atoms by an overenthusiastic artillery officer with an M107 twenty miles away or a kid high on some blotter acid sent to him in the mail by a stateside friend chucking a grenade into your foxhole because he thought you were a bloodsucking zombie demon trying to eat his brains. And none of all that prepared you for the bugs, the snakes, the foot rot and the mud. Vietnam hadn't been a war; it had been the mother of all nightmares with the jungle as its dark, gloating heart.

Holliday squinted up the trail. Enrique was out of

sight. The line was strung out; too much space between each man. He stopped. For three hours a dissonant choir of birds had screeched, whistled, hooted and rattled in the trees around and above them. Now it was silent.

'Shit.'

'What is it?' Eddie turned.

'No birds singing.'

'*Singao!*' Eddie hissed. '*Estamos jodidos!*' He turned forward and let out an earsplitting whistle.

Instantly, Domingo turned.

'*Qué!*'

'*Emboscada!*'

They rose like the floor of the jungle come to life, four Swamp Things with dangling shreds of foliage and rust-colored and mottled strips sewn and woven into nylon netting that covered them from head to toe, each armed with an MP5 submachine gun or something like it. Holliday's twitching memories of his teenage horrors in Vietnam and Eddie's shrill whistle had given the three men on the trail a tenth of a second advantage, but it wasn't much.

Acting on nothing but old instincts and adrenaline, Holliday's thought process was: 'ghillie suit – Interceptor body armor – neck-groin.' He thrust the sharpened staff in low and just to the left of the crotch. The lower flap of the Interceptor vest covered the genitals well enough, but it didn't do much for the femoral arteries running up the inner thighs on both sides.

The staff cut through the camouflage ghillie suit, glanced off the Kevlar groin flap and went a good three inches into the Swamp Thing's leg. The creature gave a high-pitched screech, dropped his weapon, grabbed his leg and toppled over.

Ahead of Holliday a high, sweeping slash from Eddie's machete had decapitated one man and a whirling backswing had taken off the right arm of a third. A single round from Domingo's .308 had taken the fourth man in the chest and even with a vest the hydrostatic shock had blown the man six feet back into the jungle. The whole thing had taken less than ten seconds.

'*Madre de Dios*,' said Eddie, staring down at the one-armed man as his blood pumped out onto the ground. Hundreds of small red ants were already climbing over the wound, and a long, thick trail of them was marching out of the jungle's interior for the alfresco feast.

'Where the hell is Enrique?' Holliday asked. He pulled back on the slide of the MP5 he'd collected from the man bleeding out at his feet.

'*Enrique se ha ido, el hijo de puta*,' said Domingo. He stepped into the undergrowth and began hauling the man he'd hit back onto the jungle path. '*El bastardo nos traicionó.*'

'He betrayed us,' said Eddie. 'He knew they were waiting here.' He picked up one of the MP5s and frowned. 'The weapon has the safety on.'

'*Estupido*,' grunted Domingo, heaving his victim onto the path. The man was still alive, groaning in pain.

'Maybe they weren't supposed to kill us,' ventured Holliday, thinking.

'They were not here to welcome us,' said Eddie.

'No, but they might have been here to take us prisoner.'

'Enrique must have told them we were coming,' said Eddie. 'That much is *muy evidente*, but how could they know who we were?'

Having bad memories about a past time and place was bad enough, but having those old nightmares spring to life in front of your face and make you take yet another life to save your own had torn something deep within Holliday that he thought had been dead and buried forever, and now it was back and he was angry. 'Someone must have told them,' he said, his expression grim. He unsheathed the bowie knife at his side and stepped up the trail to Domingo's prisoner. 'Let's find out who.'

Kate Sinclair walked down the long dock toward the seventy-two-foot Grand Banks Aleutian yacht berthed at its end. The name on the yacht's transom was *Rey Azucar* – *King Sugar*. They were on the inside passage side of the wealthy community and she could see West Palm Beach half a mile away on the mainland side of the channel.

Sinclair was escorted by a young man wearing a faux nautical officer's uniform, but there was no doubt from his demeanor, his dark glasses and the slight bulge on the left side of his pure white jacket that he was in fact a bodyguard to the boat's owner, Julio Lobo, the so-called Sugar King of Florida.

Lobo's monstrous two-story wedding-cake mansion stood behind her with its arched colonnades, bell towers that contained no bells, sculptured topiary gardens tended to by an army of black groundskeepers, most of them Dominican, and the requisite turquoise swimming pool that no one ever used but which was a nice focal point for over-the-top cocktail parties.

The elderly woman reached the end of the dock and allowed the bodyguard to help her up the companionway ladder to the open afterdeck of the yacht. She sat down on the long white leather banquette that ran around the stern of the yacht. Two things happened almost immediately.

The engines fired off and they began to ease away from the pier and a white-jacketed steward appeared with a plate of hors d'oeuvres, which he set down in front of her, and then he took her drink order.

Just to be irritating, she ordered a Bloody Caesar, a mixture of Clamato juice, Worcestershire sauce, Tabasco and vodka rimmed with celery salt – a drink almost unknown in the United States. Three minutes after placing the order, her drink appeared over ice in a tall glass garnished with a stalk of celery just as it was supposed to be. She gave it a sip and found that it was perfect.

Two minutes after the drink appeared, a stocky man in a business suit stepped out of the salon and onto the afterdeck. He had a deeply tanned face carved from granite, a square jaw, high cheekbones and an aquiline nose beneath a broad forehead creased vertically with four deep worry lines. The eyes were black under heavy brows and he had a head of snow-white hair in a widow's peak swept straight back in the old-fashioned way. He was clean shaven except for a perfectly trimmed mustache as white as his hair. He had to be in his later seventies, but he looked as fit as a man of forty.

Approaching the place where Kate Sinclair sat, he paused, gave an almost military bow, then eased himself down into a chair across from her. He extended a hand across the table. The hand belonged to a butcher or a prizefighter. The fingers were short and thick, the knuckles scarred over, the nails short and blunt. The watch on his thick left wrist was an old Stauer Graves with a sweat-stained leather band. Somehow the look didn't fit with the huge yacht and the Baskin-Robbins McMansion. Kate Sinclair knew that somewhere half-hidden in his past, Julio Lobo had been a hardworking simple man. She took the extended hand and Lobo shook it, careful not to squeeze her old bones too hard or for too long. He released his grip just as carefully and sat back in his chair.

'Senor Lobo,' she said.

'Senora Sinclair,' he replied. His voice was as dark and deep as his eyes, the Cuban accent strong even though he had not set foot in his native land for more than fifty years.

'You are a great traveler,' said the elderly woman.

She sipped her drink and placed it back on the table. 'You have homes in New York, London, Madrid, Buenos Aires, even Geneva. I was lucky to find you here.'

The steward reappeared with a tall glass of something clear and bubbly on the rocks. Perrier or Pellegrino or perhaps just soda water. The steward placed the glass in front of Lobo, but he ignored it.

'I was born in Colombia, raised on a sugar plantation in Cuba, went to school in England and returned to Cuba only to be exiled once again. I am the archetypical Wandering Jew, senora; I am a stateless man, a restless soul with no home.' He paused and released a small grim smile. 'And you are a woman of great power with resources enough to find me no matter where I was. The real question is, why were you looking for me in the first place?'

Kate Sinclair knew that Lobo was descended from Sephardic Jews who were expelled from Spain in the fifteenth century. She also knew that he had not set foot in a synagogue since 1959 when Fidel Castro entered Havana.

'I came to offer you a job, Senor Lobo,' said Sinclair. She took a long swallow of her drink and lit a cigarette.

The steward appeared out of nowhere with an ashtray as well as a small humidor, a cutter and a lighter for Lobo. He chose an H. Upmann Number 2 Torpedo, sliced off the pointed tip and lit it, all the while keeping his eyes on the aristocratic woman across from him.

Kate Sinclair felt a small shiver of fear at the look.

She knew that Lobo's name translated as 'Wolf' and she knew he lived up to his name in more ways than one. It was well known that his father, Alonzo 'Pepe' Lobo, had been in league with the Camorra in Naples, and who was to say that his son didn't have equally sinister connections? She was certainly well aware of the truth of the Balzac quotation that 'Behind every great fortune there is a great crime' when it came to her own family, so why not Lobo's?

'I am an old man and I am a billionaire several times over,' said the Cuban expatriate. 'What job could you offer me that I could possibly be interested in?'

Kate Sinclair paused. It wasn't a question to answer lightly. 'I want you to become the minister of economic development for the Republic of Cuba.'

Lobo studied her for a long moment, puffing on his cigar. The yacht reached Peanut Island and followed the channel markers around it. Ocean Point and the passage to the sea stood on their right.

'I will tell you a story, Senora Sinclair. On the morning of January the second, 1959, the day following Fidel Castro's entry into Havana, I had to go to the National Bank to get some papers my father needed. Che Guevara was sitting in the president of the bank's office. I was twenty-four years old. Guevara asked me the same question.

'What he really wanted to know was if I would be willing to run my father's fourteen sugar mills and refineries after they had been nationalized and my father exiled or worse. I could either become a *comunista* or remain a capitalist pig. Do you know what I told Ernesto Che Guevara, the great hero of the revolution, Senora Sinclair?'

'I can guess.'

'I told him to go fuck himself, senora. So who are you to waste my time with such foolish questions? Such offices within the República de Cuba are not yours to give.'

'Less than a week from now, on June the twenty-first, St Lazarus Day, at some time in the afternoon, Fidel Castro will die at his estate in Punta Cero at the hands of the Knights of the Brotherhood of Christ, of which your father was a member. It is a fact that through the Brotherhood and your father's connections to it, you have managed to rebuild his empire, an empire that now spans continents. If a man sugars his coffee in Moscow, Madrid or Mumbai, he is probably using your product.'

They had come around Peanut Island now and were heading home again. Peanut Island is a local Palm Beach park with campgrounds, a marina and beaches. It was also the location for JFK's fallout shelter during his winter visits to the family estate in Palm Beach. They even gave ten-dollar guided tours.

'Even if this was true and Fidel was to die when you say, why do you think anything would change?'

'Because it will be made to change.'

'By the Brotherhood?' Lobo laughed around the stub of his cigar.

'By the Brotherhood and outside interests that

would like to see Cuba's transition from being a pseudosocialist military dictatorship to a true democratic republic be accomplished as bloodlessly as possible. As I am sure you are aware, the Cuban military is effectively impotent and we have taken . . . steps to see that its remaining counterinsurgency is otherwise occupied.'

'These outside interests. Your interests, Senora Sinclair?'

'America's interests, Senor Lobo.'

'Given that this "change" as you call it were to take place, what would my interests be, senora?'

'All properties and land holdings owned by your family before 1959 would be returned to you, including the fourteen refineries you operated. At one time your family controlled more than half the sugar output of Cuba; if those refineries were operated by anyone other than yourself, it would be disastrous for the sugar industries of Florida, Louisiana, the Dominican Republic and Hawaii. Under your guidance, that could be prevented. That is roughly eight million tons of sugar annually under your control. Effectively you would control the world cane sugar industry.'

'If such a radical and at this time completely hypothetical event was to occur, I would need further incentives,' Lobo said.

'Such as?'

'As you are probably aware, I own a majority interest in both Royal Tropicana and Tropic Sun Cruise Lines, both of which are based out of Fort Lauderdale. I also own several large construction companies here in Florida. When this "change" of yours occurs, one of those companies will be hired to build a cruise ship terminal in Havana Harbor and my ships will be given the first licenses to dock there.

'Furthermore I wish to be made chairman of the first gambling commission in Cuba when it is established, and to be given ten licenses to be distributed as I see fit. If I am minister of economic development, it will also be a fundamental part of my mandate to control any and all resource development in Cuba, including agriculture, mining and tourism. None of this is negotiable.'

'You drive a hard bargain, Mr Lobo.'

'My father used to play poker with Meyer Lansky back in the Fifties. I had excellent role models.'

'I thought perhaps that I might have caught you unawares with my offer, Senor Lobo, but I see now that you have given this a great deal of thought.'

'Senora, for many years now Cuba has been a ripe plum ready to fall from the tree. I knew someone would come along eventually and I would make my deal with the devil. You are simply the first devil to come along.'

'No patriotism to stir your heart? No revenge for the indignities done to your family?'

'Wave your flags elsewhere, senora. Patriotism is a sickness only bloodshed will cure. It is nothing more than men putting real estate above principle, and revenge is for idiots. This is about money, Senora

Sinclair. Cuba has always been about money, nothing more, I'm afraid.'

'So we have a deal?'

'Why not?' Lobo said. 'I've never owned my own country before.'

23

The flight of six MiL 8 transport helicopters hammered over the jungle and wildwood-covered hills and valleys of the Sierra del Escambray on their way to the town of Aserradero. Lieutenant Colonel Roberto Marquez Orozco sat in the cockpit of the lead helicopter, scanning the ground five hundred feet below them. Nothing to see but treetops, rock crags and the glitter of a meandering mountain stream. Behind him in the rear of the transport, twenty men in full gear sat huddled in jump seats against the bulkheads. Orozco's helicopter swept over the Habanabilla Reservoir and into the Aserradero Valley. The town and its eight thousand peasant inhabitants lay dead ahead, the single thread of a narrow highway cutting the town in half.

'There,' said Orozco, pointing to a large open meadow just north of the town. It was really the only clear space to land in.

'*Sí*, Colonel,' said the pilot. He toggled a switch on the radio set into the control panel above him and relayed the information to the other pilots in the flight. All of the big helicopters altered course along with Orozco like giant obedient bumblebees.

Orozco's helicopter landed first, touching down on the slightly inclined meadow, its tripod gear hitting the dark earth in perfect unison, the huge rotors flattening the tall grass in a perfect circle. The main door opened and the pilot threw the rotors into the off position; it would take some time to unload the men and equipment, and the turbine ate up fuel at a terrible rate.

Behind them the five other helicopters landed in formation, in line with a hundred yards between each machine. When all the rotors had ceased turning, the clamshell rear cargo doors and ramp opened and the men began to file out.

Hidden in the woods two hundred yards to the south, Lieutenant Colonel Frank J. Turturro watched as the helicopters landed and then he quietly gave an order into his headset microphone.

'Lasers on.'

Around the large upland meadow, twelve of Turturro's men, each with an ordinary green-light laser pointer duct-taped to the telescopic sights of his Vietnam-era M40 rifle, switched the little devices on, aiming at the upper turbine chamber above and just aft of the cockpit. None of the twelve men was a sniper-grade marksman, but none of them needed to be; their only task was to keep the small spot of laser light aimed at the helicopters.

Turturro turned to his radio man and told him to switch frequencies. When the man nodded, Turturro spoke into his microphone again. 'This is Bravo. Come in, Flight Leader.'

The response was clear and almost instantaneous. 'Flight Leader here, Bravo.'

'What's your distance from X-Ray please?'

'Four kilometers.'

'Approach southwest, course one eighty. Targets are in line and painted. Fire at will, Flight.'

'Roger that, Bravo.'

From four kilometers away the sound of the three Super Tucanos was no more than the faint, indistinct sound of a swarm of hornets, and it was only at the very last second that Orozco's pilot saw the glittering of sunlight reflecting from the canopies of the distant turboprops, followed almost instantly by blurred belches of smoke and flames from the turboprops' underwing pods as each of the aircraft launched four Hellfire air-to-ground missiles at the green patch of meadow two and a half miles away.

'Colonel . . .?' The pilot pointed out the south-side window of the cockpit.

The Hellfire missiles, traveling at roughly two thousand feet per second, reached their targets – the green light reflecting from the laser pointers – in about the time it took for Orozco to turn and follow the directions of the pilot's finger. All twelve missiles made contact and the six MiL 8 helicopters and the men remaining inside them were incinerated instantly. Eight seconds after the missiles struck, the three

Super Tucanos flew in over the meadow at an altitude of a little over two hundred and fifty feet, raking the meadow with their twin .50-caliber machine guns, obliterating the few dozen men already out of the six helicopters and fleeing toward the woods. Wagging their wings, the three Super Tucanos peeled off and climbed out of sight. Six of the elite Avispas Negras unit managed to evade the missiles and the machine-gun fire before they were fired upon at point-blank range by Colonel Frank Turturro's men. Within less than a minute, two-thirds of the Cuban air force's helicopter transport capabilities had been destroyed along with a full one-third of the army's Special Forces, including their commander.

Turturro stared at the meadow turned killing field. It was an abattoir of torn flesh and bullet-ridden bodies, their lifeblood draining into the tall grass and the dark earth upon which they lay. The air smelled of hot metal, melting plastic and the rich-sour barbecue char of roasting human beings. The sound was a sighing blast furnace's breath and the snap, crackle, pop of dying machinery. Black greasy clouds blossomed into the sky. Beside him, Turturro heard his radio operator retching. Turturro, a man who had seen several wars and more than enough death to last a lifetime, simply watched. He began to whisper words he hadn't spoken since childhood.

'Hail Mary, full of grace. Our Lord is with thee. Blessed art thou among women, and blessed is the fruit of thy womb, Jesus. Holy Mary, Mother of God, pray for us sinners, now and at the hour of our death. Amen.'

'Son of a bitch!' Holliday yelled, ducking as the returning flight of the three jungle-camouflaged aircraft roared overhead just above treetop level. If it hadn't been for the thunder of the turbine engines, they could have been something straight out of the Battle of Britain; they looked remarkably like old-fashioned Spitfires or Hurricanes or even the American P51 Mustangs. The only thing missing was the shark's mouth painted on the noses. Holliday recognized them immediately – they were Brazilian-made Embraer EMB 314 Super Tucanos, nominally used to patrol Brazil's Amazonian borders but probably the best counterinsurgency fighter-bomber on today's market. Rebels or pesky natives who won't relocate where you tell them in your jungles? Call Embraer and they'll fix you right up. He also knew that Kate Sinclair, mother of the late Senator Sinclair, head of the secret society known as Rex Deus, was owner of Blackhawk Security, one of the largest private military contractors and armies-for-hire in the world, which had recently purchased a number of the Brazilian turboprops. She was also insanely power-hungry and a first-rate bitch into the bargain, as Holliday knew from personal experience. The Furies from Roman mythology could have learned a thing or two from Kate Sinclair.

'It would appear that the unhappy soldier we

captured on the path to Aserradero was telling the truth,' said Eddie.

'I wonder if he was telling the truth about the prisoners they're holding at that old airfield.'

'Domingo was cutting off the second finger of his hand with that old machete of his. He was telling the truth, *sin duda alguna, mi amigo* – there is no question about it.'

'Then we have to save them,' said Holliday. 'It's the only way.'

'I don't understand,' said Eddie. 'I thought our plan was to get to the coast and take a boat to the Bahamas.'

'Maybe that's still what we'll do, but if we arrive at the U.S embassy in Nassau with a couple of CIA agents, they might take us a little more seriously when we tell them about a few leftover missiles from October Sixty-two, don't you think? Remember, amigo, you and me and embassies aren't the best of friends.'

'This is true,' said Eddie. Their last interaction with a U.S. embassy had involved crashing through the front gates of the Moscow embassy in a snowplow and running it up the front steps and through the entrance. Total damage: $3.5 million, eventually paid by the Russian government since it was their dead snowplow operator at the controls, but nevertheless a distinct black mark when it came to embassy relations with Holliday and Eddie.

'Those aircraft were heading northeast,' said Holliday, turning to Domingo. 'Any idea where they were going?'

'The only airfield close to here is at an old abandoned finca about five miles from here. It belonged to a wealthy Havana doctor who liked to fly his friends in to hunt *jabali*.'

'*Jabali?*'

'Wild boar,' explained Eddie.

'How long to get there?'

'There are no roads,' replied Domingo. 'Through the jungle, two, three hours maybe.'

'Then we better get moving,' said Holliday. 'I want to see this place before it gets dark.'

In the end it took almost four hours to find their way to the ridge across from the airstrip that had once belonged to Dr Enrique Gomez Martinez, the high-society Havana abortionist in the time of Fulgencio Batista.

Using Domingo's powerful Soviet-era binoculars, Holliday scanned the covert military installation a few hundred yards away across the steep, narrow valley that lay between them. On the next of the multiple ridges was the burnt-out ruins of a large hacienda, almost invisible in the jungle undergrowth.

On the occupied ridge, he could make out the camouflaged hardstands for the Tucanos, perhaps twenty well-hidden tents and the old crumbling building almost overgrown with vegetation that had probably been used as some sort of control tower. Between the net-covered enclosures for the aircraft, there was a large fly tent, also covered with camouflage net, that was almost certainly the command post for the installation. At the extreme western end of the narrow plateau was the overgrown wreckage of an old DC-3.

Holliday swept the binoculars along the length of the ridge. From end to end it was about half a mile long. There were two-man pickets posted every two hundred feet along the length of the dirt runway and two guards in front of the control tower front door. Everyone was armed with sidearms and MP5s like the men they had intercepted.

'They're using the old building to keep the prisoners in,' said Holliday, lowering the binoculars.

'What about that hacienda on the ridge beyond?' Eddie asked.

'Burnt out and abandoned,' said Holliday.

'There was a road from the hacienda to the airstrip,' said Domingo. 'It is most probably *cubierta por la selva*, covered by the jungle, but it will still be there. It will lead us up to the camp, I am sure.'

'You seem to know a lot about this Dr Martinez,' said Holliday.

Domingo shrugged. 'We were the *lucha contra bandidos*; it was our job. Martinez was high on our list.' The white-haired man paused, eyes staring at something a thousand miles away and decades in the past.

Holliday thought for a moment, then gave the camp another scan with the binoculars. The jungle between the two ridges was deep in shadow now and the sun was a fireball in the west.

'All my life I am working for the Revolution,' said Domingo, shaking his head. 'And now I go to rescue *Americano* CIA agents. This I would never have dreamed. *Increíble!*'

Holliday stared across at the darkening ridge. 'We wait until dark and then we go.'

PART FOUR

Punta Cero

24

William Copeland Black sat at the table in the crumbling building beside the dirt airfield and tried to think his way out of their present problem. Laframboise, the pilot, and Arango, their supposed guide, were both on the floor, snoring away. Carrie Pilkington was staring up at the ceiling. Finally she looked down, staring at Black.

'Some analyst I am,' she said angrily. 'I couldn't analyse my way out of a wet paper bag.'

'Analysing information isn't the same thing as figuring out how to escape from a windowless jail in the middle of the jungle surrounded by armed men,' said Black. 'The era of Richard Hannay and James Bond is over.'

'Richard who?' Carrie said.

'The first fictional heroic spy of the twentieth century,' said Laframboise, coming out of his doze. 'He was the star of several books by John Buchan. The most famous was *The Thirty-Nine Steps*. Alfred Hitchcock made it into a movie in the nineteen thirties. Buchan was also known as Lord Tweedsmuir, the governor general of Canada.'

'Good Lord,' said Black.

'I had the best paper route in Ottawa,' said Laframboise, sitting up and yawning. 'Governor generals to the British high commissioners with half a dozen embassies, the prime minister's residence and City Hall, all on the same street. Learned a lot of history that way.' He shook his head, smiling as he remembered. 'At Christmas the prime minister and the French ambassador used to compete to give me the biggest tip. I made out like a bandit.'

'Cute story,' said Carrie. 'Irrelevant but cute.'

'Divide and conquer?' Will Black said.

'Something like that,' said Laframboise.

'I don't get it,' said Carrie.

'Five or six hours ago we heard a lot of activity – orders being bawled out, soldiers moving around,' said Laframboise. 'Then an hour ago three of those fighters out there took off and half an hour later they were back. Somebody's making a fuss out there and I don't think anybody's thinking about us.'

'They have not thought of us since we landed here like flies in a spiderweb,' snorted Arango. 'They knew they were going to kill us from the start, or at least *el Italiano* did.'

'Then why aren't we dead?' Carrie asked bluntly.

'Poker,' said Lafamboise. 'That Turturro guy's an old soldier. We're bargaining chips in case it all goes wrong.'

'Mr Laframboise is probably right.' Black nodded. 'Turturro's a firm proponent of what my late father referred to as the "snafu" principle.'

'*Qué?*' Arango said.

'Situation Normal, All Fucked Up,' explained Black. 'These people aren't playing at being rebels in the mountains trying to stir up the locals; this is an attack force. Something big is in the works, and if there's a snafu, Turturro wants something to trade on.'

'Us,' said Carrie.

'Us.' Black nodded.

'So what do we do about it?'

'One way or another, all of us are going to be an embarrassment, whether it's Turturro's people or the agency,' said Black. 'We're going to get swept under the rug, so to speak. I say we get out and we get out now. Turturro's probably off with those soldiers we heard gearing up this afternoon. It's getting dark. They should be bringing us something to eat pretty soon. It might be our only chance.'

'What chance?' Carrie asked. 'We're going to stab them with plastic forks? These guys have got guns!'

'There is a loose floorboard in the toilet,' said Arango. 'Pull it up. There might be nails in it. Rusty ones. A weapon of sorts.'

'I saw a kid in high school throw a cafeteria table at a teacher once. Caught him by surprise.' Laframboise shrugged. 'Might work.'

'I'm stuck back at plastic forks,' said Carrie.

'We use the chairs,' said Black. 'Carrie and I stand on opposite sides of the door, each with a chair folded up. Arango has the piece of floorboard and both he and Laframboise heave the table at the first guys through the door. If we're lucky we'll catch them off guard and manage to disarm at least one of them.'

'And if we don't?' Carrie said.

'Then we probably die,' said Laframboise.

It was seven sixteen in the evening and the last of the sun was disappearing over the western sea as *Sandpiper* arrived at the Marina Hemingway. Father Ronan Patrick Sheehan hit the air horn, requesting entrance through the breakwater passage. Receiving approval, Sheehan piloted the Hatteras Express to the harbormaster's office at the main jetty, where he was boarded by a customs officer and a harbor official.

He offered Des Smith's papers for inspection, had them stamped and was then given a berth after paying an appropriate 'document fee.' At the berth across from some sort of low-rise hotel complex, another set of officials boarded the boat, gave it a cursory inspection and were also handed what they called an 'inspection fee.' The whole process took an hour.

Throughout the various official inspections, Sheehan had worn a plastic surgical boot on his right foot and ankle and had limped around using a very solid-looking knobkerrie walking stick. When asked, he told the officials he'd sprained his ankle doing a favor for a friend. Nobody questioned his story and they didn't examine either the boot or the walking stick.

By the time Sheehan was alone again, it was fully dark. He had a quick, cold dinner of a tinned corned beef sandwich and a bottle of Kalik beer from the galley fridge, then lay down in the comfortable berth in the owner's stateroom and was asleep almost instantly.

The door to the old hut at the airfield was kicked in with the wet sound of splintering, rotten wood, and as the first man came through the opening Montalvo Hernandez Arango swung the eighteen-inch-long floorboard with a pair of three-inch nails at the end like a major league hitter belting a home run out of the park with a Louisville Slugger.

'*Mueren, pedazo de mierda!*' Arango screeched.

'*Santa puta Madre de Cristo!*' Domingo Cabrera raised his machete defensively with Arango's medieval bat less than an inch from his skull. At the same time Pete Laframboise heaved the table toward the doorway, dipped his shoulder like a hockey player making a body check and heaved himself forward. As Holliday and Eddie stepped into the hut, both Carrie Pilkington and Will Black swung their folded chairs.

The table and Pete Laframboise hit Holliday square-on and Eddie was struck high and low by the chairs. Everyone went down in a heap except for Arango and Domingo, who just stared at each other, dumbfounded.

Pete Laframboise found himself staring into the angry face of a mud-spattered, scar-faced, one-eyed man with an MP5 machine gun pointing at him. Eddie staggered to his feet and Carrie Pilkington stared. 'Oh my God!'

'Who the hell are you?' Laframboise asked, sprawled

in the broken remains of the card table he'd driven into Holliday.

'I'm the goddamn U.S. cavalry,' answered Holliday. 'Now get up.'

'You're Colonel John Holliday,' said Carrie Pilkington. 'And this is your friend Eddie Cabrera. I recognize you from the photographs in your file.'

'We've got two dead guards outside and about five minutes before the shit hits the fan,' said Holliday. 'So if you're all finished with the Marx Brothers routine, can we all get the hell out of here?'

25

Lieutenant Colonel Frank J. Turturro returned from his mission to Aserradero still shaken by the slaughter he had seen in that mountain meadow. He was no stranger to death in war, but his conflicts had come in places where men died in ones and twos, not by the hundreds. The fight at the police post a few days before had been one thing, but he knew the wholesale slaughter he'd seen today would give him nightmares worse than he had ever known. A warrior was a man who fought other men and where the better warrior vanquished the lesser; it wasn't a farmer slaughtering sheep. Blackhawk was paying him a fortune to lead this unit, but no amount of cash was going to help him carry this stone that now rested so heavily in his heart.

When he arrived back at the airfield just after dark, things went from bad to worse as his old friend and master sergeant Anthony Veccione reported the situation regarding the escape of the prisoners.

'How long ago?'

'An hour.'

'How many of our men did they kill?'

'Just two – the guards at the door, both cut down with a machete. They knocked out a man on picket duty.'

'Did he see anything?'

'There were three of them. Two black men, one white. They were all armed with MP5s just like ours. One of the blacks had a sniper rifle. An old one, he said. Russian maybe.'

Three men, just the way his contact had told him. The MP5s had to belong to Woodward and the ambush team he'd sent out. 'Shit.'

'Who were they?' Veccione asked.

'The ones the bosses asked me to keep my eyes out for. An old soldier named Holliday and two of his buddies. With those prisoners of ours they could mean big trouble. Have you sent out anybody after them?'

'In the dark? In the jungle?' Veccione shook his head. 'We'd be sitting ducks.'

'First light, then,' said Turturro. 'Just a few men. You and Nick Cavan take the lead. I need guys who've had real combat experience on this. No more than four or five men or they'll hear you coming from a mile off. Report in on the hour.'

'Yes, sir.'

'This is serious, Tony. Catch these sons of bitches or we could really find ourselves in the weeds.'

'Yes, sir.'

Ramiro Valdes, director of the Cuban Ministry of the Interior, sat eating dinner in his executive suite at the Hotel Inter-Continental in Caracas, Venezuela. Eight floors below, the evening traffic swirled along the Avenida Principal, while through his dining room window the man with the white, military brush cut could see the looming ranks of the Avila Mountains rising in the distance, blacker shapes against the night sky.

The chief of the Cuban Secret Police sliced a piece off his lobster tail with surgical precision and popped it into his mouth, chewing slowly. As he chewed, he carved a small piece from one side of the blood-rare Kobe beef tenderloin. He looked across the starched white tablecloth at his dinner guest, the sour-faced Brigadier General Luis Perez Rospide, head of Gaviota, the corporation that oversaw every aspect of Cuba's tourism industry. Between them they had an enormous amount of power, and both the Valdes and Rospide families had long been members of the Brotherhood.

'I cannot convince Raul to build a cruise ship terminal. The man is impossible,' said Rospide, eating his *pabellón criollo*, the Venezuelan version of *ropa vieja*, or '*old clothes*' – a dish of rice, beans and shredded beef that had once been famous in Cuba but had disappeared over the past thirty or forty years for lack of beef to shred. 'I gave him the numbers – three ships a day, two thousand passengers a ship, each spending two hundred dollars. That is one point two million dollars a day, Ramiro. A million dollars a day! The cruise ship season lasts from December to May. That's billions of dollars being thrown away!'

'Brother Raul is too old and too sick and too stupid. All he wants to do is retire to that ranch of his in Spain before the people rise up and hang him from a lamp-post in Revolución Square. That idea of selling off everything in the museums of Havana last year was the last act of a desperate man,' Valdes said. He sliced himself another piece of lobster meat. 'At any rate, we have more important things to think about. That is why I called you here.'

'I am always glad to get away from Havana these days,' said Rospide. 'It is claustrophobic. The Germans laugh and my staff steals chickens from the kitchens.'

'The American colonel just called me. The CIA agents he caught have escaped. From the description given by one of the guards, there were two blacks and a white man. One of the black men sounds like it was Domingo Cabrera.'

'Espin's bodyguard? The one who disappeared?'

'It would seem so.'

'Why would Cabrera rescue these men? How would he even know about them?'

'One of the companions of the CIA people was Montalvo Hernandez Arango.'

'So?'

'Montalvo Hernandez Arango was Domingo Cabrera's *capitaine* during the War of the Bandits. He knew as well as anyone where the Cuevo del Muerte was, the cave where the missiles of San Cristóbal were stored.'

'Maybe it is just a coincidence,' said Rospide.

'It might be but I doubt it,' said Valdes. 'The American colonel described one of the CIA people as being from England and speaking fluent Spanish. He sent a photo by telephone. The man could well be one of the people who picked up Dr Sosa in Dublin. He is MI6.'

'Then we are ruined!' Rospide said, pushing his plate of food away as though it had been poisoned.

'Ruined, no, but we must be careful. As you well know we have powerful Americans on our side. The question is, how much can we trust them? One of my surveillance agents in Florida reported to me that the woman who owns Blackhawk was seen in the company of none other than Julio Lobo.'

'*Maldita sea!*' Rospide exclaimed. 'She wants to put him in power instead of us?'

'I would not be surprised.' Valdes dipped another morsel of lobster into the silver bowl of garlic butter. 'The woman is a two-faced bitch, and worse, she is an American two-faced bitch.'

'Is it too late to stop all of this? To abort the operation?'

'No, it has gone much too far for that, I am afraid.'

'Then what do we do, *compañero*?'

'We kill them,' said Ramiro Valdes. 'We kill them all.'

Cardinal Spada and Father Thomas Brennan walked slowly through one of the old sections of the Vatican Gardens that covered most of the Vatican Hill. The early-summer sun was at its zenith and Spada wore a wide-brimmed red felt 'galero' to give himself shade. Brennan was bareheaded and smoking one of his inevitable cigarettes.

Spada liked the quiet here; the tourists generally

went to the Belvedere Gardens at the Vatican Museums, and only the gardeners and people going to and from their offices at the Vatican Radio Station and the Academy of Sciences used these old paths.

He liked the herb gardens especially; the smell of thyme and marjoram, oregano and sage brought him memories of the country and innocence and youth, none of which he had anymore except here as faint tastes on his palate and breaths in his nostrils. They walked past a lilac bush and it rushed back like warm summer rain on his upturned face.

He sometimes thought it strange that lives could be condensed into such small sensory things, but it was true; the smell of lilacs reminded him inevitably of the first girl he had kissed and that would never change, nor did he ever want it to.

Her name had been Lucretia and her lips had tasted as sweet as the grapes her father grew in his vineyards. Every summer his family vacationed in her district and they had great plans for a life together, all of which came crashing down at the age of fourteen when his father deemed it politically wise for his oldest son to join the Church. But even more than half a century later, lilacs spoke of her, and a grape fresh-picked from the vine burst with the flavor of her cool, soft mouth.

'Cardinal?' Brennan asked.

'Yes, Thomas, I beg your pardon. An old man's mind wandering.'

'I was speaking of Cuba.'

'What about it?'

'It is becoming more and more like the last days of Rome in the times of Caesar, I'm afraid. It is not simply a case of betrayal but a question of who is betraying whom.'

'It sounds like the Vatican,' said Spada. 'There are more sharpened daggers here than in any cutlery shop, I can assure you.' The cardinal secretary of state sighed, thoughts of Lucretia gone. 'Is this about Ortega and Musaro?'

'There are faint rumors that our jet-setting nuncio Musaro will denounce you to the Holy Father as the man behind the assassination of Castro and will also quietly denounce Ortega to the Cuban Secret Police just before the event happens.

'Ortega will be ruined or perhaps worse. You will be removed as secretary of state, leaving the position open for Musaro. The Holy Father would have no real choice if he wanted to avoid a great bloody internal scandal. You'd just quietly go away to your estates in Tuscany and never be heard from again. I'd probably end up having a suitable "cardiac event" in my bed one night.'

'You think he'd dare?'

'I do, indeed.'

'Then perhaps we should dare first, Father Brennan.'

'Which means?'

'You have your man in Havana now?'

'Yes. He's waiting for orders.'

'Have him deal with Musaro before the event and

Ortega afterward. That solves a multitude of problems, don't you think?'

'You mean kill both of them?' Brennan asked, a little surprised at Spada's ruthlessness. He was well aware of the cardinal's illness and thought it might have softened him. Apparently it had not.

Spada reached down and plucked a few leaves from a knee-high plant on the edge of the path and crushed them between his fingers. He held the crushed leaves in his palm and breathed inward deeply, his eyes closed, then offered the palm to Brennan, who took a tentative sniff.

'Very nice,' said the Irish priest, being diplomatic since he couldn't smell anything at all.

'*Ocimum basilicum,*' Spada said. 'Sweet basil, the herb of Italy. Cloves, earth, sweet tomatoes, all the good things of the countryside.' He took a last sniff of the leaves in his cupped hand and then let them fall to the ground, crushed and forgotten. 'There have been a great many holy events in gardens,' the cardinal said mildly. 'Eve's betrayal of Adam in Eden, Christ's agonies in the Garden of Sorrows, his betrayal by Judas Iscariot in the Garden of Gethsemane.' Spada stared at the hillside gardens all around them. 'I wonder how many betrayals there have been on this bloody soil in the past two thousand years.'

'Bloody soil?' Brennan said, looking down at the gravel beneath his scuffed old lace-up shoes.

'Oh yes.' The cardinal nodded, continuing down

the pathway. 'Long before the time of Christ, this place was a temple to Vaticanus. God only knows how many spring lambs and newborn calves bled to death in the light of the full moon for that unholy creature. The Vatican Hill on which we now stand was once the site of Nero's Circus, the place where the first Christians were martyred. Somewhere near here St Peter himself was crucified upside down by his own instruction. Historically the blood of the three crucifixions on Golgotha by St. Helena, as well. Truly a bloodstained place.' Spada smiled pleasantly at his companion.

Brennan, a man who had never quite given up the strange superstitious soul that is threaded into the DNA of every Irishman, despite a thousand canings by the Holy Ghost Fathers at Blackrock College, stared back at his master and suddenly had the queasy feeling that the dying old bastard could actually read his thoughts. Thank bloody feckin' Jesus that he'd chosen Cardinal Moisint, the deaf old bugger, as his confessor and not Spada.

'Well, isn't that an interesting bit of history?' said Brennan. 'But I have my duties, so I should be off, if you'll beg my pardon, Cardinal.'

'You have it, Father Brennan,' said Spada. 'And may you go with God, for in Him the world is saved, man is reborn and the dead rise again to life.' The opening words of a Catholic funeral Mass, as Brennan well knew. Perhaps he'd heed the warning.

'Thank you for the blessing, Your Eminence, and if that'll be all I'll be on my way.'

'Certainly,' said Spada. Brennan hustled off, looking over his shoulder only once. Spada gave him a little three-fingered wave – a blessing at a distance, or perhaps a curse. He waited until the Irishman was out of sight before he took the encrypted cell phone from his pocket. He tapped a number on speed dial that was answered immediately.

'Luca? I want a watch put on Brennan, day and night. I think he has gone over to Musaro. The little *bastardo* worm has turned at last, just as I knew he would.'

Holliday and the others made good time through the dense forests of the Escambray during the night of their escape. Laframboise and Eddie had both studied celestial navigation academically for their work, and Holliday knew his stars, both above and below the equator, simply for the sake of survival: there is no moss growing on the north side of trees in the jungles of Vietnam, and the hills and valleys of Afghanistan look pretty much alike in the dark when the battery to your GPS has run out, your radio can't get a signal and your compass needle keeps on whirling around with all that cobalt and nickel ore all around you. Knowing your ass from Polaris had helped all three men from time to time.

They kept moving, always a little east of north, hoping to reach the Atlantic coast of the country with a two or three days' march. From there Eddie and Domingo were almost certain they could steal a boat or bribe a fisherman to take them either to the Dominican Republic or, better yet, the Bahamas.

Holliday and the others paused for a few hours of sleep just before dawn, and as early-morning light cut weakly through the ghostly, drifting mist, he thought he might have heard a small helicopter in the distance, but it could just as easily have been the remnants of a dream, so he put it out of his mind. He woke before the others and found a small stream tumbling through the forest. He drank his fill, then splashed his face and neck. Eddie joined him and knelt down by the stream.

'Arango has gone. *El culo mierde* took Domingo's rifle.'

'I hope your brother hasn't gone after him.'

'He wanted to,' said Eddie, 'but I convinced him against the idea. We have the MP5s and the pistols we took from those men who tried to ambush us and two of those rather nice rifles we took from the guards at the airfield.'

'The M4s.'

'Yes, more than enough to start our own bandito war.' Eddie grinned.

'You're enjoying yourself, aren't you?' laughed Holliday.

'Goddamn too right, I am enjoying this, my friend, and so are you, Doc. Don't lie to me about it!'

Eddie bent over the little stream and began scrubbing his face, singing as he splashed water:

> When a man's an empty kettle
> He should be on his mettle
> And yet I'm torn apart
> Just because I'm presumin'
> That I could be a human
> If I only had a heart.

'What on earth was *that?*' Holliday laughed, stunned.

'It is from *El Mago de Oz*, of course,' said Eddie, coming up for air. 'When it rained, *El Hombre de Hojalata* got rusty and could not move. That is us, *compadre*, tin men who are rusted. This is oil for our squeaking joints. *No estamos en Kansas, Toto, esto es Cuba, mi amigo*,' added Eddie.

'*Edito! Venir aquí ahora!*' Domingo's voice rang out urgently. Eddie sprinted toward the sound of the voice. Heart pounding, Holliday followed on his heels.

A hundred feet from the small clearing where they had made their rough little camp, Pete Laframboise was standing statue still, his legs slightly spread, his hands in front of his crotch and his back to them. Domingo was kneeling in the grass, his fingers gently following an almost invisible strand of nylon fishing line to a sapling on Laframboise's left.

'Oh, shit,' whispered Holliday. It was an old Vietnamese trick; tie the line to the lever of a hand grenade, pop the pin and put the grenade into a tin can that it just fit into. Hit the line the grenade pulled out of the can, the lever popped and say adios. Sometimes if the path was wide enough they'd put a can at each end of the line. Simple, cheap and deadly. Laframboise had obviously gone to empty his bladder and felt the line against his legs just in time.

Holliday could see that all Domingo had to cut the line was the machete. He could also see Laframboise's knees shaking. 'Domingo,' Holliday said calmly but loudly enough to hear. The white-haired Cuban cautiously turned his head. Holliday took the bowie knife from its sheath and flipped it deftly to land beside the older Cuban's right foot, the long, razor-sharp blade cutting into the dark earth like butter.

'*Bueno,*' said Domingo, laying down the machete. '*Le doy las gracias, amigo.*' Domingo slid the big-bladed knife out of the dirt and sliced through the fishing line with a single downward swipe. Holliday held his breath and he felt Eddie stiffen beside him, but nothing happened. Laframboise's knees stopped shaking and he zipped up his fly.

'That was a close one,' he said, half turning toward the others. Domingo took a step toward him and then his eyes widened with horror.

'*Ay no!*'

There was a harsh swishing sound as a sapling bent back on itself, whipped back into place, and six sharpened bamboo stakes, each eighteen inches long, impaled both Domingo and Laframboise where they stood. Holliday saw that the sapling was weighted at the end by a small, curved rectangular object that he recognized instantly: it was an MMI 'MiniMore,' a smaller version of the much larger Claymore fragmentation mine.

'Hit the dirt!'

Holliday dropped, the gentle pinging as the second trip line pulling the ring on the mine tinkling melodically before the main charge exploded and its load of shrapnel exploded in a twenty-foot arc at roughly waist level. It sounded like a small sharp thunderclap followed by an acrid cloud of smoke and then something like the pitter-patter of hail as the projectiles within the mine hit the jungle. Then there was silence and the smoke began to clear.

Holliday stood up. 'Anybody hurt?'

Will Black and Carrie Pilkington, coughing as they appeared out of the smoke, shook their heads. Eddie was already at his brother's side, huge tears running down his cheeks. The MiniMore had missed Domingo's face but had blown off much of his left arm below the elbow. Four of the six bamboo stakes had found their mark, taking the older Cuban through the belly and the midriff, but he was still alive – barely. The MiniMore had decapitated Laframboise. Blood and tissue were splattered everywhere.

'Help me, Doc,' pleaded Eddie, his voice broken through his tears.

As gently as he could, Holliday bent back the sapling long enough for Eddie to pull his brother out of his grotesque embrace with Laframboise's headless corpse.

Eddie then eased his brother off the vicious sharpened stakes and laid him down onto the dark earth.

Blood was pouring from his wounds, but Eddie had already torn off his shirt to stanch the gaping rents in his belly and Holliday made a quick tourniquet above the elbow using his belt. Even so he knew it was just delaying the inevitable. The stakes had pierced Domingo's liver, kidneys and intestines. He didn't have much time left.

'*Te amo, hermanito,*' whispered Domingo, blood bubbling between his lips.

'*Permanezca tranquilo y descanse Domingo,*' hushed Eddie, his tears falling onto his brother's face.

'*Explicar a Mamá Lo siento por todo, Edito, prométeme, mi pequeño vampiro.*'

'*Prometo.*' Eddie wept. Domingo smiled through bloody teeth, his breath coming in rapid gasps. He turned to Holliday.

'They mean to start a war,' said the dying man. 'You must stop them.'

'The missiles, you mean?'

'There are no missiles. Only the warheads remained. The Chinese made three suitcase bombs for us from the old fissionable material. Two have been taken to Orlando. I know nothing of the third.' He coughed a great gout of blood.

'Dear God,' Holliday whispered.

Domingo brought up his good right hand and gripped his brother's shoulder, pulling him down. He whispered urgently into Eddie's ear, his breath failing with every word. Then his head fell back and with a long, terrible sigh he died. Eddie began a soft keening wail as he wept over his brother's body. He reached out and with his thumb and forefinger closed Domingo's eyes. He stood then, gathering up the fallen machete and the bowie knife.

The keening sound of Eddie's mourning grew louder and suddenly, horribly, Holliday could make out the tune to 'Auld Lang Syne,' the song from Eddie's days as a Young Pioneer and the same song Holliday had first heard before Eddie had gone on his murderous rampage in the jungles of Central Africa. Eddie's killing song, his hymn to death.

'Bury him deeply so the animals do not get him,' said Eddie, and then he was gone.

'Eddie! Come back!' Holliday yelled, but there was no answer. He turned to Will and Carrie, his eyes burning with killing fury. 'Bury these men and don't make a move away from here until I get back.'

And then Holliday was gone as well, disappearing into the dawn mist, following his friend to whatever fate awaited them.

26

'This shit is not going down quite the way we thought it would,' said Max Kingman, taking a large bite out of his foie-gras-topped Kobe beef cheeseburger. Chewing, then swallowing, he nibbled at a fresh-cut French fry, first dipping its end into a silver salver of Dijon mayonnaise.

He took a sip of his Château de Malleret, Haut Médoc, and leaned back in his buttery-soft leather armchair. Somewhere behind him the twin engines of the Gulfstream G560 purred. Across the table from him, Joseph Patchin took a tentative bite of his own burger. Kingman smiled. 'If God had a wife, that's what her ass would taste like,' he said.

The CIA deputy director took another bite of the admittedly tasty burger and tried not to think about Kingman's somewhat blasphemous description. Mirroring Kingman, Patchin took a sip of the extremely smooth red wine. 'Exactly what shit are we referring to?' Patchin asked. He glanced out the window. The sun was setting behind them and there was nothing but water below them, so he assumed they were somewhere over the Atlantic. Kingman hadn't mentioned a destination so far.

'The Cuban shit, of course,' snapped Kingman. He

picked up half a dozen French fries in a bunch, dunked them into the yellowish mayonnaise and stuffed all of them into his mouth.

'Any particular part?' Patchin asked.

'Your part.'

'How is that?'

'I've had one of my best teams hung out to dry by this ex-army officer of yours and his nigger Cuban commie fucking pal. Not to mention the fact that those two have apparently managed to fuck things up further by rescuing your analyst bitch and that limey you sent in for a look-see. And if that wasn't bad enough, our people are getting some hard intel that this fucking Housein-Sosa character was a goddamn, son-of-a-bitching Trojan horse.'

'What sort of Trojan horse?'

'The kind that's a plant,' said Kingman. He took another swallow of wine. 'They *let* you have the stupid bastard in Dublin. They gave him to you on a silver fucking platter.'

'I don't believe it. He wasn't a walk-in. He wasn't even one of ours – he was a gift from MI6.'

'Yeah, like they've never had a few fucking commies hiding in the woodwork. Jesus! Talk about moles! You've got nothing on those guys, yet you took the doctor at face value.'

'What did he have to gain?'

'He gets to go and live in Miami or wherever the hell he's been squirreling away money for the past fifty years. He passes on the message he's supposed to and then he gets his get-out-of-jail-free card.'

The two bites of foie-gras burger were sitting in Patchin's gut like ball bearings. He was getting raked over the coals by a fat, blasphemous bastard and he didn't understand what the man was talking about. 'I'm not sure I'm understanding all this,' said the deputy director.

'Christ on a crutch, man, are you that dumb? The doctor was a signal flare that said "we're just about open for business." It's a palace coup d'état, my friend. Castro's going to be offed, Raul's going to get in that jet he's got permanently fueled and ready to go at Libertad Airfield and head for the hills and the generals will be running the show.

'The way we're hearing it, Raul's son Alejandro will be top dog, at least as long as he can fight off the competition.' He grinned. 'It's going to be the biggest fire sale since they brought down the Berlin wall.'

Kingman paused, took another big bite of his cheeseburger and washed it down with more wine. 'Setting the doctor loose was a red flag, Mr Patchin. Get your bets down and get them down early. If I was you, boy, I'd start selling sugar futures short and tobacco futures high. The only thing in the way of it now is this guy Holliday and your two employees.' He paused, gesturing toward Patchin's plate. 'Eat up your burger, boy. That thing would cost you fifty bucks at any decent restaurant inside the Beltway and you're going to need a full stomach by the time we get there.'

'Get where, exactly?'

'Geneva. Talks with Mrs Kate Sinclair, our own big *jefe*. And you got a lot of 'splainin' to do, my friend; the old bitch is not at all happy with the way this is all going down.'

Holliday heard the deep, resonant buzzing before he saw anything. A sound like the humming of an industrious swarm of bees around a hive. But it wasn't bees and it wasn't a hive. He was on Eddie's heels within a few moments of his friend leaving his brother, but it had taken him more than an hour of fighting his way through the jungle to catch up with him.

Throughout the chase he'd expected to hear bursts of gunfire, but there was nothing but the raucous sounds of the birds in the trees and the faint, distant thunder of what seemed like a summer storm approaching.

The scene he came upon abruptly in the small clearing was like something out of *Lord of the Flies*. The three men were arranged in a triangle, their headless naked bodies impaled upside down on long bamboo stakes pounded into the ground, the sawn-off heads thrust onto the tops of the poles, eyelids slashed off, dead eyes covered with crawling flies.

Their tongues and genitals had also been hacked off and rested together at the base of each pole. All three of the men's bellies had been slashed open, the bloody purple coils of intestine cascading onto the ground.

Kneeling in the middle of the triangle, stripped to the waist, his face covered in streaks of blood, was Eddie, chanting softly but clearly, his hands, also bloody, held outstretched and palms up. His eyes were closed and his head was tilted back as the flies swarmed all around him and his terrible trophies.

Ochosi Ode mata obá akofá ayé o unsó iré o wa mi
Ochosi omode ache.
Ochosi Ode mata obá akofá ayé o unsó iré o wa mi
Ochosi omode ache.
Ochosi Ode mata obá akofá ayé o unsó iré o wa mi
Ochosi omode ache.

He kept repeating the long phrase a dozen more times and then stood. His head came forward and his eyes opened, looking at the three dead men around him. Then he noticed Holliday standing silently at the edge of the clearing and came toward him.

'I was saying a prayer to *Ochosi*, the *Orisha* of Justice, the justice which these men have been given. They killed my brother and the pilot, Pete, the way you would kill an animal. There is no honor in that, so they died without honor themselves, and animals can eat them where they stand. Let the flies use them as nests for their maggots, for that is all they are worth.' He turned back to the grim assembly of dead flesh behind him. 'There were four of them, but one escaped. His time will come, though, *compañero*, I promise it.'

'These men died hard,' said Holliday, his voice soft.

'Does it offend you?' Eddie asked.

'No, your brother died hard, as well, but at least he died with great honor. He was trying to save Pete's life.'

'Thank you,' said Eddie. He looked at the dead men and spat in their direction, then turned back to Holliday. 'Sometimes the old ways are the best ways.'

Holliday had no answer for that. He put out his hand and touched Eddie's bare shoulder. 'Time to leave here, *amigo*, and get back to the others. What your brother said before he died makes it even more important that we get away from here.' His brother's secret was America's worst nightmare, the code above all codes that would send a shiver up the spine of any military figure or president who heard it, no matter how battle-hardened that military figure was or how stalwart and valiant the president: PINNACLE-NUCFLASH. The detonation or possible detonation of a nuclear weapon that creates the risk of an outbreak of nuclear war.

The man moved slowly through the deep mangroves of the Everglades, guiding the lightweight fiberglass kayak through the dark green tunnels of foliage. A mile or so behind him, his partner was waiting patiently on the airboat, ready to whisk them both back to civilization.

When the man reached the optimum distance according to his GPS unit, he backwatered with his double-bladed paddle and stopped. Reaching down between his legs, he hauled out the sixty-pound ruck-sack containing the RA-115-01 submersible device and dropped it over the side. The device could last for years underwater, so the man had no fear for its safety. With the bundle safely out of sight, he backpedaled out of the mangrove tunnel and headed back to the airboat.

27

'As Benjamin Disraeli, the British prime minister, once said a long time ago, "The world is governed by very different personages from what is imagined by those who are not behind the scenes." How true it is,' sighed J. Hunter Kokum, the sixty-three-year-old national security adviser to the president, magically elevated to that position after the untimely retirement of the previous adviser, General George Armstrong Temple, for 'reasons of health,' a common White House ailment that seemed to bring down so many great men. Perhaps, Kokum thought, smiling, it was some kind of power flu that only people in high positions caught.

Behind Kokum's back in the hallowed halls of the White House West Wing, Kokum was often called the Gray Ghost. His hair was gray, his suit was gray and his face was gray. He even wore a gray silk tie and had a gray silk puff in the breast pocket of his jacket. He wore gray eel-skin Romano loafers and carried a Geoffrey Beene stingray-skin billfold, also gray. This led to his other nickname, Reptile Man, which he rather favored for its superhero overtones.

Kokum left his office, turned right and trotted up the short flight of steps. He passed the closed door of the vice president's Ceremonial Office – rarely used – passed the closed door of the vice president's secretary – rarely there – and turned into Harley McGraw's office, the president's chief of staff.

Unlike Kokum's tornado-struck office, McGraw's office was as neat as a pin, and so was McGraw. He was the same age as Kokum but much more robust. He had a wide face, a three-quarters bald head and the broad nose of a sixth-generation Mick from Chicago, which is exactly what he was.

His grandfather had been a cop, his father had been a cop and, not one to be typecast, Harley McGraw became a banker, and a good one. By the time he was thirty he was a millionaire, by the time he was forty he was the whispering wizard giving the mayor a direction to go in and by the time he was sixty he was another kind of wizard, whispering into the ear of a presidential candidate.

The whispers must have been the right ones, because his candidate won and he was made secretary of commerce for his efforts. During the wholesale slaughter of the West Wing staff after what had become known as the Kremlin Khristmas and with the elections looming, the president, like every other president before him, wanted Chicago in his pocket, so Harley McGraw was made chief of staff.

'So,' said Kokum, sitting down across the wide desk from McGraw. 'Who would have figured it? Of all the gin joints in all the towns in all the world, she walks into mine.'

'Our friend the doctor was a plant, I understand.'

'Looks that way, although I can't get in touch with Patchin; he's pulling one of his cloak-and-dagger things. It looks like that Pilkington girl of his was right from the start – he was never a defector at all.'

'Smart to lay it off on the Brits. He comes under the auspices of MI6 all wrapped up with a ribbon and a bow.'

'They knew which beaches we were going to hit in the Bay of Pigs before we did. Every president since Eisenhower has thought of them as uneducated peasants, but these guys have been around since Columbus. Havana was a thriving city when Peter Minuit picked up Manhattan from the Indians for next to nothing.'

McGraw sighed and leaned back in his chair. 'I would have thought it was going to be Pakistan, or Yemen, or even Iran, but Cuba?'

'Americans don't like thinking about Cuba,' said Kokum, who'd thought a lot about the subject recently. 'In the schoolyard when you get tricked out of your lunch money by the smart kid, the bully gets upset. We had our favorite Christmas toy stolen and Fidel won't give it back.'

'And we can't take it back because that would make us bullies,' said McGraw. 'The old bastard with the beard really put one over on us.'

'I'm not quite so sure of that,' pondered Kokum. 'Since Kennedy's promise that the United States would never invade Cuba and the embargo after the missile crisis, think what it's done for the economy. It's perfect protectionism. Under the mask of political idealism the embargo keeps Florida and Louisiana sugarcane growers happy, not to mention Hawaii. It protects the California produce industry – it would be a hell of a lot cheaper to ship avocados and tomatoes and all sorts of other fruit and produce ninety miles across the Florida Straits rather than three thousand miles across a continent. Not to mention keeping Las Vegas and Atlantic City and all those idiotic Indian casinos alive and kicking.'

'So we just let Cuba die a natural death?' McGraw asked, lightly scratching the top of his shiny bald skull.

'It's not going to be a natural death. It's going to be a bloody palace coup and maybe even another revolution. There's a group of rebels in the mountains who call themselves Zapatistas after some dissident who starved himself. They seem to be doing some serious damage. It's starting to look like we might have a brand-new Libya right in our own backyard.'

'And no chance of a coalition to go in and calm things down, I suppose.'

'Who?' Kokum asked. 'Half the tourists in Veradero are Canadians, Mexico is so corrupt we could never trust a word they said, Venezuela hates our guts and Brazil and Argentina couldn't give a shit. Who do we join up with, Barbados? The British Virgin Islands? Haiti maybe?'

'So you're telling me we're going to have a military dictatorship down there for another fifty years?'

'Or a series of them,' said Kokum.

'Who gets to tell the president?' McGraw asked.

'This could be worse than the BP spill, and in an election year. Shit!'

'You're the chief of staff,' said Kokum. 'You tell him.'

'You're the national security adviser. You tell him.'

'I'll flip you for it,' suggested Kokum.

'We'll both tell him.'

'Jesus wept,' said Colonel Frank Turturro, staring down at the hideous image on his iPad. The image, sent from the Desert Hawk III mini-drone he'd sent out twenty-four hours after the last time his men had reported in, left nothing to the imagination. The men, all equipped with under-the-skin RFID – Radio Frequency Identification Devices – in their biceps, had led the tiny drone to them within half an hour of the aircraft's launch.

The pictures had been uploaded to the requisite satellite, the signal boosted to take it to the Blackhawk Security Systems Compound War Room and then relayed back to him. The three headless corpses were barely identifiable, but the heads weren't decomposed enough to make it impossible, despite the spawning maggots: the one on the left was Nick Cavan, the one in the middle was a corporal named Dick Rush and the third man was Toby Greer, an old combat veteran Turturro had worked with in Afghanistan. There was no sign of Anthony Veccione, the 'Therapist.'

'Do we have a signal on Master Sergeant Veccione?'

'Yes, sir,' said the young communications officer

standing stiffly at attention in the camouflaged operations tent. 'Loud and clear, sir.'

'Good, get me a GPS fix on him as soon as possible. If he's heading back in this direction, I want an escort sent to meet him along with a medic.'

'Yes, sir. Anything else, sir?'

'Yes,' said Turturro, thinking hard. 'Send me Ed Broadbent.' Broadbent was the best of the Tucano pilots. If anyone could find the son of a bitch who'd desecrated his men's bodies, it was him.

The old man with the frayed straw hat and wearing the white cotton shirt and the torn cotton pants sat side-saddle on the swayback of the tired-looking gray burro, giving it an occasional slap across the neck with a long willow switch when it began to slow as it shuffled slowly along the dusty road carrying its bound bundle of cane across its ancient rump.

The burro – whose name was Graciano, which meant 'pleasing and agreeable,' which he was not – came to a dead halt when he saw the four people step out of the jungle and onto the road. Three men and a woman, all heavily armed with very modern-looking weapons. The *nèg* carried a very old machete in his belt that was brown with rust or dried blood, and the *blanco pirata* with the ruined face had a large knife in a sheath.

The old man, whose name was Federico Fernández Cavada, stared at the four people and wondered for a moment if this was the day God wished him to die. He mentally shrugged his shoulders. Who cared? He had lived in the world longer than he could remember, had a wife, watched her die, had children, watched them forget where they came from, heard of a revolution that was supposed to change his world but had done nothing one way or another, even heard stories of men on the moon and Cubans on the teams of the American major leagues, but what of it? If God meant him to die today, then so be it, as long as somebody took care to feed Graciano.

'*Señores buenos días y la dama,*' said Federico politely.

The black one answered, 'Good day to you, as well, my friend.' He smiled.

Federico found it somewhat interesting that the man did not call him 'Comrade' as the officials in Hatillo or Moron did, but then again, it had been a long time since he had been to either one of those places. Maybe things had changed. It was also interesting that the man's accent marked him as originally coming from Havana. He decided to remark on it.

'You are a long way from home, my friend,' said Federico.

Graciano's body squirmed and he farted, then blew air from his nostrils. 'This is true, but I would very much like to know how far away I am.'

'And how could I tell you that?' Federico said.

'If you told me where I was, then I would know,' said the black man.

'You are lost?' Federico said, a little incredulous. What were people like this doing lost in the jungle?

'We are lost and hungry,' said the black man.

'There is lots of food to be had in the jungle for people with such weapons as yours.'

'We have been trying to be discreet in our movements, old grandfather.'

Federico nodded. They were being pursued by others like them. He would be a fool to put himself between such people, but the black man was very polite and it was obvious he was well educated. 'Who looks for you?'

'Bad men, old grandfather,' said the black man.

And there was the age-old question of course, thought Federico. Bad men never thought they were bad, but everyone thought they were good. 'And how am I to know that you are not the bad men and the people pursuing you the good?'

'You are a wise man, old grandfather, to ask such a question, but the answer is an easy one.'

'And what is the answer?'

'If we were the bad people, we would have blown you off your old burro by now and butchered his stringy old flesh for our dinner.'

The black man smiled.

Federico smiled. 'That is a good answer,' he said. 'Come with me to my home and we will talk and I will give you some food.' He put the willow switch lightly to Graciano's neck and the burro moved slowly off again. Eddie and the others fell in behind him.

'That didn't sound like any Spanish I ever heard,' whispered Carrie.

'That's because it wasn't Spanish – it was Cuban

Creole,' said Black. 'It's the second language here and it goes back a long way.'

'Could you understand what Eddie was saying?'

'No, but it was obviously all the right things.'

28

Alfonsito's finca, or farm, was located at the very end of the narrow little road in the mountains. There was a small cluster of plaster-covered single-story buildings that looked as though they had been a work in progress for a hundred years or so, a broken-backed small wooden barn and a pigpen with half-built walls of concrete blocks. The house was roofed with loose squares of rusted sheet metal, and the barn was thatched with woven banana leaves and cane.

Several small fields climbed up the slope behind the house and outbuildings. Holliday could see tobacco, tomatoes, potatoes, something green like spinach and even a spiky field of pineapples.

There were a pair of avocado trees ripe with fruit giving shade to the doorway of the farmhouse, and underneath one of the trees was a 1941 half-ton Dodge pickup that looked as though it might have been black at one point but which was now covered with a coat of uniform mud gray house paint.

The old Dodge was in excellent shape except for the frighteningly bald tires, and with a little work Alfonsito could probably get more money for the truck than for his entire farm. A dozen chickens poked about in the front yard, pecking at nothing. Off to the right was an adobe fire pit with a grease-encrusted grill. Heat was rising from it, which meant the coals had been lit some time ago.

Alfonsito slid off the burro, tying it to a low branch of one of the avocado trees. He led them into the main room of the house and threw open the shutters of the two windows to let in some light. There was a homemade table, four wooden chairs and a small bed in the corner.

Alfonsito spoke to Eddie. 'Take the table and chairs outside. We will eat under the tree where it is cooler.'

'Certainly,' said Eddie. He explained what the old man had said and they began moving everything outside. Alfonsito stepped into a back room, disappearing from view.

'You think we can trust him?' Carrie asked.

'He's offering his hospitality,' said Eddie. 'That is trust enough for me.'

They took the table and chairs outside into the shade of the avocado and Alfonsito appeared a few moments later with a split and eviscerated suckling pig, which he laid on the grill.

Alfonsito disappeared again and came back in a few moments with a burlap sack and five tall plastic cups held in his spread fingers. The cups were old McDonald's *Batman Forever* giveaway cups with the images mostly faded and scratched off.

He opened the burlap sack and ceremoniously removed five cool bottles of blue-labeled Mayabe beer. He set one bottle and one cup before each of his guests. He found an old wooden crate beside the door, upended it for a stool and then passed an old rusted bottle opener around the table. When all the beer had been passed around, he stood and lifted his bottle.

'*Bweson zanmis!*'

'It means "Drink, my friends,"' translated Eddie. The others all raised their bottles. '*Onè Respè!*' said Eddie, toasting Alfonsito. The others all followed suit without having any idea what it meant, but whatever they'd said, it made the old man smile. Behind them on the grill, the smoky sweet smell of barbecuing pork began to fill the air.

By early evening the team of scouts sent out by Turturro had returned with Veccione in tow, exhausted and suffering slightly from exposure but otherwise intact. Broadbent the Tucano pilot had searched until the light began to fail, but all he could find was an abandoned campsite and a clear trail heading northwest.

'They're heading for the coast,' said Veccione. 'I'd bet on it.' The 'Therapist' gave a little wince of pain and his face darkened. 'I'd like to get my hands on the savage son of a bitch who did that to Nick and the others.'

'Why didn't he get you?'

'I was getting some kindling for a fire. I heard the commotion, so I bellied down and got as close as I could. It was too late. One against three and he took them all out. There was nothing I could do.'

'You had a sidearm.'

'It was holstered. He would have heard.'

'So you just watched him kill my men?'

'Fuck you, sir. They were already dead with their guts pouring out and their heads on poles. I didn't think getting myself killed was going to be particularly useful.'

'So you bellied away?'

'I didn't move a muscle until they were gone.'

'They?'

'The guy with the eye patch showed up about half an hour later. The black guy went off with him. I split.'

'Why do you think they're headed for the coast?'

'Where else would they go? They know we're after them. They flew in here with a crop duster, for Christ's sake! They're not equipped to get through army check-points on the highway, so they sure as hell aren't going back to Havana.'

'The guy with the eye patch and the black came by boat up the Agabama River. What's to stop them from doubling back?'

'They'd have to double back. They gotta know they'd run into us. Not to mention the fact that it's almost a hundred miles downriver to the south coast. With this Viva Zapata shit we've stirred up, every Cuban patrol is going to be on edge.' Veccione winced again and moved on his cot to get more comfortable. He shook his head. 'They have to be heading for the north coast. By now they're not more than twenty-five or thirty miles from the Atlantic side.'

'Where?'

'Caibarien,' said Broadbent, the pilot, speaking for the first time. 'I was studying the maps and charts when I got back. It's the only place they could find a boat.'

Turturro looked at his watch. Forty-eight hours now before Point Zero, the code name for their operation, to begin in force. Holliday and the others had to be caught before then. 'All right,' he said finally, 'Caibarien it is.'

They ate roasted suckling pig and drank beer in the dying sun, and then Alfonsito found blankets and bedding enough and took them to the big tobacco drying shed, where they bedded down for the night. Tomorrow they would help him gather enough produce in the cool of the morning for him to take to the market in Caibarien and he would be more than happy to give them a ride.

The coastal town had once been known as La Villa Blanca, the White Town, famous for its port, its hotels, its *parrandas*, or *carnivals*, and its white-sand beaches arcing around the Bahia de Buena Vista. Now the town had fallen into disrepair, the fine old nineteenth-century hotels crumbling, its two sugarcane mills long closed down and most of the piers and other port facilities rotted, sunk or destroyed by decades of hurricanes sweeping over them.

On the eastern side of the decaying town, there was still a small fishing fleet, specializing in lobster and other crustaceans and a small but active sponge fishery. It was here, suggested Alfonsito, that they might be able to find someone willing to rent out his boat.

The old farmer woke them before the sun had truly risen and they found themselves in a ghostly universe of early mist that hugged the ground and drifted, shredding through the trees on the hillsides all around them. Alfonsito gave them a breakfast of harsh black *café Cubano*, fried eggs and crisp pieces of succulent *lechon* from the night before and then they went to work in the fields, following the old man's directions and filling basket after basket with fresh-picked produce and even two or three dozen already ripe pineapples.

By the time they were finished, the mist had burned off and the hot sun was rising in the sky. The baskets were loaded in the truck and then Alfonsito disappeared into the old house. They packed away their weapons among the baskets of food and waited for the old man to reappear.

'Bloody hot work, that,' said Will Black, sitting on the open tailgate. 'I really am a city boy, I suppose. Never was one for all that "bringing in the sheaves" silliness.'

'We spent our whole summers doing it,' laughed Eddie, stretching his arms and yawning. '*Trabajo voluntario*, whether you volunteered or not. Two months gathering tomatoes only to see them rotting on trucks because there was no gasoline.'

'What gets me is the quiet,' said Carrie. 'A few birds,

the wind in the trees. Nothing. I haven't heard a car in weeks, it seems. A bit spooky.'

'Is this where I'm supposed to do the John Wayne bit and say, "Yes, ma'am, just a little too quiet?"'

Alfonsito appeared in the doorway, a transformed man. His white stubble had been shaved off, he was dressed in a clean white shirt and pants and he sported a clean yellow straw hat on his head and a bright blue sash around his waist. There was an old pistol stuffed into the sash. Alfonsito posed, smiling in the doorway, showing his tobacco-stained teeth.

'*Magnifico!*' Eddie explained, clapping his hands and grinning.

'*Muy guapo!* Very handsome,' Will Black said, smiling as well.

'The senoritas will swoon for you, grandfather,' said Eddie in Creole. Alfonsito, despite his years, colored like a beet.

'Why does he carry a gun?' Carrie whispered.

Eddie asked the question in Creole and Alfonsito smiled, hauling the old revolver from his sash. 'He says there are pirates on the highways as well as the seas.'

'May I see the weapon?' Carrie asked eagerly.

Eddie asked the question to Alfonsito and the old man looked a little querulous. He responded with his own question in Creole and Eddie translated. 'He wishes to know why such a pretty senorita would like to see the old *pistola* his father gave to him.'

'Because I am interested in such things,' said Carrie. 'I shoot pistols as a sport.'

'This is true?' Eddie asked, surprised.

'Of course it's true,' responded the young CIA employee, a little acid in her tone and perhaps more than a little pride. 'I was first in the women's rapid fire at the European Championships in Belgrade two years ago and second in the Pan American Games in Guadalajara last year. I'm also on the U.S. Women's Olympic team.'

'Good Lord,' said Black.

'It's not all sugar and spice and everything nice, you know,' said Carrie.

Eddie spoke in rapid Creole and Alfonsito nodded. He approached Carrie and slipped the revolver out of its place in the sash and handed it to her ceremoniously. She held the weapon reverently in her hands.

'It's a forty-five-caliber Colt New Service double-action revolver,' she said, turning the weapon over in her hands. 'It looks like it's in perfect condition. It's got to be at least a hundred years old.'

Alfonsito said something to Eddie with pride in his voice and Eddie translated. 'He says his father fought with Teddy Roosevelt at the Battle of San Juan Hill at Santiago de Cuba during the Spanish-American war . . . when the United States and the Cubans were friends, not enemies.'

'Does it still work?'

Eddie asked and Alfonsito answered.

'He says of course it still works and that you may try it if you wish.'

'Tell him I am honored.'

*

The screaming of the Super Tucano's Pratt & Whitney turboprop engine came out of nowhere as Ed Broadbent, the Blackhawk pilot, brought the old-fashioned-looking fighter plane around the hillside, screening Alfonsito's farm from view.

He'd gone out early from the old landing strip deeper in the mountains, hoping to catch the fleeing group before they broke camp, and he wasn't prepared to see his targets unarmed and standing in the open. He instinctively realized he was flying too high and moving too fast to get a shot, so he immediately threw the aircraft into a rolling climb to drain off his air speed, flipping the yoke switch for the twin Herstal .50-caliber machine guns in the wings.

He peeled out of the climb and came back on the group from the opposite direction, nose dropping and losing altitude quickly. There were five of them gathered around an old American pickup, all of them staring up at him, their faces a white blur. The Heads Up display was putting them right in his sights and he barely hesitated before his thumb hit the firing button for the twin .50-calibers. The hesitation killed him.

Before he could activate the brutal firepower in the wings, he watched dumbfounded as the five-bladed aluminum propeller seemed to bend, blur and disintegrate right before his eyes. His left hand reached for the ring-pull of the Martin-Baker ejection seat just as the fourth big-caliber round from the revolver gripped by Carrie Pilkington seventy feet below him struck the auxiliary fuel pod directly beneath the cockpit and the eight-million-dollar aircraft turned into a fireball. The solid-fuel rocket charge and the explosive in the ejection seat exploded, hurling the blazing, torchlike stick figure of Ed Broadbent through the glass cockpit cover and into the cool clear air.

'*Guete!*' Alfonsito whispered in Creole, eyes wide as the flaming twisted remains of the fighter plane roared over his little house and crashed into his tobacco field.

Carrie popped open the cylinder of the big old revolver and started ejecting the spent brass. She grinned at Alfonsito. 'Yup, still works.'

29

The fishing fleet in Caibarien was located in a small bay on the eastern edge of the decaying but once vital old town. There was one rotting concrete pier and several short, wobbly wooden docks jutting out into the clear shallow water, but it looked as though most of the fishermen brought their catches to shore in small luggers and dories, which were pulled up onto the stony beach and unloaded there.

Alfonsito parked his truck on the dusty road and told them to wait for him to return. Holliday, seated in the bed of the truck with the others, watched the old man and Eddie go, then looked out over the bay. Most of the dozen or so boats were in the fifty-foot range, old, tubby and in need of paint, single-masted with a squat, flat-roofed wheelhouse set far back in the stern. None of them carried radar dishes and only one or two had rudimentary radio antennas strung up the forward mast and boom. All of them had great folds of brown net hung out to dry over the gunwales. Breathing in, Holliday inhaled a potent aromatic mixture of the fresh produce around him on the bed of the truck, the salt tang of fresh sea air and the bitter grunge of diesel oil. A seabird of some kind swooped down out of the harsh blue sky and settled on the forepeak of one of the boats.

'That reminds me,' said Holliday, turning to Carrie. 'I never congratulated you on your Annie Oakley demonstration this morning. Pretty amazing shooting down a fighter plane with a hundred-year-old six-gun.'

'Aw, shucks, Shurrif, 'tweren't nothin', really,' she drawled. 'It wasn't. I'm not kidding. There's more than one military analyst who called the Tucano and the Texan II and the 67 Dragon flying coffins. They don't have enough armor and probably the first shot at the prop would have been enough. Throw a five-bladed prop even a fraction out of sync and it'll rip the whole airframe apart. They're for nostalgia buffs who wished they'd flown Spitfires in the Battle of Britain.'

'It was still pretty impressive,' said Holliday.

'Agreed,' said Will Black.

'Do I detect a little "impressive for a girl" chauvinism in there somewhere?'

'Not a bit of it,' answered Holliday. 'Gender doesn't matter a crap when it comes to having your ass hauled out of the fire. I said impressive and I meant it. We'd all be dead meat if it wasn't for you.'

'That old double action was what did it. The Tucano's coming at about a hundred knots; the Colt has a muzzle velocity of about seven hundred feet a second – when that big fat .45 round hit the prop, it was the equivalent of a Canadian goose going through the fan of that jet that went down in the Hudson.'

'Except this time the pilot wasn't as good,' Holliday said. 'Or as lucky.'

'No, I guess not,' said Carrie, a faraway look in her eyes and her tone dark. 'It was a horrible way to die. I've never killed anybody before; it was always just paper targets and gongs. This was real.'

'That's right,' answered Holliday. 'It was real and you'll never forget it until your dying day, but it still doesn't change the fact that you saved five people's lives and maybe a hell of a lot more than that if we actually get out of this.'

Eddie and Alfonsito reappeared atop the path leading down to the beach. 'How did it go?' Holliday asked Eddie as they approached the pickup.

'He will do it. His name is Geraldo López-Nussa. His son, Ricardo, is his partner. The son is his only family. If you can guarantee to speak for him to the people of American *Inmigración,* he would be most grateful.'

'I can pretty much guarantee him citizenship for himself and his son if he can get us outside Cuban territorial waters,' said Holliday.

'We meet him on the beach. His boat is Corazon de Leon, the *Lion Heart.* It is the one with the red stripe.'

Holliday looked quickly out onto the calm waters of the bay. It was the boat with the bird on the forepeak. Maybe it was an omen.

'Got it.'

'It is already late in the day for the lobster boats to head out to sea. Four strange people on Geraldo's boat will have people talking, especially when three of them are obviously *yumas*. The police will know quickly. We must move, and fast, if we want to get away cleanly. Geraldo says there has been a Zhuk patrol boat seen in the area.'

'Then we should get a wiggle on,' said Black. He picked up the burlap sack containing the weapons and they followed Geraldo down to the beach. His son, Ricardo, was waiting by a dory already pushed halfway into the water. They climbed in, Ricardo shoving them off and then leaping into the stern to handle the rudder as his father took the oars.

'How many of the patrol boats are there?' Holliday asked. Eddie relayed the question to Geraldo as he pulled at the oars.

'He says they used to be in every harbor in Cuba, but now there are only a dozen or so. Mostly they patrol the Florida Straits looking for people trying to get to Miami.'

'Did you ask him about the other thing?' Holliday asked.

Eddie nodded. 'He has some . . . not very much. Red.'

'Good enough,' said Holliday.

Geraldo rowed while Ricardo steered and a few moments later they arrived at the permanent wooden buoy where the Corazon de Leon was anchored. They scrambled aboard while Ricardo tied off the dory. The deck of the boat was littered with strange-looking boxes made from mangrove branches. The boxes were three feet on a side and open-ended.

'*Casas para los langouste,*' explained Geraldo. '*Nosotros les fuera cosquillas con cañas de bamboo.*'

'They are little houses for the lobsters. They sink them in the sea and then – how do you say, "tickle"? – them out with long bamboo poles into their nets.'

Geraldo took them to the wheelhouse, which was larger than it had seemed from shore. There was a small room behind the wheelhouse itself, which had a set of bunk beds, a table, chairs and some rudimentary cooking facilities including a portable propane stove and some pots and pans. A porthole on either side of the little cubicle provided light. Both portholes had been opened wide and a pleasant cross breeze riffled across the room. Geraldo spoke some rapid-fire Spanish and Eddie nodded.

'Geraldo wants us to stay here until we are beyond the *cayos* and in the open sea.

'No problem,' replied Holliday. They settled themselves into the small galley. A few moments later they heard the throaty cough of a diesel engine and seconds after that the *Lion Heart* began to move, heading toward the open sea and perhaps, at long last, freedom.

Bruno, Cardinal Musaro, papal nuncio to Cuba, sat in the dining room of the nunciate in the Miramar District of Havana waiting for the midday meal to be served. He sat at the head of the table, which looked directly out the open French doors onto the beautifully tended Orange Garden. The trees were all valencia, the true Mediterranean *Citrus sinensis*, not the American hybrid usually associated with the name. Each of the trees was between six and ten meters high and pruned so that it was broad and bushy. Even though it was early in the season, the fruit was already visible among the branches.

As usual he ate alone at the seventeenth-century lyre-legged walnut table. His lunch had begun with half a dozen fresh oysters followed by conch fritters and a lovely avocado salad, and he was now working his way through a satisfying *medianoche,* or *midnight,* sandwich consisting of roast pork, ham, mustard, Swiss cheese and dill pickles, served on a soft challah-style bread and pressed in his beloved George Foreman Grill. When the sandwich was finished, he would end the meal with a Flan de Guayaba y Queso, cream cheese and Guava flan with coffee to follow. He liked to eat lightly at luncheon since he was often required to attend lavish dinners given by Havana's high society, which generally meant the more Catholic members of the military hierarchy. Tonight, for instance, it was a pre-St Lazarus Day feast being given by Brigadier General Ulises Rosales del Toro, a Hero of Cuba, the vice president of the entire country, the effective head of the sugar industry and one of the men most likely to succeed if Fidel died and Raul abdicated, which was the most likely scenario. Little did Del Toro know how soon that would be.

One of his attendants brought in the flan and after he'd departed a second priest appeared. He wasn't familiar to Musaro and the papal nuncio frowned. Strangely the man had a limp and carried a heavy, old-fashioned root-wood cane, polished to an almost glassy shine.

'I don't mean to interrupt your meal, Eminence, but I have an urgent message from the Vatican.'

Musaro's frown became a grin. This was the news he had been expecting. He'd seen that bastard Spada's medical files and he knew the timing was perfect. 'Yes?'

Father Ronan Sheehan raised the head of the knob-kerrie, its large upper handle weighted with an extra ten ounces of lead, and struck Musaro hard on the right side of his forehead at his temple, instantly crushing both the frontal and the sphenoid bones. He caught the dying cardinal by the scruff of the neck and dragged him to his feet. He gently kicked the man's ankles out from under him, then let go of his collar. Musaro dropped heavily to the ground, striking the right side of his head against the corner of the table before he hit the Persian-carpeted floor. The hit on the edge of the table had opened the wound nicely so that blood from the corner of the table began dripping down on the body, more fluid, brains and blood oozing out onto the rug. Sheehan paused just long enough to take a breath of the ripening oranges outside, then turned and left. Half an hour later he was back at the Marina Hemingway, guiding the late Des Smith's boat in the general direction of Key West.

30

After rounding Punta Brave, the Corazon de Leon puttered slowly southwest heading for the shallow channel between tiny Cayo Boca Chica at the end of its much larger brother, Cayo Fagoso, on the port side and Cayo Frances to starboard. Beyond was the open sea. Geraldo and his son, Ricardo, stopped the engines briefly beside an old wreck of a molasses ship, the SS *San Pasqual*, blown onto the reef in 1939.

The crystallized molasses still threw off a terrible odor, but the old concrete ship was exactly the kind of place where you caught the best lobster and it took less than twenty minutes for the father-and-son team to bring up several dozen of the enormous creatures. It also gave them a chance to see if anyone had shown any interest in their leave-taking.

Eddie and the two Cuban lobstermen met briefly on deck, and then Eddie reported back to the little galley aft of the wheelhouse. 'They say that from here we can go two ways: to Key West or to Billy's Cay in the Bahamas. If we go to Key West we have to travel along the coast for more than seventy miles, but Billy's Cay is one hundred and seventy miles and almost due north. They are suggesting Billy's Cay and ask for your thoughts on this.'

'How long before we're beyond the twelve-mile limit?'

'From the wreck . . . perhaps forty-five minutes.'

'No sign of the Zhuk patrol boat?'

'Nothing. The sea is ours.'

'I agree with Geraldo and Ricardo. We head for Billy's Cay.'

'*Bueno.*' Eddie nodded. He turned and left the galley.

'Time to get to work,' said Holliday.

Paul Smith, senior analyst and interpreter for the Central American Division of the National Geospatial-Intelligence Agency, sat in his small office in the new Fort Belvoir complex. It was Saturday, Smith's usual day for golf, but here he was, at the express order of Mrs Leticia goddamn Long, director of the agency, to repurpose the new GeoEye 2 satellite as well as run a series of four overlapping and continuous RQ-170 drones over Cuba. The RQ-170 was tasked to fly at mid altitudes, but it was felt that although one had been recently brought down by the Iranians, the Cuban electronic defenses were not sophisticated enough to cause any problems. He had six computers running simultaneously on his workdesk and a huge eighty-inch monitor on the wall giving him a larger, high-definition view from GeoEye 2.

To make matters worse, not only was he to retask the satellite and oversee the drone flights out of Creech, but he was to personally maintain twenty-four-hour surveillance and see to it that there was always someone watching the screens. Under no circumstances was he to leave the gigantic building, which meant some kind of hideous dinner in the food fair mall in the Atrium and a night in one of the 'suites' the agency maintained for just this kind of situation. The 'suites' were somewhere short of a room at a Motel Six. It was worse than being an on-call intern in a hospital. Smith yawned and let his eyes flicker back and forth across the screens with an occasional glance at the big screen on the wall. His headache was getting worse by the minute. It was going to be a long day and an even longer night.

Father Thomas Brennan sat at one of the small tables outside the Osteria Dell'Angelo on the Via G. Bettolo, eating a small plate of *ciambelline* aniseed doughnut-style biscuits and enjoying a glass of sweet Vin Santo dessert wine after a pleasant dinner. Finishing the last of the biscuits, he lit a cigarette and watched the traffic squeeze down the narrow roadway a few blocks from the Holy City.

All in all, the Irish priest was feeling quite content. He had photocopied Spada's personal medical file to those concerned and was now waiting for the almost certain results.

Spada had less than a year, and probably no more than six months, left to live, which would give Musaro plenty of time to establish himself to take over the position. He chuckled to himself; the pope was primed, so to speak. With Musaro in position – a much more aggressively active man in the role of Vatican secretary of state Soladitum Pianum and the entire Vatican intelligence apparatus would finally be used to assert its real potential.

The endless sex scandals, the Vatican Bank scandal and the cloud that still hung over the death of John Paul I – a plan Brennan had advised against from the beginning – had all conspired to lower the Vatican's prestige and political power. Now, with Spada gone and the Holy Father seriously thinking of resigning, perhaps that would change. Within the next year or so, there was going to be a shift in power in the Vatican and Brennan was assuring himself a position on the winning side.

Finishing his cigarette, Brennan lit another, waved to Angelo, the retired rugby player and owner of the restaurant, and walked back to his little apartment on the Via Mazzini. He stopped off at the Caffè Della Rosa for a final espresso and made a quick call on his cell phone. Twenty minutes later he reached his building and trudged up the three flights of stairs to his apartment.

He quickly stripped off his clothes, took a shower and put on the old velvet robe and slippers that were his usual form of dress when he was at home. Fifteen minutes later, there was the shrill sound of his doorbell and without even switching on the intercom he buzzed the downstairs door open. A few moments later, there was a quiet knock at his door and he let his guest in. As usual it was Mai Phuong Thúy, his favorite, the compact portable massage table almost as big as she was.

'*Buổi tối cha tốt,*' she said politely.

'And a good evening to you, as well, my dear,' the priest answered. He stepped aside to let her pass, then followed her down the short hall to his comfortable book-lined living room. She set up the massage table, draped a sheet over it, then helped Brennan remove his robe and slippers.

He climbed up onto the table, facedown, while Mai took her oils out, and then he gave in to forty-five minutes of her excellent ministrations. At the end of the forty-five minutes, the massage stopped and Mai disappeared into the one-bedroom apartment's kitchen. Brennan heard the pinging of the microwave oven that meant she was heating her small towels. It was his signal to roll over on his back, which he did.

The microwave pinged again and a few seconds later the Irish priest heard the small sound of Mai's feet on the living room rug. He closed his eyes and she laid one of the towels over his face. A few seconds after that, her hand began to massage his flaccid organ, magically arousing it to all of its five-and-a-half-inch hooded length.

'*Không cảm thấy người cha tốt?*' Mai asked.

'Wonderful,' wheezed Brennan, his voice thick with pleasure.

'*Jak to cítí, zrádce?*' said Daniella Kay Pesek, the widow of Czech assassin-for-hire named Antonin Pesek, the man who had been hired by Brennan less than a year ago to kill John Holliday and who had failed, dying in the process. Daniella slipped her usual weapon, a seven-inch hard plastic hairpin, into Brennan's right ear, penetrating the outer ear, then penetrating the middle ear and finally through the temporal bone to the brain via the internal auditory nerve canal.

The movement was almost surgical in its precision, and it killed Thomas Brennan instantly. She gave the hairpin a swift circular twist and then withdrew it quickly. There wasn't even a drop of blood. 'Can you clean up?' Daniella said to Mai in passable Vietnamese. She handed the woman an envelope containing the twenty-five-thousand-dollar fee requested.

'*Tất nhiên.*' Mai nodded.

Daniella gave the young masseuse a smile and left the apartment. When she reached the outside, she made a quick call on her cell phone. Spada would want the news immediately.

Paul Smith was mentally choosing between a Burger King Triple Whopper and Cheese with a side of onion rings and a large Diet Coke and a KFC Big Hungry Box Meal with a large Diet Pepsi when he saw it on screen four of the array on his desk. 'It' was just a blob on the screen, but it had put out an anomaly ping, so he zoomed and tightened up the RQ-170 image.

The drone was on the far edge of the pattern and if the pattern hadn't been just so, the image wouldn't have appeared and it was doubtful GeoEye 2 would have read it as an anomaly from that height. Eyes bugging out, he slapped the keyboard, throwing the image up on the eighty-inch screen, recalibrated and zoomed in yet again, filling the giant plasma surface with an enlarged version of what he had just seen.

Any ideas of fast food vanished. This one was going to take him right up to the executive dining room in perpetuity. He grinned; it was also so far above Leticia Long's head that it was in the stratosphere.

'Holy shit!' Smith whispered reverently. He reached for the telephone, got the operator and gave an order as clichéd in the movies as 'follow that car.' Paul Smith said, 'Get me the White House.' And the operator did.

31

The Zhuk-class patrol boat appeared on the aft horizon approximately five hours after the Corazon de Leon had left the lobster grounds around the wreck of the SS *San Pasqual*. By Geraldo's calculations they had been traveling at an average speed of twelve knots per hour, which put them sixty miles from the wreck and well outside Cuban territorial waters.

'How far?' Holliday asked Eddie, who was staring at the distant shape of the old-style patrol boat.

'Fifteen miles, maybe a little more,' replied Holliday's friend. 'Perhaps twenty.'

'How long?'

'It is hard to say, *mi compadre*. The Zhuk was rated at thirty knots maximum speed, but that was when they were new. The Cuban boats are from the Seventies. I doubt that they can maintain twenty knots now, if that.'

'What can Geraldo give us?'

'No more than fifteen.'

'That means they'll gain five miles each hour.' It was three in the afternoon; the patrol boat would be within range by seven in the evening – just about sunset at this time of the year – but it wouldn't be fully dark until eight thirty or nine. They barely had a chance of getting away in the dark.

Looking to the other horizon, they could all see that dark storm clouds were gathering, high, bruised-looking thunderheads.

'Tell Geraldo to pour it on and tell him to pray for rain. It's our only chance. Now.'

32

The tropical dusk was quickly turning to darkness when Colonel Frank Turturro's forward team reported to him that the burnt-out remains of Broadbent's Tucano had been spotted smoldering in a farmer's field forty-five miles east of Caibarien. There was evidence that his prisoners had escaped from the farm in a truck of some kind and had either managed to steal or hire a boat or were now hiding in the town itself. Fifteen minutes after that, he wasn't surprised to get the Abort code from the Mount Carroll Compound.

'*Figlio di puttana,*' he cursed, reverting to the language of his Brooklyn youth. The Abort involved two major operations. First, the retreat of the remaining Tucanos to the fallback position on Isla Guanaja, a nearly uninhabited island a few dozen miles off the sometimes deadly Honduran coast. The individual pilots would then refuel and fly back to the United States and the Blackhawk-owned private airfield in Arizona.

The second part of the Abort mission was considerably more complicated. Splitting into platoon-sized units, the almost fifteen hundred men scattered around the Sierra del Escambray would make their way to the Caribbean coast, where they would reassemble close to the nearly empty beaches to the north of Playa Inglés, a small run-down resort town. Two refitted freighters would stand offshore for three nights just beyond the twelve-mile limit and when signaled would send in enough inflatables to remove all the troops.

It all sounded well and good, but Turturro had sat through most of the planning sessions for Operation Cuba Libre, and the least attention had been placed on aborting. Apparently failure wasn't an option for people like Swann and Axeworthy. When push came to shove, Turturro gave fifty-fifty odds if there would be any freighters offshore when the time came.

The whole thing was beginning to sound like a reprise of the Bay of Pigs. Then, as now, air support made all the difference. Without the Tucanos they were a hit-and-run guerrilla force not much bigger than Fidel's band of brothers in the Sierra Maestre back in '58 and '59. Sighing, Turturro got up from behind his desk in the command tent. He went and stood outside, breathing in the sweet-rot stick of the jungle. Desert winds or jungle swamps, failure always smelled the same.

'Tha-tha-that's all, folks,' he whispered to himself, wondering if he was going to get off this island alive.

Max Kingman and Kate Sinclair sat in the study of the ex-ambassador's Georgetown house discussing recent events in Cuba. Kingman was drinking too much. By Sinclair's estimation he was at least three Scotches ahead of her one. He wasn't pleased by the way Operation Cuba Libre was going at all.

'It's starting to smell bad, Kate, I'm warning you. This Holliday is more than a monkey wrench in the works. He's a mother-humping Sherman tank.'

The elderly woman smiled. 'You're showing your age now, Max; nobody's used Sherman tanks since Castro at the Bay of Pigs.'

'Very funny. We've got everyone on our side now. Lobo, Bacardi, DuPont, all the hotel chains. We've made promises, Kate, and if we can't pay the piper we're going to be in some very hot water.' The ruddy-faced man took a long pull at his drink.

'Come now, Max, the country is imploding. Its economy is a black hole, for God's sake. How long can Raul survive by selling off the contents of the State Museum to keep the country stumbling along? He's released a crowd of criminals along with the dissidents from his prisons because he simply couldn't afford to feed them. The country's being run by Alzheimer's patients.'

'Worked for Reagan,' grunted Kingman. 'For a little while, anyway.'

'Relax,' said Kate Sinclair. 'Tomorrow Fidel dies. Raul and his family will be on his jet to Spain within hours of his brother's demise and the Brotherhood will be in charge.

'And try to remember, Max – Lobo, Bacardi and all the rest are paying us huge sums of money for a chance to reclaim their properties, and with the Brotherhood's agreement they've also hired Blackhawk Security as a counterinsurgency force during the period of "transition." Relax, Max. We've just won the lottery.'

'We're killing a lot of people to do it, Kate.'

'Having second thoughts, Max?'

Kingman shrugged. 'I never did like Orlando much.'

'They're suitcase bombs. Nuclear firecrackers. The estimate if both of the bombs go off is fewer than two hundred thousand people dead, maybe less – Lake Buena Vista or whatever it's called is twenty miles away from town.'

'And the one in the Everglades?'

'Backup. The point is the bombs are the key that opens the door. It's going to make nine-eleven look like a house fire.' Sinclair raised her glass. 'The bombs are the rationale for an invasion that should have succeeded fifty years ago.

'They'll rewrite the Patriot Act; they're going to be hiring private police forces, shoot-to-kill border patrols. Think of it as one big business opportunity. Those bombs are the keys to the magic kingdom, Max, and we'll be the ones sitting on the royal thrones.'

'No, you won't,' said Joseph Patchin, entering the study. A nine-millimeter Glock 19 was held firmly in his right hand.

'How the hell did you get in here?' Kingman said, half rising from his leather chair.

'I'm the director of operations at the CIA, you fat old bastard,' answered Patchin. 'I've still got a few chops.'

It was clear to Kate Sinclair that Patchin was at least as drunk as Kingman. She calmly opened the bag on her lap, took out her lighter and cigarettes and lit one. 'Perhaps you could enlighten us on the reason for your presence here.'

'Sure, Ms Psycho Sinclair, you crazy bitch.' Patchin closed his eyes for a second or two and swayed slightly. 'There's been a Pinnacle Nucflash alert for Orlando. Where do you think that came from? Three guesses, and the first two don't count. It's your old goddamn pal Holliday – that's who. The president, in all his great fucking wisdom, has asked for NEST teams to descend on Florida like locusts. The signal traffic between the American Interests Office at the Swiss embassy in Havana is burning up the airwaves. The jig is up, as they used to say. I think what it really means is we're screwed. We're all going down.'

'NEST?' Kingman asked, his face slack and his brow furrowed, not quite getting it.

'Nuclear Emergency Support Team,' said Kate Sinclair. 'They find lost atomic bombs and the like.'

'Full marks, sweetie.' Patchin grinned drunkenly.

'But . . . but there must be something we can do!' Kingman said.

'Sure there is,' said Patchin. 'We can die.' He fired two quick shots, one into Kingman's chest and another into his throat, killing him instantly and blowing him back even more deeply into his chair.

Remarkably his drink stayed firmly gripped in his hand. Blood began to spread across his starched white shirt and bubble from his mouth in little pops and burbles as the life drained out of his body. Patchin watched for a moment, fascinated, then swung around to face Kate Sinclair. 'Your turn now, Lady Crazy, and then I'll join you in hell myself.'

'I'll take a rain check, Mr Patchin.' She slid her little Khar PM45 pocket pistol from her purse and shot Patchin once, taking out his left eye and blowing his brains out through the door and into the hall outside the study. Patchin collapsed like an empty suit of clothes.

Sinclair stood, walked over to Patchin and took the handkerchief from the breast pocket of the man's suit jacket. She wiped off her own handprints from her pocket pistol, then went and placed the weapon in Max Kingman's dead right hand, squeezing his index finger into the trigger guard and pressing his other fingers around the grip.

She took the Scotch glass from his other hand and put it on the table beside him. She finally retrieved her own glass, emptied its contents back into the Scotch decanter, then wiped and dried the glass before putting it into the bar cabinet with a dozen or so others just like it.

Sinclair looked around the room, nodded once, then left the room, careful to step over the mess Patchin's brains had left in the front hall. She paused at the front door, took out her cell phone and made a quick call.

'File a flight plan for Zurich. I'll be there in half an hour.' She closed the cell phone, put it back into her purse. Using Patchin's handkerchief, she turned the doorknob and stepped out into the muggy evening air. She closed the door, put the handkerchief into her purse.

'Goddamn it to hell,' she said quietly, then headed for M Street and a taxi to take her to the South Capitol Street Heliport.

So far the growing storm had kept the Zhuk at bay, the high, choppy waves throwing both the patrol boat and the Corazon de Leon around like a kid's bath toys. She had come abreast of them but was standing about a mile away, the red, angled stripe on her hull occasionally visible as she rode the crest of a wave.

Every ten minutes or so, there would be the popping, tearing sound of the twin forward and aft machine-gun turrets, but so far they hadn't done much more than blow off the upper portion of the mast and boom and splinter a few of the piled lobster traps on deck.

Eddie was at the wheel while Geraldo and his son were belowdecks checking out the boat's sluggish response to the helm. Will Black was in the galley trying to prepare them something to drink and eat while Holliday stood beside Eddie, staring through the binoculars.

Carrie was clutching a bulkhead and trying to keep her feet under her as the bow of the lobster boat smashed into a wave, then rose to the crest and then dropped into the trough on the other side. The sky was black and what they could see of any horizon was dark gray. The rain beat down furiously, drumming on the deck and the roof of the wheelhouse.

'I don't understand,' yelled Carrie, raising her voice above the bluster of the storm. 'She's been over there for an hour. Why haven't they blown us out of the water?'

'The machine guns can only traverse to a certain angle. If she got any closer she'd be shooting over our heads, *comprendez*?' Eddie said. 'And they probably have very little ammunition.'

Eddie hauled over on the wheel as they hammered into another wave, then rode it upward. On the downward slide he hauled in the other direction, trying to keep the Corazon de Leon from slewing broadside into the next wave. 'Besides, they are probably afraid, as well. They are a long way outside Cuban waters.'

'Pretty soon they'll figure out that the only way they can deal with us is to ram us, and that'll be that,' said Holliday, lowering the binoculars.

'Brew up!' Will Black called as he staggered out of the wheelhouse, somehow managing to balance a tray of mugs in one hand. He began handing them out. 'Coffee, strong, hot and sweet.'

'Shit,' said Holliday.

'That bad?'

Holliday shook his head and pointed to the windscreen of the wheelhouse. The rain was streaked with shades of pink. 'The paint is coming off the roof. We're done.'

Geraldo stumbled into the wheelhouse through the starboard-side hatchway. He spoke to Eddie in rapid-fire Cuban.

'Well?' Holliday asked.

'The boat is leaking badly,' translated Eddie. 'Ricardo is trying to make repairs, but we're taking on a lot of water.'

'Double done,' said Holliday.

Suddenly the storm clouds above them split wide, casting down a huge, golden swath of dying sunset light and blue sky like something out of a Rembrandt painting or one of the apocalyptic horrors of a John Martin canvas. It was simultaneously beautiful and ter-rifying at the same time.

'*Están cambiando de dirección!*' Geraldo yelled, eyes wide and pointing in the direction of the patrol boat. The Cuban crossed himself. '*Madre de Dios,*' he whis-pered.

'He is changing course!' Eddie said as they topped another wave. It was true. As well as it could, the Zhuk was angling itself slightly across the breaking seas, her bows taking a terrible pounding, spray flying far above their bridge. It would take a while, but within no more than ten or fifteen minutes they would be on a colli-sion course and that same steel bow would crush the Corazon de Leon into splinters.

'Bloody hell!' Will Black said.

'What can we do?' Holliday asked Eddie.

'Nothing, *mi compadre*. If we try to do the same thing

away from them, we will capsize. We are wood. They are steel.'

'Then it's over,' said Holliday, staring out at the terrible sunlit sea.

Following the establishing of the PINNACLE NUC-FLASH ORLANDO message on the Corazon de Leon's wheelhouse roof by Paul Smith and the further knowledge that a Zhuk-class patrol boat was following it led to a predictable chain of events that moved up and down the chain of command with remarkable efficiency.

When the first aerial NEST team flying over the Orlando area reported an anomalous and extremely large radiation signal originating in the Lake Buena Vista area and since the Zhuk was both of Cuban military origin and well outside both Cuban territorial waters and even beyond its economic fisheries zone, it was deemed both prudent and proactive to send up one of the new Predator C Avenger drones from Creech Air Force Base in Nevada for a look-see.

After a four-hour flight the Avenger, at an elevation of just under sixty thousand feet and using its highly sophisticated Advanced Low-observable Embedded Reconnaissance Targeting, or ALERT, system, spotted what was deemed to be hostile intentions from the Zhuk, and this information went rapidly back up the line to the Pentagon and from there to the Situation Room, where the president and several other notables were gathered around the same monitors they'd watched Osama bin Laden ascend to Paradise on.

Based on the fact that one of the NEST ground teams had discovered two suitcase nuclear devices in a Disney hotel parking lot, the president of the United States had no compunction at all in his next order.

'Do it,' he said firmly, simultaneously wondering if he was guaranteeing his reelection or sending it around the toilet bowl.

And the Avenger did what it was told, releasing its single two-thousand-pound BLU-109 Penetrator laser-guided bomb normally referred to as a 'Bunker Buster.' The needle-nosed bomb sliced down through the full sixty thousand feet at ten minutes before sunset, its perfectly calibrated systems guiding in toward the heat signal coming from the Zhuk's engines.

The Penetrator bomb was traveling much too quickly for the human eye to follow, but the explosion that followed was spectacular. Riding up to the crest of yet another wave, Holliday saw the Zhuk disintegrate in front of his eyes. He also knew exactly what was going to happen next. 'Everybody, down!' Holliday bellowed, dragging Eddie down off the wheel.

There was a brain-rattling concussion and a split second later all the glass windows in the wheelhouse blew out. Suddenly the interior wheelhouse was being flooded by sheets of stinging rain and salt spray.

Eddie struggled to his feet and grabbed the wheel as

they heaved down into a wave trough. When they rose to the crest of the next wave, the Cuban Zhuk had completely disappeared.

'What was that!' Carrie Pilkington asked, squinting her eyes.

Holliday grinned, relieved. 'That, Miss Pilkington, was the U.S. cavalry.'

'*Dios mio!*' whispered Geraldo.

33

Fidel Castro died right on schedule, shortly after his private celebration of St Lazarus Day at his Punta Cero estate. By that time the president of the United States, the president of Mexico and the prime minister of Canada had agreed on a joint occupying force of Cuba based on the incontrovertible evidence of a planned nuclear attack by Cuba on the United States, an unprovoked act of war by any definition of the term.

The occupying force would be under U.N. observation until the first untainted and uncorrupted democratic elections in the country since 1933 and the Revolt of the Sergeants, which left Fulgencio Batista as the de facto leader of the country ruling through a series of puppet governments until he took over the presidency himself.

The uncovering of the suitcase bombs, and a day later the bomb in the Everglades, put the president's numbers through the roof, virtually guaranteeing his election despite the state of the economy. As predicted by Kate Sinclair, plans were immediately drawn up to increase governmental and police powers under the Patriot Act.

The deaths of Max Kingman and Joseph Patchin never made it onto the news cycle, and as the huge corporate conspiracy involved in the plot became known to the White House, that, too, was swept under the rug, at least for the time being, hanging people from meat hooks having become politically incorrect and not good for the incumbent president's image.

Lieutenant Colonel John Holliday and Eddie Cabrera lay on identical lounge chairs under the shade of an umbrella on Cable Beach, sipping Kalik beer. They had been keeping under the radar at one of the smaller hotels, waiting for things to blow over. Holliday knew it couldn't last forever; eventually there'd be a closed Senate investigation and he at least would be subpoenaed. Until then he'd rest as best he could.

'I'm sorry about your brother, Eddie,' Holliday murmured.

His friend shrugged. 'I am sorry, too, but he is dead and I am alive. This is Cuba, my friend.'

Holliday's new cell phone beeped at him. He knew who was calling because he'd only given the number to one person. He took out the phone. Lines of text began to appear on the screen.

'Uh-oh,' said Holliday.

'What is this uh-oh?' Eddie asked.

'Where my cousin Peggy is involved, it usually means trouble.' Holliday shook his head, laughing. 'Apparently she and Rafi found the secret diaries of

Colonel Percival Harrison Fawcett. They're arriving in Nassau on the ten o'clock flight.'

'Faucet, this is the tap to get water, yes?' Eddie asked.

'The water part's right, but don't think of tap water. Think of the Amazon.' He switched off the phone. 'I think we're in for another wild ride, my friend.'

EPILOGUE

The two old men sat on the porch of the older man's farm in the mountains of the Spanish Sierra Morena and looked out over the hills.

'It is pretty here, don't you think, brother? Nice and hot, like home.'

'Pretty enough,' said the older of the two. Behind them in the house, he could hear the sound of the evening meal being cooked. 'Pretty enough and hot enough for my old bones, but it is not home, is it?'

'No, but you can rest here. There was no peace at home – you know that.' The younger brother laughed. 'And here you can watch your own state funeral on the television while your nation mourns you. This is an opportunity given to very few men, *compañero*.'

'Poor Benito. He was with me for many years. I pray he did not suffer too much.'

'It was very quick,' the younger brother lied. In fact, the man's death had been excruciating and had taken hours.

'And that *mariquita pedófilo*, Ortega?'

'He had a heart attack shortly after your death. Between the eyes.'

'*Bueno*,' sighed the older brother sleepily, his eyes closing. '*Muy bueno*.'

The younger brother waited for a few minutes, listening to his brother's steady breathing, and then tiptoed back into the cool shadows of the porch.

And the old man slept and dreamed of the bright stars on a dark, cold night, a toboggan ride and making angels in the snow.

Read on for a special preview of
Paul Christopher's next thriller

Lost City of the Templars

Available from Penguin in January 2014

If you were looking for a word to describe Peggy Blackstock's mood as she walked down the strand in the seaside English town of Torquay, 'bored' would have sprung to your lips, immediately followed by 'If I see one more ye olde English pub advertising the best fish and chips in Torquay, I'm going to hurl.'

She'd been in town for two days, and there were still three more to go until Rafi's World Archaeology Congress convention was over. She was already at her wits' end. Being in Torquay was like being in Coney Island without Nathan's, the Cyclone or the bumper cars. There were just as many people, but the sand on the few beaches was muddy and dirty, the English Channel water was freezing cold and most of the food tasted like library paste.

It wasn't that she wasn't interested in her husband's work. In fact she was more than interested – she was fascinated. Rafi specialized in the archaeology of the Crusades in Israel and it took them both to dozens of sites from Jerusalem and Jaffa to Turkey and Turin, from Bosnia to Berlin and just about everywhere else in Europe. The Crusades had covered a lot of ground from the tenth century to the fourteenth century, and they had reached as far as Sweden in their scope.

On her far-flung trips with Rafi, Peggy had become an accomplished archaeological photographer, and she had landed more than enough freelance assignments, contributing pictures to the *New York Times Travel Magazine*, *Bon Appétit*, *National Geographic* and half a dozen other periodicals.

But something was missing, and Peggy knew exactly what it was: she craved the adrenaline rush of the truly unknown. Since coming back from Africa and losing track of her cousin Doc, she'd missed the . . . excitement and adventure that seemed to follow the ex-U.S. Army Ranger. It had been like that even when she was a girl.

It was Doc who'd taught her not to be afraid of heights and had calmly and efficiently taught her the skills of rock climbing in the Adirondacks. It was Doc who'd also taught her to hunt and fish and use a gun.

It was their uncle Henry the professor who'd given Peggy her first camera and taught her how to use it, but it was Doc who'd given her the courage to reach the places where'd she'd taken the first photographs that really mattered to her: the summit of Mount Skylight, the fourth-highest mountain in the Adirondacks; at sunset, a lone gray wolf in the winter at Yellowstone; and a hibernating twelve-hundred-pound Kodiak bear in Alaska. It was Doc who'd started her on a lifelong quest for adventure, and somehow she knew the quest wasn't over yet.

One thing was sure: no one was going to find the adventure of a lifetime on the main street of Torquay.

So, at the next corner, she turned left, away from the sea, and began climbing a narrow residential street of low attached bungalow-style dwellings that climbed up a seriously steep hill. It was not the most likely path to any kind of adventure at all, but the kids in the Narnia books had found it through a cupboard door, and Harry Potter had found it on platform 9¾ in King's Cross Station, so you never really knew, then, did you? Anyway, the exercise would do her good; she'd had one too many orders of ye olde fish and chips in the past few days.

There were a few shops on her way up the street; the English version of a 7-Eleven, with ads for fruity-flavored vodka coolers in the window. There was a hairstylist called British Hairways, where the customers under their dryers looked as though they were all in their eighties. And a prosthetic store called Lend You a Hand had a single bright pink artificial leg in an otherwise empty window. Peggy would probably find the Bates Motel around the next bend.

What she did find was Weatherby and Sons Auction House, a ragtag assembly of a plastered bungalow attached to something at the rear that might have been a two-story carriage house turned into a commercial garage and a third stumpy-looking building with a pair of firmly closed barn-sized doors.

Between the stumpy building and the garage lay a paved driveway that seemed to be doubling as a parking lot. At the end of the drive there was an overhead aluminum door, slid three-quarters open. The roll-up door had a sign over it that read AUCTION TODAY. The car in the parking lot was a Jaguar XKR convertible, this year's model. The auction business was doing well by somebody. Peggy turned down the drive and ducked under the aluminum door.

The interior of the auction house was like the biggest, most chaotic yard sale in the world: rowboats sat in the rafters; chandeliers and harpoons were hanging from the beams; a stack of twisted narwhal tusks lay in one corner along with an equal number of ancient-looking bamboo fly rods and an enormous stuffed Scottish stag with a rack of eighteen-point antlers. The stag looked dusty, the glass eyes cloudy. Probably not a lot of buyers for stuffed giant Scottish stags in these days of fiscal responsibility. There was a stage at the front of the hall, with perhaps a hundred or so folding chairs in front of it, most of them filled with people waving numbered paddles around as they bid on one item after another. Easels were set up on the stage to display works of art. There were a movable display wall full of hanging musical instruments and several tables with smaller and medium-sized objects to be sold. The auctioneer stood at a podium in the center of the stage, and a crew of workers, male and female, carted things on and off the raised platform. An old man with grizzled stubble and thin hair slicked back with something that looked like Vaseline handed her a paddle and said, 'There you go, dearie. Have fun.' Then he pointed her to an empty seat at the end of an aisle halfway to the auction stage. She took her seat and noticed that the number on her paddle was 666 – not a particularly auspicious number for someone who'd shivered her way through all five of the *Omen* movies.

The items went by quickly: six Regency chairs for twenty-two hundred pounds, the lot; a Georgian silver porringer for a thousand; a Royal Winton circus jug for three hundred sixty pounds . . . The list went on and on. Throughout every lot that went up, Peggy noticed that the paddle in the lap of the man beside her never twitched. He was in his fifties, with the high cheekbones and dark deep-set eyes of a Russian or a Slav. His hair was too long – well over his nape. But his salt-and-pepper beard was perfectly groomed, and his suit looked very expensive. The man's hands were strong, well-manicured, but with the raw knuckles and the calluses of someone who had spent a lot of time outdoors. He certainly didn't give the impression of someone who'd be interested in silver porridge pots. After fifteen minutes, he made a frustrated grunting sound, stood up and left.

The next lot was a hodgepodge of household effects from a man named Raleigh Miller, who, according to the auctioneer, had lived to the ripe old age of one hundred and ten in a room at the back of the Hole in the Wall Pub on Park Lane for as long as anyone could remember. He would come down to the pub each evening for a bottle of Samuel Smith's Imperial Stout and an order of fish and chips, both of which he took back to his room.

The room must have been sparsely furnished

because there weren't too many household goods being offered and even fewer being auctioned. The final lot was a small steel footlocker, padlocked and rusted shut with a faded first-class travel sticker that said RMSP *ALMANZORA*. The apparent journey the box had taken was from Montevideo, Uruguay, to Southampton, arriving on August 26, 1928. Peggy did the math. If Miller had been a hundred and ten years old when he had died, that meant he had been born in 1903. He'd been just twenty-five years old when he had departed on the RMSP *Almanzora*. What had a twenty-five-year-old British kid been doing in Uruguay, and where had he gotten the money for a first-class cabin? Interesting questions. The first price from the podium was two pounds. Peggy held up her paddle. No one else bid, once, twice, thrice, and it was hers. She went down to the stage, paid her two pounds, filled out the appropriate paperwork and received her prize. It weighed a ton, and Peggy asked if they could call her a taxi; walking back to the convention center would have been an impossibility. Not only did they call her a cab – they put the box on a little hand truck and called one of the younger assistants to haul it out to the curb for her.

'You know anything about this old guy Miller?' Peggy asked as they went up the main aisle.

'He was a bit of a loon, I know. Least, that's what my uncle told me.'

'Your uncle?'

'Bert. He's one of the barmen at the Hole in the Wall.'

'Why did your uncle Bert think he was crazy?'

'He was forever getting newspapers, not proper English ones but foreign – the *El Observadorio* or something. And *A Vozey da Serra*, sounded like.'

'Interesting,' said Peggy.

They reached the roll-up doors and went out into the sunlight. The dark man who'd sat beside her briefly in the auction room was smoking a cigarette, leaning on the rear fender of the Jag. He watched silently as the young assistant tipped the box off the hand truck and eased it onto the pavement.

'There you go, missus,' said the assistant. When she took a heavy one-pound coin and pressed it into the young man's hand, he handed it back. 'Not necessary, missus, but thank you all the same.' The young man smiled at her and headed inside the auction hall.

Peggy smiled back; it was the most politeness she'd received from a stranger since she'd done a photo essay for the *New York Times Magazine* on the Amish.

'How much did you pay for the box?' asked the man leaning on the Jaguar. His accent was cultured but definitely Eastern European. At a guess she'd have thought Russian or maybe Czech. Whatever the accent, she didn't like the tone.

'Why do you care?' Peggy responded.

'It should have been mine.'

'You weren't there to bid on it.'

'A call of nature,' said the man.

'Well, I can't help that,' said Peggy. She looked up the street, wishing the taxi would come.

'The box should have been mine,' the man repeated, a little more insistently.

'You mentioned that,' said Peggy.

'I will pay you for it,' said the man.

'I'm not selling it.'

'I will give you a hundred pounds for it. You will make a profit.'

'I don't want a profit,' said Peggy, irritated. 'I want the box, and it's not for sale.' Why the hell did the guy with the Jaguar want a footlocker from 1928?

The taxi arrived, a boxy red Renault minivan with Price First Taxi on the sliding door. The driver got out, opened the sliding door and hauled the footlocker inside. The man leaning on the Jaguar stepped forward and handed Peggy a business card.

'If you change your mind,' said the man. 'My cell phone number is there. Anytime, day or night. I will await your call.' The last bit had a slightly sinister edge to it, as though something bad would happen if the call didn't come.

'Don't lose any sleep waiting.' Peggy took the card and got into the cab.

'Where to, missus?' the cabbie asked.

'Palace Hotel, please,' said Peggy.

'Right you are, missus.' The cab moved off.

Peggy looked at the card:

Dimitri Antonin Rogov
Expeditions
Custos Thesauri

'*Custos Thesauri?*' Rafi Wanounou laughed, staring at the card Peggy had handed him. 'That's ripe coming from a man like Dimitri Rogov! *Latro Thesauri* would be more like it.' They sat at the breakfast table in their room at the Palace Hotel, the rusty footlocker between them.

'So what does it mean? Who is he?' Peggy asked her archaeologist husband.

'*Custos Thesauri* means 'keeper, or guardian, of the treasure' in Latin. *Latro Thesauri* is the opposite: the 'thief of treasures.' Dimitri Rogov would make Lara Croft look like an amateur and your beloved Indiana Jones a bumbling boob.'

'How dare you cast aspersions on my secret love!' Peggy laughed. 'You should look so good in a beat-up fedora.'

'You're sounding more like my mother every day,' said Rafi, smiling back. The truth was, of course, that when Rafi had brought home a girl named Peggy Blackstock, his mother hadn't been impressed. He told her the name in Yiddish was Schwarzekuh, but that didn't seem to help much either.

'Seriously though,' said Rafi, 'Rogov is infamous. He's a tomb robber, a smuggler, a forger and an all-around thief. If he wants something, he'll do just about anything to get it.'

'Well,' said Peggy, 'maybe we should find out what's inside.'

It took the better part of an hour. A hammer and chisel borrowed from hotel maintenance, as well as spraying around the edges of the lid with something called Cillit Bang, which came in a bottle with a bright pink label, finally did the trick.

The first thing out of the footlocker was the bundle of very frail-looking pinkish notebooks with faded designs on the covers. Rafi gently cut and removed the string. Then, putting on a pair of the latex gloves that he carried with him everywhere, he carefully opened the top notebook.

'*Benn-zonna!*' Rafi swore, his eyes widening as he stared down at the words in faint sepia-colored ink.

Being the Private Journals of
Lt. Col. (R.A) Percival Harrison Fawcett
in Search of the Lost City of Z

'I think it's time we gave your cousin a call,' said Rafi slowly. 'I think we're going to need him.'

He just wanted a decent book to read ...

Not too much to ask, is it? It was in 1935 when Allen Lane, Managing Director of Bodley Head Publishers, stood on a platform at Exeter railway station looking for something good to read on his journey back to London. His choice was limited to popular magazines and poor-quality paperbacks – the same choice faced every day by the vast majority of readers, few of whom could afford hardbacks. Lane's disappointment and subsequent anger at the range of books generally available led him to found a company – and change the world.

'We believed in the existence in this country of a vast reading public for intelligent books at a low price, and staked everything on it'
Sir Allen Lane, 1902–1970, founder of Penguin Books

The quality paperback had arrived – and not just in bookshops. Lane was adamant that his Penguins should appear in chain stores and tobacconists, and should cost no more than a packet of cigarettes.

Reading habits (and cigarette prices) have changed since 1935, but Penguin still believes in publishing the best books for everybody to enjoy. We still believe that good design costs no more than bad design, and we still believe that quality books published passionately and responsibly make the world a better place.

So wherever you see the little bird – whether it's on a piece of prize-winning literary fiction or a celebrity autobiography, political tour de force or historical masterpiece, a serial-killer thriller, reference book, world classic or a piece of pure escapism – you can bet that it represents the very best that the genre has to offer.

Whatever you like to read – trust Penguin.